KEEPING IT REAL

A MILWAUKEE MAYHEM NOVEL

TRACY SOLHEIM

Sun Home Productions

For Patrick 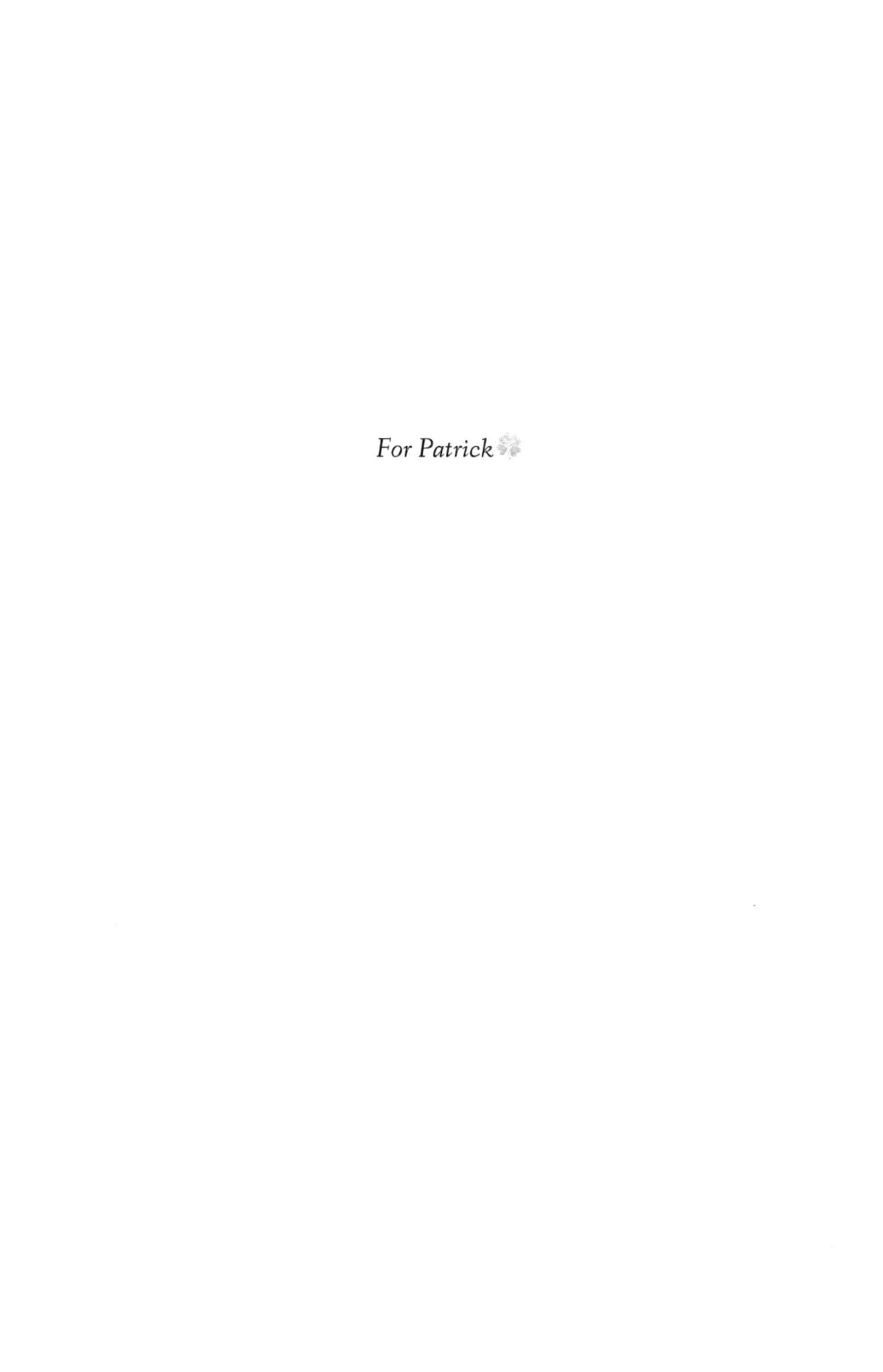

"LOOK OUT!"

Alek Bergeron jumped out of the path of a pint-sized boy wielding a hockey stick just as the kid slammed into the boards. None the worse for wear, eight-year-old Gunner Ferguson let out a frustrated groan, his tongue visible through the gap where one of his incisors had yet to grow in. The expression on the boy's face was a lot like his father's, the Milwaukee Mayhem's star center Denis "Gus" Ferguson, after Gus lost the puck to a rival player.

"You need to learn to *feel* the puck with your stick so you can keep your eyes focused ahead," Alek advised Gunner. "Otherwise, your sister will deke you out of your skates every time."

The boy's younger sister sprinted past them, skating as though she were born wearing blades. Given that she'd been chasing her father and older brother since she could walk, it was no surprise that five-year-old Grace was a natural on the ice. She took the corner of the rink like a speed skater, hanging on to her balance as well as the puck right before she shot it toward the net.

"That's my girl!" Gus called from the other end of the rink despite the puck veering wide right of the goal.

Gunner snorted. "Dad told me I had to let her steal the biscuit at least twice today. That way, she wouldn't whine the whole way home."

"You're a good big brother." Alek patted the top of Gunner's helmet.

"Yeah. But now I'm going to show her how it's done." He raced off to grab the puck as it rebounded off the far boards before shooting it into the empty net with a perfect flick of his wrist.

"Well played, Gunster." Timothée Valentine, the Mayhem's right winger and league heart throb, skated over to high-five the boy.

Two tween girls, likely belonging to someone in management, trailed Valentine, the pair sporting adoring looks. The team had broken training camp that day, and everyone within the organization was at the practice facility getting in some last-minute downtime with their families. The grueling seven-month regular season would kick off the following week.

"Excellent shot," Gus praised his son as he weaved his way through the other players and their kids enjoying the free skate on the practice ice.

Grace snowplowed into her brother, nearly decapitating him with her stick when she went to wrap her arms around his neck in congratulations. The siblings' playful camaraderie brought to mind a similar brother and sister Alek had known once upon a time. His chest burned at the thought. He quickly squeezed his eyes shut to keep the memories from seeping in and destroying the balance he'd carefully cultivated over the past decade.

"There are treats in the canteen," Gus said to his kids as he guided them to where Alek leaned against the boards next to the exit gate. "Go snag one of Mom's chocolate peanut butter cupcakes for me before they all get eaten."

Gunner tossed his stick to his father and raced off the ice, barely pausing to put on his skate guards. Gus lifted Grace onto the bench behind the glass, kneeling to unlace her skates.

"Do you want a cupcake too, Uncle Alek?" Grace asked.

Alek stepped off the ice amid a stream of his teammates who were headed in the direction of the dressing room. "You betcha." He bent down to remove the cumbersome pads that guarded the goalie's legs. "I never pass up anything your mom bakes."

"Hey! What about me?" Valentine asked, his fan club having skated off in the other direction.

Grace giggled. "You're not my godfather."

Valentine made a show of clutching his chest. "But I thought I was your boyfriend, Gracie?"

If looks could kill, the stink-eye Gus leveled at his teammate would have incinerated him. Not that Valentine cared. His long lashes, matching dimples, and glossy dark curls got him out of as much trouble as they got him into.

"Okay. I'll save you a cupcake, too," she promised before racing off in her stocking feet, calling for her brother to wait. She blew a kiss in the direction of her father before she disappeared.

The adoring grin Gus wore as he and Alek followed Valentine into the dressing room had Alek's chest twitching again. Almost as if he envied the guy or something. Which was ridiculous.

Both men were at the top of their game on a team poised to make a strong run for the Cup this year. Sure, when Gus left the ice, he went home to his magazine-cover-worthy family. His wife of ten years kept the home fires burning during the season, raising their two amazing kids while working as an occupational therapist.

When Alek went home, it was to an empty house. Just the way he liked it. Everything within his place was exactly what he wanted and where he wanted it.

His twin sister accused him of being a neat freak. His teammates joked he was an old fart who lived in a mausoleum. Alek ignored them. So what if he lived his life in an orderly and predictable way? He spent half of every week on the road constantly surrounded by nineteen teammates. The solitude his house provided helped to ground him, allowing him to focus on what was really important: hockey.

That didn't mean he was a monk. Companionship was easy to find for a professional athlete with his notoriety. If his sister was to be believed, Alek's "piercing blue eyes and thick sable locks" didn't hurt when it came to attracting the opposite sex, either. And if he wanted to experience the chaos of family life, he had plenty of kids to play "funcle" to, including his sister's year-old twins.

But his relationships were always on his terms. And never if they interfered with his goal of winning the Cup. After all, that had been the mission from the moment he picked up his stick as a professional. It had eluded him for seven seasons so far, and Alek was starting to get a little twitchy.

It didn't help that his dad was recently diagnosed with early-onset Parkinson's Disease. While most guys at thirty still saw their lives spread out before them, his father's illness was a gut-punch reminder that there were no guarantees in this world. Given everything his parents had done to help him get to this level of play, Alek wanted his dad to share in the joy of hoisting the Cup.

Before his dad's health issues, the only ticking clock was how long Alek's body would allow him to play. Now, though, the clock seemed to be a lot louder and faster. He sat on the bench in front of his stall and tugged at the laces of his skate in frustration.

"What's eating you all of a sudden?" Gus asked as he shoved his kids' hockey sticks into his equipment bag. "If I know my wife, she's already packed a to-go box of cupcakes for you. Not to worry."

Which was likely true. Claire Ferguson never missed a chance to feed Alek as if he were one of her own children. Unlike with her kids, however, cupcakes didn't make everything better.

"Nothing," Alek replied, trying to muster up a smile. His funky mood was on him, not Gus. "Just focused on getting my head together ahead of the season."

Valentine groaned. "Oh, man, Ice-Berg. The season is still a week away. No need to be a fun sucker and queue up your speech about putting in the work. Every guy here knows you never miss a practice, a morning skate, a training session, or a game unless blood is spewing from some part of your body." Valentine bowed. "Believe me, we all strive to emulate your work ethic. It's just that some of us have a life outside the rink."

Alek had a life. So what if his looked a little lonely to the guys because he didn't have a family or girlfriend constantly distracting him? He wasn't like Valentine or most of the other hockey players in the room, who all possessed unlimited talent. Alek never believed he'd make it to the pros. It took him twice as much grit and hard work to earn a job between the pipes.

The nickname Ice-Berg didn't just refer to his glacier-colored eyes, but also his menacing single-minded focus. And being the best had his undivided attention for the time being. That and winning the Cup.

Gus paused from wiping his skate blades, shooting Alek a compassionate look. He was the only person within the organization aware of his father's prognosis. His friend knew how much Alek wanted to go all the way this season for his dad.

"We've got this," Gus said with quiet conviction.

"You know what you need, Ice-Berg?" Zach Picard, the Mayhem's captain said from across the dressing room. "You need a woman. Someone to help you relieve all that preseason . . . *tension*." He punctuated the last word with a waggle of his eyebrows.

Alek shook his head at his teammate. Sex seemed to be the captain's answer to everything. Picard was a "no strings attached" player with a puck bunny eagerly waiting for him in every city. Alek found it hard to believe that all the women were cool with it. Yet Picard skated from ice rink to ice rink with no drama impeding his game.

The Mayhem's newest addition, Brad Merriweather, looked up from his dressing stall. "Bergeron had a woman, except he let some pro football player steal her away. Oh wait, it wasn't a steal. Bergeron practically walked her down the aisle and handed her over to the guy."

Every man in the room suddenly stopped what they were doing. Merriweather had a reputation for being brash and a bit of an asswipe. Since joining the team this summer, the defenseman had lived up to that hype.

Unlike Picard, Alek's recent love life had not been drama-free. The Milwaukee media had a field day when the woman Alek had been seen around town with ended up marrying the Growlers quarterback. It didn't help that punches were thrown at a charity gala that both men attended. No one cared that they were defending the woman's honor. Instead, social media managed to make more of the incident than was necessary. As usual.

The silence stretched as everyone waited to see if Alek would react.

"You're misinformed, Merriweather." Valentine's French Quebec accent was much more clipped than normal as he jumped to Alek's defense. "Bergeron and London are friends. That's all. She and the quarterback were high school sweethearts."

While Alek appreciated the save—Valentine was more than just a pretty face and a wicked stick handler—his recitation of the facts wasn't entirely accurate. Alek had thought he'd found "the one." And it still stung. Not the part about her choosing another guy over him. Alek begrudgingly had to admit London and Trey were meant for each other.

The idea that he had been so off base about London's feelings made Alek question whether or not he was cut out for a long-term relationship. After all, he'd been wrong about a woman's love once before.

The tidbit about him and London remaining friends was true, however. The best part about it? Alek continued to be a thorn in the side of the Milwaukee Growlers quarterback.

"If you're ready to get back out there," Valentine continued as he tugged a Mayhem hoodie over his curls, "the influencer I'm dating has a friend. I'm happy to set you up."

Gus covered up his laughing gasp with a cough. Valentine's content creator girlfriend had the annoying tendency of adding a rising inflection to the end of everything she said. Carrying on a conversation with her felt like a game of twenty questions. No doubt her friend was the same.

And the last thing Alek wanted was to get involved with a woman whose day revolved around social media. As one of the league's premier goalies, he already spent enough of his life in the very judgmental public eye. It turned out that once a player signed a lucrative contract, every fan felt it was their God-given right to pile on when that player had an off game. After the Mayhem didn't make it out of the first round of the playoffs last season, fans—and more than a few hockey pundits—blamed Alek despite the team being short two starting defensemen.

"I think Ice-Berg is interested in something more substantial." Picard eyed Alek critically. "In fact, I think something more long-term might do you some good."

Here we go again.

"For the hundredth time, I'm not getting a dog," Alek told them.

"What's your beef with dogs?" Valentine demanded. "Why do you hate them?"

"I don't hate dogs."

Gus laughed. "He tolerates ours just fine."

"We are on the road half of every week," Alek argued. "There's no way to take care of a dog."

It was his standard argument. The fact of the matter was he wasn't a dog person. For some reason, though, that made him some sort of monster.

"You're just afraid a dog would mess up your neatly ordered mausoleum," Valentine accused.

"Will you guys shut your pieholes? I wasn't going to suggest a dog," Picard interjected, quieting the room. The captain turned to Alek. "Now that you've officially entered the dirty thirties, you probably should get serious and start looking for a wife."

The rest of the guys laughed while Alek shot his captain the bird. "You're only a year younger than I am."

"But I have the stamina of a nineteen-year-old," Picard declared. "I don't need a wifey to tuck me in at night yet."

This was met with a chorus of guffaws.

"You know, there's a lot to be said for settling down," Gus argued. "For one, it's easier to concentrate on the game when you know who's warming your bed at night."

"Why would any guy want to settle down?" Merriweather

sounded as though someone had told him the hockey season had been canceled. Given that the guy was married with two little kids, Alek found his teammate's reaction odd. Judging by the looks the other guys were doling out, he wasn't the only one.

"What?" Merriweather shrugged. "Don't lie and tell me you married guys aren't chomping at the bit to escape from under the honey-do list and get back out on the road. To sleep through the night without being woken up by your whining kid. Or to not have to listen to your wife tell you she's 'too tired' when you want some." He winked at Alek. "The ladies are never too tired on the road, am I right? Why give up a sure thing for a ball and chain at home? In fact, I'm happy to be your wingman this season. Not to brag, but I do pretty well with the chicks myself."

The strained silence was back except for a whispered exchange between the two Swedish players. Alek didn't speak the language but whatever they said was uttered in a tone laced with disgust.

When no reply was forthcoming, Merriweather hefted his equipment bag onto his shoulder. "Suit yourself. But my offer stands. Later," he called before sauntering from the dressing room.

Picard heaved a sigh. "Something tells me that guy could be a handful this season."

For the most part, the players tried to police bad behavior within the confines of the dressing room. The guys liked to keep the outside distractions to a minimum. It helped them play better as a unit. A rocky marriage during the season could seriously mess with the team's mojo, though.

"Yeah. I feel sorry for his wife. She's already got her hands full with two kids under the age of three." Gus grabbed his bag, exchanging a look with Alek. "Do you want to come by the house for dinner?"

Alek appreciated the offer, even if it was a pity ask. As much as he enjoyed spending time with the Ferguson family, he had no intention of butting in on one of their last nights of togetherness before the season.

He shook his head. "Thanks, but no thanks. I have some stuff to take care of at home."

Picard laughed and gestured to Alek's longish hair. "He's got to wash his flow tonight."

Gus looked like he was going to call him out on his lie. Instead, he released an exasperated sigh. "Stop by the canteen to pick up your cupcakes before you go."

He and Picard headed in the direction of the party. The Swedes followed them out.

"I'm going to tell that jerk-off Merriweather that you already have a wingman," Valentine said as he made his way to the door. "And it's me. Picard's right. You need a woman. Leave it to me. St. Valentine will find you the perfect happily ever after this season."

Alek scoffed loudly in the now empty dressing room. As much as he appreciated his teammates having his back, he didn't need them focused on finding him his "happily ever after." He was resolved that one wasn't in the cards for him. Besides, the Mayhem's number one priority this season was to win the Cup. End. Of. Story.

He reached for his cell phone and keys right as the phone buzzed. It was likely Claire demanding that he join them for dinner. Except when he went to slide the phone to talk, the number on the screen wasn't hers.

It was one he thought he'd blocked nine years earlier. A number that belonged to the guy Alek expected to stand up for him at his wedding to his college girlfriend. Until that same guy ran off and married her himself.

Alek swore as he hit the Do Not Accept button. For the first few months, Jamie called repeatedly. Alek never picked up. He had nothing to say to his former best friend. The calls only stopped when he blocked Jamie's number.

A hazy memory stirred. He vaguely recalled unblocking Jamie after consuming too much alcohol to numb the pain the night he'd learned of his father's diagnosis. Fortunately, he'd fallen asleep before any drunk dialing could take place. Well, he'd remedy this situation right now.

He was opening the phone's screen to reapply the block when Jamie's number popped up again.

"Ah, what the hell? He's never going to get the hint without hearing it directly from me," Alek mumbled before sliding his finger across the screen. "What do you want?"

The line was quiet for a long moment before a small voice spoke up. "Is this really Alek Bergeron?"

Alek immediately regretted his ugly tone. It wasn't Jamie. Just some random kid.

Except why is he calling from Jamie's number?

"Yeah," he said cautiously. "Who's this?"

There was an excited gasp before the boy spoke again. "I'm Finn. Finn Cobert. And I'm your biggest fan."

Right.

Jamie had a son. Alek's mom had mentioned that at some point during the past nine years. The boy must be somewhere around Gunner's age. Leave it to Jamie to use his kid to weasel his way back into Alek's life. He was going to be disappointed, though, because it wasn't going to work.

"Good to know. Hey, Finn, if you're calling for an autographed stick or sweater, have your dad reach out to my publicist. I'll be glad to send you one of each." It wasn't the boy's fault his father had screwed Alek over.

"Cool! Thank you. But that's not why I called."

Of course it wasn't. He could almost sense Jamie hovering in the background, waiting for Alek to take the bait. The guy had never met a stranger and couldn't stand it when anyone was miffed at him. He was used to being the beloved center of attention. A cool breeze brushed against the back of his neck as if Jamie was saying, "Gotcha."

"Look—"

"Please don't hang up." Finn's excitement had dimmed. "I feel like I know you. My dad and I watched all your games whenever they were on the hockey channel. Even on school nights. He always told me bedtime stories about all the crazy things you got up to when you were roommates in college. Especially when you traveled overseas to play against each other in Europe." Finn paused to suck in a breath. "He said they were the best days of his life. Well, except for when me and him were doing something fun together."

The boy's voice cracked before it trailed off. His use of the past tense had Alek instinctively bracing his shoulder against the wall.

"Finn, can I talk to your dad?"

The boy ignored him. "Dad told me that if he couldn't be here and I ever needed anything, I should get in touch with you. That you were him in a different place. And you would always have my back."

The room felt like it was spinning. Alek dropped onto the bench. "Finn, put your dad on the phone. Please."

The boy was silent for so long, Alek thought he had hung up. Until he said the words Alek wasn't prepared to hear.

"I can't. My dad and my mom are dead."

TWO

SHERIDAN COBERT'S heart raced as she hurried from room to room. While it was nice to know that particular organ was still functioning after everything she'd been through the past several days, she wasn't pleased with the universe for giving her a reason to bring it back to life. Apparently, the universe didn't have a mercy rule. It simply continued to test her.

A fine sheen of sweat broke out on her forehead. Her nephew was the only other living member of her immediate family, and she'd already lost him. It wasn't like Jamie and Madison lived in a mansion anymore. For the past several years, their house was a modest rancher with three bedrooms and two baths. Sheridan knew all its nooks and crannies intimately because she'd grown up inside it. Given the amount of grief its four walls had endured over the past two decades, it was a wonder the place was still standing.

There was no sign of Finn in the kitchen. Not that there was room to move in there anyway. Neighbors stood practically shoulder to shoulder, trying to organize the fridge and freezer so they could cram in the never-ending stream of casseroles that kept appearing at the side door.

She peeked into the den, where the late afternoon sunlight flickered off the wall of trophies belonging to her brother. Jamie's friends congregated in the room, drinking and reminiscing about his short-lived glory days. Some of the people gathered were from as far back as middle school and his junior team. Others were regulars from their father's bar, where Jamie held court every night.

Make that *used* to hold court.

She pressed her palm against the wall as another wave of sorrow washed over her. It had been like this since she'd gotten the news of the fatal car accident three days before.

This can't be happening.

Except it was. And not even her library of self-help books seemed to be of any use to her right now. The only thing she knew for certain was that she had to be strong because there was a little boy who was hurting likely more than she was.

If only she could find him. She'd looked in every hiding place in the house. Finn wasn't in any of them.

Sheridan stepped outside to check the backyard. The kids from the local hockey team Jamie coached milled about aimlessly, trying in vain to look cool despite their shock and heartache. Finn worshipped those kids, shadowing them everywhere. Except not today.

That left her with only one other place to look. Behind the door she had been dreading opening since she arrived back in New Hampshire yesterday.

Jamie and Madison's bedroom.

She forced herself to turn the knob and was rewarded with the muffled sound of her nephew talking to someone. Hattie, the family's big Bernese Mountain dog, greeted Sheridan with a forlorn sigh and a swish of her tail. The dog didn't bother lifting her head from where it rested on Jamie's favorite sweatshirt.

Sheridan dragged in a rough breath. The poor animal was hurting, too.

She glanced over at the display of photos on the dresser, her eyes immediately drawn to a photo of Jamie and Finn she'd taken years earlier when her nephew was a rambunctious towheaded three-year-old. She'd expected his hair to have darkened to the same brunette shade as hers and Jamie's, but so far, it hadn't.

Her brother's hazel eyes, so similar to her own, were shining with the unbridled joy of a man at the top of his hockey career. It had been a long time since she'd seen Jamie look that happy. She choked back a sob, realizing she never would again.

Finn's voice filtered out from the partially opened closet door.

"My dad and mom are dead," she heard him say.

"Finn!" she cried as she yanked the door all the way open to find him huddled beneath his mother's dresses, still hanging neatly from the rod. He had a cell phone pressed to his ear. "Where did you get that phone? And who in the world are you talking to?"

God, she sounded like the worst kind of shrew. Not exactly how her interactions with her nephew usually went. She was supposed to be Finn's favorite aunt. Never mind that she was his only aunt. But she had no idea who he was telling such delicate and personal information to. She'd watched enough *Dateline* to know how easily someone sinister could prey on a grieving little boy.

"It's Dad's phone," Finn replied, his tone defensive. "The policeman brought it back this morning while you were at the funeral home."

She swallowed roughly. Finn had begged to go with her. To not be left among a house full of mourners. But picking out caskets was not something an eight-year-old boy should ever have to do. She knew that firsthand. Her father had been too distraught to do it when her mother died eighteen years ago. She and Jamie had done it for him.

Sheridan forced her features to relax so as not to scare Finn any more than he probably already was.

"Okay. Why are you hiding in a closet? And who are you talking to?" Those were fair questions. He couldn't hate her for asking, could he?

"It's Alek Bergeron."

His curt answer had her reaching out to steady herself with a hand on the doorjamb. She pressed the other hand to her roiling belly.

Alek Bergeron.

He'd been such a fixture in her life during Jamie's college years. She'd had such a crazy crush on the guy. *More than a crush.* She believed he was her forever love—right up until he became the source of her greatest humiliation.

She hated how much she still missed those penetrating light blue eyes of his, and how, when he focused them on her, Sheridan used to feel like she was the center of the universe.

At least his universe.

And how many times since their mortifying last encounter had she longed for that easy smile of his? The one that always seemed to make everything better. She was a little bit ashamed, thinking what she wouldn't give to have it aimed at her right now. To have him help shoulder the grief and the pain of this unbearable loss. Always the steady one, Alek would know how to navigate through the tough days and months ahead with more certainty than she could muster.

Except that wasn't ever going to happen. The friendship they once shared had dissolved beneath the weight of some very bad decisions made nearly a decade earlier. Guilt for the part she played in the drama gnawed at her chest.

"He wants to talk to you," Finn said, refocusing her attention on the here and now.

A painful lump formed in her throat as she took the phone from Finn's outstretched hand and pressed it to her ear.

"Hello?" she croaked.

"Sher."

Hearing the deep timbre of his voice again made her knees buckle. She slid down the wall to the floor, landing beside the dog.

"Christ, Sheridan. Is it true? Are they . . . are they gone?"

Tears burned the back of her eyes. She nodded forcefully before realizing he couldn't see her.

"Yes," she managed to utter. "It's true."

Alek's sigh sounded tortured. She could picture him running his fingers through his thick hair like he always did when he tried to come to grips with a difficult situation.

"When? How?" he asked.

She cleared her throat, but the pain remained. "Thursday evening. They were coming home from Finn's back-to-school night."

He gasped. "Finn wasn't with them, was he? Is he injured?" he demanded.

The concern for her nephew, a boy he'd never met, was so like Alek that the knot strangling Sheridan began to loosen. She was thankful the man she knew and adored was still there. Even after everything that had happened.

"No. He was with a babysitter."

She glanced at Finn, still sitting in the closet, his arms wrapped around his knees as he listened intently.

"Thank goodness," she added as she shot him a soft smile.

"Yeah," Alek agreed. "How is your dad taking it? And you?" His voice softened. "How are you, Sheridan?"

Of course he wouldn't know about her father. Why would he? The break nine years ago had been clean and permanent.

"As my dad predicted, he didn't live to see his sixtieth birthday," she told him.

Alek made an agonized noise, and she immediately felt sorry for hitting him with more bad news.

"He was never the same after my mom died. It literally broke his heart when Jamie had to step away from the game," she explained.

It had broken all our hearts.

Jamie, leading the league for points scored during his fourth season, took a punishing cross-check from an opposing player. He went down hard on the ice when a teammate tripped and landed on the back of Jamie's neck. Her brother was lucky that the only damage was a loosening of the first and second cervical. Doctors were able to fuse the two using part of Jamie's pelvis. But it was the end of his promising career. No team would take a chance on their star player receiving a hit that could paralyze him.

She swallowed roughly. "The one consolation was my dad passed away in his sleep."

His fractured breathing was the only sound audible on the other end of the phone.

"It's okay, Alek," she reassured him in much the same way she'd comforted her older brother for most of their lives. "We're okay."

She reached over and laid her hand on Finn's forearm.

"We're going to be just fine," she said as she gently squeezed.

Finn shook off her hand and jumped to his feet, startling the dog.

"He needs to be here," he demanded.

Hattie barked in solidarity as she stood, too.

"Dad would want him here. Alek, will you come? Please?" He was shouting now, his face growing blotchy red as his bottom lip curled in defiance.

Confused, Sheridan struggled to stand. Her nephew was the most even-natured kid she knew. "Finn, you need to be reasonable. Your dad and Alek were friends a long time ago."

"*Best friends!*" Finn yelled. "And a best friend would come to his best friend's funeral. I know Dad would have gone to his."

Somehow, the thought of Alek dying made her chest ache even more than it already did. She'd barely survived him breaking her heart years before. Yet knowing he was no longer walking on this earth would be even more unbearable, she realized.

"Finn," she said, wondering how best to reason with the boy whose world was already turned upside down.

"I'll be there," Alek announced loud enough for her nephew to hear.

She'd forgotten for a moment that he was on the other end of the phone.

Oh no. No, no, no.

Sheridan was hanging on by a thread as it was. Seeing Alek again would likely unravel the shred of equilibrium keeping her sane right now.

"The service is tomorrow afternoon." She tried to dissuade him. "I—I doubt you'll be able to get a flight."

"I said I'll be there, Sheridan. And I will."

The line went dead. Finn jerked his chin up and down once, then he turned on his heel and stormed out of the room. Hattie gave her a pitying look before trotting after him.

Sheridan's knees gave out, and she plopped down on the bed, mystified by what had just transpired. How had Finn known to call Alek? Were he and Jamie communicating again? Was that the reason for the recent strain in Jamie's marriage?

Surely, Alek wasn't trying to resurrect his relationship with Madison?

But why not?

He'd loved Madison first. He'd planned to propose to her. Sheridan had even seen the ring. And the fact that he remained single all these years could mean he was still in love with her late sister-in-law. For all she knew, Madison could have remained in contact with Alek all this time. The very thought had her doubling over on the bed.

"Oh, honey." Her aunt swooped into the room and was suddenly beside her, wrapping Sheridan in her arms.

"You'll get through this," Aunt Eileen reassured her. "You have to do what you've always done. Take things one day at a time."

She rested her cheek on the older woman's shoulder. "Yeah, but I always had Jamie to hold me up."

"The way I remember it, it was always *you* holding *him* up. And your dad, too," her aunt said with an exasperated huff.

Sheridan sighed. "Thank goodness for you and Uncle Alan riding to the rescue."

Shortly after Sheridan's mom passed away from a long battle with leukemia, her father's cousin and her husband relocated from New York to help Ed Cobert raise his young children and run his popular bar. It took her father more than a year to recover from the loss of his wife. His son's prowess on the hockey rink was the bright spot that eventually got him out of bed in the mornings. It didn't take long for a young Sheridan to realize she needed to do everything she could to make Jamie's life as easy as possible so he could continue his success on the ice. It was the only way she knew how to patch her broken little family back together.

"I think Finn hates me," Sheridan whispered.

"Don't be silly. He doesn't hate you. He hates the situation.

You, of all people should be able to relate. It's easier for him to take it out on you because, deep down, he knows you'll always be there for him." She chuckled softly. "At least that's what the therapist used to say to me about your brother."

Sheridan sat up and swiped at her eyes. "Jamie was a beast that first year, wasn't he? I guess I know what I'll have to look forward to then."

"Then you're going to raise him?"

She turned to her aunt, dumbfounded. "Was there ever any question?"

Aunt Eileen sighed heavily. "You've spent nearly all your life caring for one Cobert male or another while giving up so much of your dreams."

It hadn't been that bad. Sure, when most young girls were at sleepovers or cheer camp, she'd been shadowing her brother from hockey rink to hockey rink, making sure he had whatever he needed to play well. But she never thought of it as "giving up" anything. She'd loved feeling useful.

Necessary.

By the time she got to high school, her brother was playing college hockey nineteen miles away at Dartmouth. Sheridan visited campus almost daily to drop off some home cooking or Jamie's laundry. There wasn't time for Friday night pizza dates or dance parties. Not that she cared. She had already found the guy for her: her brother's roommate, Alek Bergeron. She'd been a goner the first time he'd smiled his seductive grin at her.

It was hard to believe that Jamie and Alek had become instant friends. Their personalities couldn't have been more opposite. Where Jamie was carefree and spontaneous, Alek was thoughtful and dependable. He had to work twice as hard to be the player Jamie was. In the beginning, he was the dark to Jamie's light until they started to wear off on each other. Thanks to Alek's work ethic, Jamie focused more on honing his skills.

Alek, in turn, took himself less seriously, relaxing and enjoying life more.

They somehow made sharing a room work, too, despite Alek living by the rule that everything had its place. And that place was usually out of sight. On the other hand, Jamie's side of the room looked like a nursery of raccoons lived there. It was one area Alek refused to bend and the only source of tension in their relationship.

Well, until Jamie ran off and married Alek's girlfriend.

"You're finally living for you," Aunt Eileen continued. "Helping others while traveling the world. You have the freedom to go wherever the wind takes you with nothing tying you down."

Sheridan's therapist saw things a little differently, claiming that Sheridan refused to commit to any one place or person because she hadn't yet cut the apron strings with her brother. The good doctor pointed to her string of failed relationships as evidence.

She's going to have a field day with this new plot twist.

"Finn is going to need some stability while he adjusts," her aunt pointed out as if Sheridan didn't already know that. "You're a traveling nurse. You can't uproot him every time you take a new job. And you've finally got your dream assignment in Spain. You spent a year perfecting your Spanish. Are you really going to turn that down?"

"If not me, then who? Madison's mother was fifty-two—practically a senior citizen—when she adopted her. Even if she wasn't suffering from the early stages of dementia, she's in no shape to take on a little boy."

"Of course not," her aunt countered. "It wasn't her I had in mind."

Sheridan took in her aunt's raised eyebrow and shook her head. "You'd take him? Don't be silly. I doubt an eight-year-old boy would enjoy living at The Villages in Florida," she argued.

Her aunt laughed. "Puh-lease. He's his father's son. He'd have all the ladies doting on him."

"You can't be serious?"

"Of course not." Her aunt waved a hand around the room. "Uncle Alan and I would move back here. It's not like we haven't done it before."

"Don't take this the wrong way, but you were twenty years younger then. You don't really want to trade warm, sunny Florida for winters in New Hampshire any more than I do. And for all your talk about living one's life for themselves, you're not practicing what you preach." Sheridan stood from the bed. "No. Like you said, I go where the wind blows. And that wind is blowing me home to take care of my brother's little boy again. Nurses are in great demand. And if by some chance I can't find a job, it's not like I don't know how to run a bar."

"That's a lot for a young woman to take on. Finn won't be an adult for another ten years."

Her aunt's assertion that Sheridan would likely be doing it alone stung. "I can handle it," she said with more gusto than she felt.

Aunt Eileen sighed. "Well, we will always be an airplane ride away whenever you need backup."

"Promise you won't run off anytime soon, though, okay?"

"You're not getting rid of us that easily." Aunt Eileen gave her a warm smile and linked her arm through Sheridan's. "We are here as long as you need us." They walked toward the door.

"Good. The funeral is going to be difficult enough, but coming face-to-face with Alek Bergeron again may send me into a deeper tailspin for a few days."

Her aunt stopped in her tracks. "Alek? I didn't realize you two were still in touch."

"We aren't. Or weren't. I came in here to find Finn on the phone with him."

"How is that possible?"

"I don't know. But Finn was talking to him as if they were long-lost frat brothers or something."

"That's . . . an interesting development." She gave Sheridan's arm a gentle squeeze. "It will be good to see him, won't it?"

For you, maybe.

Sheridan never shared with anyone what she'd overheard Alek saying that long ago night. It was too embarrassing. Nine years later, she still got the sweats thinking about her nearly spectacular gaffe. At least he never knew about her crush on him.

Well, she wasn't a lovesick teenager any longer. And there would be a buffer of nearly a hundred people at tomorrow's service. She could put on her big girl panties to handle a couple of minutes in Alek Bergeron's orbit without giving anything away. She had to. Because the secret she had been keeping from him all this time would likely cause him to think even less of her than he already did.

THREE

A TSUNAMI of memories threatened to overwhelm Alek as he climbed the steps to the Barn Burner bar the following afternoon. He and Jamie had spent many evenings enjoying life within its doors. Not that Jamie's father let them get into too much trouble. Ed Cobert rode Jamie harder than their coaches when it came to conditioning and training for his time on the ice. Jamie's dad toiled for years in the minor league. He was determined his son would make it to the pros.

As if there was ever any doubt that Jamie would be drafted. The right winger was a natural talent who didn't require much training, just an ice rink to showcase his skills. If that wasn't enough, Jamie's smile and "aw shucks" demeanor would put Valentine to shame if the two had ever been on the same team. Everyone gravitated to Jamie, both on and off the ice.

Coming from Canada, Alek had been grateful to have a New Hampshire local for a roommate. Their easy friendship was solidified that first day when Jamie showed up in their dorm room with a signed photo of him with Ovechkin and the latest Xbox. The fact that his father owned a bar twenty minutes from campus was the icing on the cake.

"Are you alright?" his mother asked when Alek hesitated on the final step.

He patted the fingers she had wrapped around his biceps. "I'm good."

She gave his arm a squeeze, prodding him to move forward. He stalled a moment longer, however.

"Thank you for coming with me," he told her.

Not that he had any choice in the matter. Peri Bergeron was a force of nature who rarely took no for an answer. A celebrated interior designer, she let her clients think the choices were theirs. But Alek and his dad knew better.

Once she heard the news about Jamie and Madison, she insisted on meeting Alek in Boston and accompanying him to the funeral.

"Don't you need to stay with Dad?" Alek had protested.

"Your father is still perfectly capable of taking care of himself and will be for a very long time," she'd maintained. "Jamie was practically a second son to me. I can't not be there."

It was true. In typical Peri fashion, she'd taken Alek's motherless roommate under her wing, cheering as loudly for Jamie as Alek at every game his parents attended. She'd even chaperoned their summer in Europe, attending pro hockey camps following their freshman year.

"And Madison . . ." she continued. "Well, she was important to you both."

Alek never understood the way his mother always tiptoed around the subject of his ex. She'd never come out and said it, but he got the sense that both she and his sister believed Madison more guilty of betrayal than Jamie, which was out and out ridiculous. They were both guilty. But Jamie broke a sacred man code as old as time: Never poach your best friend's girl.

Still, he was glad to have his mum by his side today. As Sheridan predicted, coordinating flights into Boston had been tricky. Alek had to wait at the airport for his mum's plane to arrive from Ottawa, putting them behind from the get-go. The funeral service was already underway by the time they slipped into the back row of seats.

At the gravesite, Alek had purposely hung back behind the crowd. He was a little uneasy about meeting Jamie and Madison's son. Not to mention seeing Sheridan again after all this time.

His relationship with her had been collateral damage from the fallout of Jamie and Madison's marriage. It wasn't until Sheridan was no longer in his life that he realized how much having her around had meant to him.

Since Alek had redshirted his freshman year at Dartmouth, he still had two years of eligibility to play college hockey left when Jamie stole his girlfriend and turned pro. One of his junior league coaches convinced Alek to transfer to Minnesota, where he'd have the eyes of more pro scouts on him. Given everything that had gone down, transferring was a no-brainer. He was happy to cut ties with everything and everyone involved with Jamie, including his little sister, who was off to Syracuse for her freshman year of college anyway.

"We don't have to go in," his mother said, offering him an out.

He shook his head. Sheridan and Finn were innocent in everything that went down back then. They deserved his condolences after such a tragic loss. The pain of losing both parents at such a young age was unimaginable to Alek. And Sheridan . . . she continued to be the supportive rock he'd come to know, keeping her hand on her nephew's shoulder throughout the burial.

But who was holding on to her?

That concern was enough to get his feet moving. He held the door for his mother and followed her inside. He wasn't surprised at the size of the crowd. Everyone Jamie met immediately became a friend.

He was glad to see not much about the Barn Burner had changed since he had been there last. Hockey sticks signed by teammates of Ed Cobert and later Jamie hung crisscrossed on the walls. Multicolored string lights wound through the glasses lined up behind the bar. High-top tables surrounded the U-shaped bar, each with a view of one of the twelve televisions mounted from the ceiling. The doors to the patio, with its outside seating and river views were flung open to accommodate the overflow of guests. The replica of the Cup gifted to Jamie's father by a movie production company that once filmed a hockey film inside the Barn Burner still stood in its place of honor next to the beer taps.

And in the center of it all was Sheridan Cobert, doing what she always did, making sure everyone else was being taken care of. She smiled softly at an elderly woman dabbing at her eyes, eventually reaching over to comfort the woman with a pat on her shoulder. Some things would never change.

Except some things about his best friend's little sister *had* changed. Gone was the overdone makeup she wore during high school. The adolescent chubbiness of her cheeks had disappeared, too. She'd grown into a refined woman who looked comfortable in her own skin. Confident even. Her brown hair no longer hung to her waist. Instead, it cascaded softly to her shoulders. The color was lighter, too, with sun-kissed strands of blond making it shine even in the bar's low light.

Alek was suddenly desperate to catch her attention. To see if her hazel eyes still had those green flecks that sparkled like emeralds when she laughed. To find out what and who made her happy. To catch up on all the things he'd missed about her these past years.

He edged through the crowd surrounding her, only to be stopped in his tracks with a waist-high body check.

"You came!" a boy cried as he wrapped his arms tightly around Alek.

There was no doubt who the boy belonged to. His blond hair and blue eyes were dead ringers for Madison's. Anyone looking at Finn would have thought Jamie played no part in his conception.

He gently placed his hand on the boy's head. "You betcha. I promised I would be here."

Finn gazed up at him with shiny, red-rimmed eyes and a bashful smile. "Sheridan said you were just being nice, but I knew you'd come."

Something about Sheridan doubting him didn't sit well with Alek. He looked up to find her studying him, her expression unfathomable.

"Sheridan, sweetheart," his mother said as she pulled Jamie's sister into a hug. "It's been too long."

"My dad hung some of your sticks on the wall." Finn gripped Alek's hand and began to tug him away. "Come on, I'll show you."

"Sure, buddy. Let me say hello to your aunt first, then I'm all yours."

Alek's mom jumped in to run interference. "Can you show me where the ladies' room is, Finn?"

The boy looked like he wanted to refuse.

"I'll be right here," Alek assured him.

Finn exchanged a look with Sheridan, who nodded at her nephew. His shoulders slumped as he sighed and let go of Alek's hand.

"Yes, ma'am. It's in the back."

They walked away, leaving Alek and Sheridan staring at each other in awkward silence.

"How are you?" Alek finally asked before plowing his fingers through his hair. "I'm sorry. That was a ridiculous question. It's just . . ."

"I'm fine, Alek," she said softly. "Finn's emotions have been all over the place. You are the distraction we didn't know he needed. Thank you for coming."

A distraction? Thank you for coming? Seriously?

Nope. That wasn't working for him. He closed the distance between them, wrapping his arms around her and pulling her body against his. She didn't resist. She didn't relax either.

"Sheri," he whispered against her hair.

His plea seemed to do the trick because the tension seeped from her body, and she rested her cheek against his chest. She gulped a sigh as her fingertips gripped the back of his shoulders. Alek lowered his head and buried his face into her neck, inhaling her floral scent.

"It's okay. I've got you." He swayed side to side as he rubbed her back.

He had no idea how long they stood that way, and he really didn't care. Having Sheridan in his arms felt like coming home from a long, stressful journey. Like a missing piece was suddenly put back into its place.

"I'm back!"

Sheridan jerked out of Alek's arms at the sound of Finn's voice. The boy stepped between them, grabbing hold of Alek's wrist again.

"I want to show Alek around," Finn told Sheridan with a touch of rebelliousness in his tone. "And to introduce him to the guys on Dad's team."

Sheridan bore it with another one of her soft smiles as she caressed her nephew's cheek.

"I'm sure Alek would enjoy that."

Alek wasn't so sure. Not if it took him away from her.

Except Finn was hurting, too. And if "distracting" her nephew helped them both, Alek would do his part.

He brushed his knuckles against the back of her hand. "We'll catch up later?"

"Of course," she replied with a guarded smile before she turned to a couple and thanked them for coming.

"This way." Finn led him through the throng of people.

Several heads turned as he and Finn walked past. Alek nodded in acknowledgment while keeping pace with Jamie's son.

"See!" Finn pointed to a collage of photos on the wall. "That one is when you and Dad were in college."

Alek recognized the photo. It was him and Jamie right after they'd won the Ivy League championship junior year. Finn's voice rose as he gestured to another one.

"And that one is when you shot a goal into the empty net when you played on Tier One hockey for Canada, and Dad played for the US." Finn laughed. "Dad said he didn't try to deflect it when it went past. That way you'd know what it felt like to actually score a goal."

Of course Jamie was still making that claim all these years later. Alek bit back a grin as he shook his head. He didn't bother to point out that Finn's father hadn't even been on the ice at the time.

He glanced at another photo from his college days. This one of a smiling Madison standing between he and Jamie at center ice, her arms draped around both their shoulders. It was one of many pictures the three took together. In this one, Madison and Jamie were sharing a smile. Feeling like a fool, Alek wondered how often they did that without him noticing.

"Dad put up some from your pro days over here," Finn pointed out.

Alek tore himself away from the picture and wandered

over to another collage. Just as Finn said, a series of photos of him defending the Mayhem net hung on the wall. He was surprised to see them there, given that he wasn't drafted into the pros until after he'd cut off all communications with Jamie.

"Ed was very proud of you, too," a familiar voice said behind him.

He turned to find Jamie's Aunt Eileen standing with her hands braced on Finn's shoulders.

"Although Jamie added to it, obviously," she continued.

"Dad has a bunch of magazine clippings in a file in the office," Finn added. "He has *The Hockey News* when you were on the cover after you won the Vezina Trophy two years ago. It's in a frame on his desk. I'll go get it."

Finn dashed off before Alek could call him back. Not that his voice was working all that well right now. He shook his head in bewilderment.

"I'm not going to apologize for Jamie and Madison. What they did was . . ." Eileen sighed. "It was inexcusable and not what you deserved. But I honestly think Jamie was naive enough to believe you'd come around and he wouldn't have to choose between the two of you." She rested her palm against his biceps. "For what it's worth, I'm sorry about the way things went. Had I known they were going to come back from the draft in Las Vegas married, well . . ."

"Don't," Alek said as he pulled her in for a hug. "If I'm being honest, Jamie did me a favor. Playing pro hockey was a pipe dream for me. I always figured those games in college would be the end of my career." He dropped his arms and returned his gaze to the photo of the three of them. "But I was so damn pissed at Jamie that I worked my ass off to get a shot at being drafted so I could stop every one of his shots on goal when we played against each other."

Eileen chuckled. "It's a good thing he didn't know that because he would have been insufferable taking the credit."

Alek laughed along with her because she was right. He gestured in the direction where Finn was fighting his way through the crowd to get to the office.

"He's a good kid," he said to Eileen. "I'm surprised he's their only child."

Eileen's face dimmed. "Madison suffered from some nasty postpartum depression after he was born. She was afraid to be alone with him. Not very convenient when your husband is not home half the time."

"I can imagine. But at least they had you to help."

Jamie's aunt shook her head. "Not me. Sheridan dropped out of Syracuse and spent two years in Boston playing nanny."

"Of course she did," he murmured.

"And now she'll be dropping everything to take care of him again." Eileen sighed. "She's been applying for a position in Spain for a couple of years. She's finally gotten it, and this happens."

"Spain?"

Eileen nodded. "She's a traveling nurse. A good one, too."

A nurse. That fit. Something that felt a lot like pride coursed through him.

"And it's just her? She's not involved with anyone?" He wasn't sure why he asked. Except Sheridan deserved to have someone taking care of her for once. Especially now.

"She's never in one place long enough." Eileen sounded a tad disappointed before she arched an eyebrow. "And you? What's your excuse for remaining single?"

Alek shook his head. "We're not going there."

Eileen opened her mouth to argue when, lucky for him, Finn arrived with the shadow box containing the magazine.

"It's heavy," Finn announced with a gasp.

"Here. Let me hold it." Alek reached out to take the big wooden box from the boy's hands at the same time as Finn lost his grip. The glass-topped box shattered on the concrete floor.

The conversations around them stopped. Finn's bottom lip began to tremble as he choked out a sob. Alek dropped to his haunches to pick up the broken pieces.

"It's okay, bud," he tried to reassure the boy. "Accidents happen. This can be fixed."

"No," Finn wheezed. "It was Dad's, and now it's g-gone t-too."

Alek jumped to his feet when the wheezing turned into gasps. Finn patted his chest as he struggled to pull in air. Sheridan was by his side in an instant.

"Finn," she said much more calmly than Alek felt. "Look at me. Focus and breathe." She pressed an inhaler to his lips. "One, two, three."

The little boy wrenched his shoulders up and down as he inhaled the medicine.

"Again," Sheridan commanded, and they repeated the process.

When he was breathing somewhat normally once again, she leaned down and whispered something into his ear. Tears began to slowly roll down his face. She pressed her lips to his forehead when Eileen stepped in.

"Uncle Alan has the nebulizer set up in the kitchen," Eileen said quietly as she steered Finn in that direction. "Let's go get some juice in those lungs, and then maybe we can find a popsicle."

As soon as they were out of sight, Sheridan wrapped her arms around her middle and sighed heavily.

"He has asthma," she explained. "All of this is exacerbating it." She turned to face Alek, a tremulous smile on her lips. "He'll be fine."

Yes, but will you? he wanted to ask.

She wobbled on her high heels when she squatted down to clean up the broken shadow box. Alek reached for her elbow and towed her back up.

"I've got this," he told her.

"Like hell you do," a very unexpected voice announced beside him.

He turned to find his agent, Collin Slater, standing there. Collin was holding a large envelope in one hand.

"Don't even think about putting those million-dollar fingers anywhere near broken glass," Collin said before shaking his head at Sheridan. "Can you believe this guy?"

To Alek's utter dismay, Sheridan gave his agent the first real smile he'd seen on her lips since he arrived. He was pretty sure his chest was going to explode when she walked into Collin's arms and hugged him enthusiastically.

Collin closed his arms around her waist before inhaling her scent, the same way Alek had earlier. Alek shot him a death glare. Collin's eyes went wide before his lips began to twitch. The dickhead took his time untangling himself from Sheridan.

"My dad sends his regards," Collin said, reminding Alek that he and Jamie were both represented by Collin's dad, Marty, at one point.

Only Jamie was no longer a professional athlete who needed an agent.

"I would have been here sooner," Collin continued. "But I was in Australia negotiating with a tennis player we want to add to our rosters."

"She must be very pretty for you to go all the way down under during football season," Sheridan teased.

Clearly, she was familiar with his agent. For some reason, the idea didn't sit well with Alek.

Collin responded with a cat-ate-the-canary grin. "She does have incredibly well-toned, *looong* legs."

Sheridan made a sound that was more snort than laugh.

"For crying out loud, Collin," Alek protested.

His agent winked at Sheridan before waving the envelope in the air. "I come bringing information." His gaze landed on Sheridan, and he sobered up. "It seems your brother asked my father to draft a will for him a few days after his son was born."

Sheridan gasped.

"Based on your reaction, I assume you were unaware it existed. Did he and Madison have anything new drawn up since then?" Collin asked.

"No." Sheridan shook her head. "I'd hoped he might have something on his laptop, but somebody broke into the bar and stole Jamie's laptop before I could check."

"Are you kidding me? People suck." Alek shook his head in annoyance.

"Probably just some kids who took advantage after learning that he'd died," she said. "We checked with everyone we knew. But no one knew if Jamie had written one."

Her answer had Collin's shoulders slumping ever so slightly.

"A will definitely makes things easier." She let out a relieved-sounding sigh. "My insurance company is making me jump through hoops to get Finn added to my policy. His inhaler alone is five hundred dollars without insurance coverage."

Collin whistled softly.

Sheridan held out her hand. "Please tell your dad I said thank you. You can leave it with me. I'm sure you've got a sporting event to get to tonight."

Collin nodded. "Monday Night Football in Boston." He leveled a smirk at Alek. "Bergeron's favorite quarterback is playing."

Alek muttered a choice word as he shook his head in disgust.

"It means a lot that you came all this way to deliver it." Sheridan reached over to take the envelope from Collin, but he kept it firmly grasped between his fingers.

"Actually, the will stipulates the contents be read aloud by Jamie's representative, which is me. I hate to pull you away, but it shouldn't take long. Can we find a quiet place?"

"You go," Alek told her. "I've got this."

Collin rolled his eyes. "What did I just tell you, moron? No touching the broken glass. You're coming with me."

Alek was seconds away from popping off on his agent. "I was going to find one of the kitchen staff to help," he ground out.

"No can do," Collin insisted. "I need you in the room when I read the will."

"What the hell for?" Alek demanded.

Collin looked a little sheepish as he cleared his throat. "Jamie left you something."

FOUR

SO MUCH FOR *only spending a few minutes in Alek Bergeron's orbit.*

In fairness, that ship sailed the minute Sheridan allowed him to put his arms around her. Fool that she was, she leaned in and hugged him back. She blamed her weak moment on exhaustion. Pure and simple. Never mind how good it felt to have him holding her for those couple of moments. He was one of her few remaining connections to Jamie, and no matter how much she wanted to protect her heart by avoiding Alek, the pull was as strong as ever.

At least on her side.

She'd grown up enough not to kid herself any longer. Alek's hug was a gesture of sympathy. Nothing more. *He was simply acting as a surrogate big brother,* she reminded herself. *Don't read anything into it.* She wasn't going to make that mistake of opening her heart up to him again.

She led Collin and Alek to the small office behind the bar. As relieved as Sheridan was to know there was a will that would keep her from having to go to court to be declared Finn's guardian, she couldn't for the life of her imagine what her brother would have left Alek. The pair hadn't spoken in nearly a decade.

No one objected when Peri Bergeron and Aunt Eileen slipped into the office behind them.

"Finn?" Sheridan asked her aunt.

"He's fine," Aunt Eileen reassured her. "His breathing is back to normal. Alan is keeping him occupied in the kitchen. What's this I hear about a will?"

Collin took the seat behind the desk. He gestured at Sheridan to take the only other chair in the room. She shook her head. Her body already felt like a wrung-out dishrag. As it was, she was holding it together by sheer force of will. If she sat down now, there was no guarantee she wouldn't slide onto the floor and never get back up. She propped her shoulder against the file cabinet instead.

"I'm good right here. Read away," she urged Collin. "You've got a two-hour trip back to Boston to make. I don't want to keep you any longer than necessary."

Alek held the chair out for Aunt Eileen as Collin pulled out several folded sheets of paper from the envelope. He cleared his throat.

"This will was executed several days after Finn's birth," Collin began. "Obviously, Jamie left everything to Finn should something happen to him and Madison. But as we all know, circumstances changed dramatically a few years later with Jamie's injury and the loss of your father."

"My father left the bar to Jamie and the house to me. I didn't need it, so I let Jamie and Madison live there," Sheridan interrupted. "Finn should be in good shape financially."

Collin opened his mouth only to abruptly close it again. He swiped at his brow before continuing. "Actually, he sold the bar to a restaurant consortium two years ago. They kept him on as an employee because his status as a local celebrity kept people coming through the doors."

Sheridan suddenly wished she'd opted for the chair.

"What?!" Aunt Eileen cried.

Collin offered up a sheepish shrug. "The pandemic was hard on a lot of places like this. And a young family has . . . expenses."

Aunt Eileen shot to her feet. "He shouldn't have done that! This bar has been in my family for nearly a hundred years. Passed down from son to son. The house was paid for. He could have asked Sheridan to pull some money out of it. She wouldn't have refused." She looked over at Sheridan. "Right?"

She was suddenly feeling sick to her stomach. "Jamie had already taken money out of it," she explained to her aunt, hating that her family's dirty laundry was being aired in front of Alek and his mom, neither of whom likely ever had a money issue in their entire lives. "Four years ago. Jamie insisted on paying off my student loans. He said he would have done it if he was still playing. We co-signed for a home equity loan. Jamie was making the payments. He wanted me to start my career debt free."

"I don't understand. Jamie had over a million dollars in the bank before he was injured," her aunt argued. "Between that, the income from the bar, and a free place to call home, he had more than enough to pay for your nursing school and still live comfortably in this small town." She glared at Collin as if this was all somehow the agent's fault. "Please tell us the idiot had a life insurance policy."

Collin nodded. "Finn is the beneficiary of a hundred-thousand-dollar policy."

"Lucky for Finn, his asshole father hadn't figured out a way to grab the cash from that yet. Otherwise, he would have screwed his own son the way he screwed over his sister," Alek said, his tone sharp enough to cut ice. "And me."

He was wrong. Jamie hadn't screwed over Sheridan. He was simply being Jamie trying to repay her for caring for Finn when he was a baby. Trying to step into their father's shoes he never intended to have to fill so soon in life. Jamie never figured he'd need a head for money, either. As for the part about Jamie screwing Alek over, well, he was being unfair there, too. Mainly because he didn't know all the facts.

And whose fault is that?

Alek took hold of his mother's elbow and steered her toward the door. "I can't listen to any more of this. Whatever he left me, I don't want it."

"It's not that simple, Alek," Collin said. "He left you his son."

"WHAT THE EVER-LOVING *FUCK*, COLLIN?" Alek shouted.

He lunged toward his agent, but Collin was already out of his chair, reaching for Sheridan, who'd gone deathly white. She swayed on her heels before Collin steadied her. He gently led her to his empty chair and guided her down into it. Alek's mum quickly uncapped a water bottle as she knelt by Sheridan's side. The only action Alek seemed capable of was dragging both hands through his hair. It was either that or punch the filing cabinet.

Dammit to hell, Jamie.

"Trust me, I'd kick Jamie's skinny ass if I could, but he's not here," Collin spoke quietly to Sheridan. "Don't shoot the messenger." He leveled a glare at Alek. "This can all be worked out in the courts."

"I-I don't understand," Sheridan whispered.

Her aunt stood on one side, rubbing Sheridan's shoulder,

while his mum remained on the other side, gently stroking Sheridan's arm. Alek felt an overwhelming urge to shove both women away and comfort Sheridan himself.

"He left you each a letter." Collin dug back into the envelope and pulled out two folded sheets of paper. He held one out to Alek, but for some reason, Alek couldn't make his arm move to reach for it.

"This is ridiculous," he said. "This is some sick prank Jamie thought up after getting wasted when he realized fatherhood was for life."

"Alek," his mother chastised him. She rose to her feet and took the letter from Collin.

"You know my dad, Alek," Collin insisted. "He wouldn't have followed through with this if he didn't think Jamie was of sound mind."

His mum arched an eyebrow at him in question. When Alek still didn't move, she unfolded the paper and cleared her throat.

"Ice-Berg," she began. "If you're reading this, then I guess I'm no longer here. I hope that you've finally answered my phone calls by now. I hope that you've forgiven Madison and me for falling in love."

Alek rocked back on his heels as if Jamie had physically punched him.

"It wasn't supposed to happen." His mother's voice cracked when she continued. "But I hope you've come around and can see how happy we are. Or *were*, as the case may be."

He swore under his breath when Aunt Eileen gasped out a sob before covering her mouth with her hand. He still couldn't find the strength to pull the letter back from his mum, though.

Mum sucked in a breath. "I'll bet you're thinking this is some kind of messed up joke. Why would the guy you hate leave his kid for you to raise? I'll tell you why. Because, even three days into fatherhood, I want the best for my son. And you, my friend, are the best. My dad barely managed to survive after my mother passed. I can't leave Finn in his care. God knows if Ed will survive this."

His mother paused for a moment as she glanced over at Sheridan.

"And leaving him for Sher to raise is out of the question."

Sheridan slammed her lips together and wrapped her arms around her stomach.

"You were right," his mum read on. "I've been taking advantage of my little sister's tender heart all this time. It was selfish to depend on her to do everything for me. I should have forced her to live her own life years ago."

"Amen," Aunt Eileen murmured.

Alek couldn't tear his eyes off Sheridan. Her normally expressive eyes had gone flat as if she'd mentally checked out of this conversation. He wished he possessed the ability to do that, too.

"So tag, you're it, Ice-Berg," Mum continued. "You're the only dude I know who will be the perfect father and role model for my son. Even if we haven't made up and you still hate me, you'd never take it out on Finn. I know you too well. Your honor is bigger than your bluster. You grew up in the perfect family, with a pair of great role models." Mum's voice cracked again. "Even if Finn turns out to be half the man you are, I know I've made the right choice. You probably won't believe this, but I love you, man."

Alek's temple was beginning to throb. He dragged his gaze away from Sheridan, afraid of what she might see in his eyes. Anger. Confusion. And something else he couldn't quite name.

His mother carefully folded the letter and tried to hand it back to Collin. The agent gestured for her to keep it. She glanced over at Alek before tucking it into her bag.

"Shall I read yours?" Sheridan's aunt asked her.

Sheridan's chin bobbed slightly. Her aunt heaved an anxious-sounding sigh, then began.

"If you're reading this, you probably want to rip me a new one. But hear me out, Sher. A very wise man has been riding my ass for several years about how I take advantage of you. About how I let you pick up all the tasks Mom would have done when you should be out enjoying your teenage years. Well, that ends here."

You picked a fine time to listen to me, you jackass, Alek thought.

"I know no one will love Finn like you will. Full stop," Eileen continued reading. "Like me, he'll be a better man for having you as his mama bear. But not if you haven't taken the time to discover who *you* are first. You're too young to be saddled with raising another Cobert hellion."

Her aunt nodded vigorously as she read on.

"I haven't told you this enough, but I love you, Sher. I wouldn't have made it to the top of the game without you by my side. I'm so grateful to have you for a sister." Her aunt swiped at a tear rolling down her cheek. "Hopefully, you will never see this letter. Once you're settled into your own life with your own happy family, I'll change this caveat. For now, though, I'll rest easier knowing Finn will be taken care of should anything happen to Madison and me. I have no doubt that together, you and Alek will give my son the very best life."

"I knew it!" Finn cried from the doorway of the office. "Dad promised you would take care of me."

An anguished sound escaped Sheridan's lips as her nephew charged into the room and stood before Alek. The color was back in his cheeks and his blue eyes danced with delight.

"I don't remember going to my dad's games when he

played," Finn gushed. "But now I'll get to see all of yours. Are we going to live at your house?"

It felt like all the air had been sucked out of the room. Probably because everyone inside it was holding their breath. Alek met his mother's gaze above Finn's head. She looked genuinely stricken. She opened and closed her mouth several times, but no pearls of wisdom emerged.

He looked back down at Finn. The little boy's cheeks began to lose some of their rosiness as the moment stretched. Alek's temple began to throb harder.

You'd never take it out on Finn. I know you too well. Your honor is bigger than your bluster.

The words were out of Alek's mouth before he could stop them.

"Yeah, Finn. You are going to live at my house."

Sheridan's groan of dismay was drowned out by Finn's whoop of excitement.

"Yes!" He hugged Alek's waist. "My dad was right. You are the best."

The reality of what he'd just done made Alek's throat grow thick.

Finn dropped his arms and headed to the door. "I have to tell Hattie we are going to live in Milwaukee." He spun back around to face Alek. "Oh, I almost forgot. Do you have a backyard?"

The question caught him off guard. "Um, yeah, sure. Big enough to build a small rink if that's what you want."

"Cool!"

Alek felt the weight of everyone's eyes on him as soon as Finn was out the door. But the only ones he was interested in belonged to Sheridan. And they were shooting daggers at him.

"How could you encourage him?" she demanded as she unsteadily rose from her chair.

Her aunt moved to placate her. "Hold on a second, Sheridan. Maybe this isn't such a bad idea in the short term."

Sheridan recoiled at her aunt's perceived betrayal. Eileen ignored her, turning to fix Alek with a hard look.

"I assume you have health insurance?"

"Of course."

The older woman nodded. "Good. Finn needs refills of his asthma meds."

"I'll call our GM and get it taken care of right away," Alek told her.

"No!" Sheridan shouted. She turned to Collin. "You said this could easily be fixed in the courts. How do I make that happen?"

"Sheri, honey. That will take some time to sort out," her aunt said. "We need to deal with the here and now."

"I'm not handing over my nephew to him." She flailed her arm in Alek's direction. "Not to someone who thinks this is a joke." She aimed her next words directly at Alek. "Because it's not a joke to me. None of this is. And that little boy is all I have left."

Alek was pretty sure his heart stopped when her voice cracked.

"I'll take care of his asthma meds," she continued. "And I'll take care of Finn."

"How?" her aunt demanded. "You can't take him to Spain. Not with his guardianship all messed up. Where will you live while that gets straightened out? The house belongs to the bank. And this bar . . ." Eileen actually growled. "Well, any income from it is lost to you and Finn, thanks to your idiot brother." She shook her head as she mumbled Jamie's name and what sounded like a few choice expletives. "You should take Alek up on his offer. If for no other reason than Finn seems happy with the situation."

"And why wouldn't he be?" Sheridan cried. "Alek just promised him an ice rink, for crying out loud! How am I supposed to compete with that?"

Eileen sighed. "This isn't a competition, sweetheart. It's the wind blowing a little course correction for you. But it's only a temporary one. Just until the storm passes."

Sheridan huffed a sigh as she sank back down into the chair.

"Would you mind giving Sheridan and me the room?" Alek asked.

The only person who looked like they might object was Sheridan. Instead, she crossed her arms defensively and remained where she was. Her aunt pressed a kiss to the top of her head before following Collin to the door.

Mum gave his biceps a squeeze. There was an odd look in her eyes. Almost as if she was proud of him. At least she didn't think Alek was as crazy as he felt at the moment.

When the door closed behind them, he scooted the second chair closer to where Sheridan sat as if she were wrapped in a strait-jacket. He cautiously lowered himself into it so he was facing her.

"I should have consulted with you first," he began. "I apologize."

His words seemed to take away some of the tension in her shoulders.

Alek sighed. "I got caught up in the moment. He's been through a lot, and I couldn't . . . let him down."

She sighed softly and nodded. "Get used to it. He has Jamie's charm, and he knows how to use it."

He chuckled. "I've been warned."

Her eyes were shiny when she finally met his. "Are you really serious about this?"

"I have a big house. I'm there only half the time. It seems like a solid plan while Collin gets the guardianship sorted out."

"And once he does? What happens then? How do I tear Finn away from hockey games and his own private ice rink?"

Alek dragged his fingers through his hair. "Yeah. I probably should have given this more thought."

She snorted. "You and Jamie both."

The harsh way she said it surprised him. He didn't like being lumped in with Jamie. This wasn't Alek's fault. Her brother was still jerking all of them around from the grave.

"One year." Again, the words were out before he even registered thinking them. "You and Finn stay with me through the end of the season. Collin will have all the guardianship crap sorted out by then. That should be enough time for Finn and me to build a solid relationship. One that will be strong no matter where life takes us. I'll be the role model Jamie wanted me to be."

She snorted again. This time, her censure stung.

"Let me do this. I want to help. And not only with Finn." He started to reach for her hand, but the stiff way she held herself had him jerking it back. "I want to help you, too, Sheridan. You were a big part of my college years. Jamie's wasn't the only life you made easier. Hell, you were practically a little sister to me, too."

She jumped from the chair and stormed toward the door. "I can take care of myself," she said without bothering to turn around.

Alek stood as well. Everything inside him was screaming *do not let her walk out the door.*

"No one is doubting that," he argued. "You're the most capable person I know. But don't you think it would be nice not to have to be everyone's keeper for once in your life? Even if it's only for a year?"

She paused with her hand on the doorknob.

"If you can't do it for yourself, at least do it for Finn." Alek was playing dirty pool. The Sheridan Cobert he once knew *always* sacrificed her happiness for the men in her family. It was in her DNA. As much as he'd wanted her to change, he took a shot that she hadn't.

Her shoulders bunched up as she drew in a slow, deep breath. She pressed her forehead to the door. "Finn is the only reason I'm agreeing to this absurd arrangement."

A rush of relief coursed through him. "Thank you."

"Mm-hmm," she replied before pulling the door open.

A dog was barking excitedly somewhere inside the bar. And not a small dog, from the sound of it.

"Someone brought a dog to a funeral?" Alek shook his head. He shouldn't be surprised by the idiotic things people did.

Sheridan swiveled her chin back in his direction. There was no mistaking the wily smile on her face. "That's Hat Trick. Better known as Hattie. She goes where Finn goes."

Shit.

A ROAD SIGN announcing the Wisconsin border in thirty-five miles flashed by the window of the leased SUV Sheridan drove. Beside her, Finn bounced up and down in the passenger seat as if their destination was a Disney theme park and not the home of the man his father had betrayed.

Not that her nephew knew anything about that. Jamie, it seemed, had built up Alek in Finn's mind so that he was practically one of the Avengers. No doubt her brother was living vicariously through the hockey accomplishments of his former roommate. It was also glaringly obvious that Jamie still cherished the friendship he and Alek once had despite the way their relationship imploded.

Sheridan's stomach churned with the guilt that had been persistently gnawing at her since her brother's death. She'd honestly thought she was doing the right thing for everyone involved all those years ago. It was true what they said about hindsight being twenty-twenty.

"I can't believe we are almost in Milwaukee." He gave a little whoop of excitement.

"Neither can I," she mumbled to herself.

The past two weeks had whizzed by in a parade of blurry memories. The only part that stood out was the hundreds of times she'd asked herself why she'd agreed to this absurd plan. An entire hockey season living with the temptation that was Alek Bergeron? She needed to have her head examined.

For some reason, she seemed to be the only one who thought the situation was a disaster in the making. Aunt Eileen and Uncle Alan had practically pushed her and Finn out of town.

"We'll pack everything up and put it into storage for the time being," Aunt Eileen offered. "You and Finn don't need the added emotional burden of that task. A change of scenery will do you both some good. Especially if it's somewhere that isn't laced with memories."

"Aren't you the one who said Finn's routine shouldn't be changed?" Sheridan had accused.

Her aunt's replying smile was a tad patronizing. "Too late now. That horse is already out of the barn." Her face softened. "And Finn really seems energized by this change. Isn't it better for him to have something different to focus on right now?"

Do it for Finn.

Sheridan hated how Alek had used those simple words to manipulate her into agreeing to this scheme. He knew no scenario in this world would have her abandoning her nephew. Even worse, he had no qualms about hitting her in her weak spot. Which was how she found herself on the home stretch of a thousand-mile drive west to Wisconsin, where she was going to spend the next months carefully guarding her heart.

And my secrets.

As if sensing her unease, Hattie leaned forward from the back seat and rested her big head on Sheridan's shoulder. Biting back a snicker, she recalled the shock on Alek's face when he realized Finn came with a dog. His mother had quickly thrown up a smokescreen, cooing and snuggling with the big dog while Alek adopted a poker face.

"You've always maintained the reason you aren't a dog person is because you've never really been around one," Peri had said. "Well, here is your chance."

Alek responded with an unintelligible grunt, likely trying to figure out a way to retract his offer to take them in. Sheridan was disappointed when he didn't come up with one. She wasn't surprised, though. As Jamie said, Alek was a man of honor. He'd put up with a dog invading his space if he must.

Fortunately for him, Hattie's only care in the world was Finn's happiness. She would be a good dog. Sheridan would also be on her best behavior. The way she figured it, sharing the same space with Alek would be a whole lot easier if there wasn't any drama.

"It looks like both of us will be flying under the radar for a while, sweet girl," she murmured to the dog.

"You're going to love it, Hattie." Finn scratched the dog behind the ear. "Alek's house is a billion times bigger than our old one. And wait until you see the yard. It's *massive*."

"How would you know?"

"Alek gave me a tour on FaceTime."

Of course he did.

Sheridan didn't have the heart to take Jamie's phone away from his son. It was paid through the end of the year, so she'd let him keep it. Not without installing a host of parental protections first, though. As far as she knew, Alek was the only person Finn used it to communicate with.

That makes one of them.

There had been a lot of details to work out between Alek and her these past two weeks. Sheridan was proud that she'd managed to keep their interactions to the digital realm. The less she heard his raspy voice or his long Os, the better. It was bad enough she couldn't stop thinking about the feel of his arms wrapped around her at the funeral. Or the sound of his heart beating beneath the cheek she'd had pressed against his chest.

Which made her a fool.

Let me step in as your spare big brother and take care of you.

He'd made it perfectly clear she was nothing more than a little sister to him. Multiple times, in fact. So why the heck wasn't her body getting the message? If she was going to survive the season, she needed to get a firm grip on her feelings. And fast.

Damn you, Jamie.

This was all his fault. Anger toward her brother was not something she was used to feeling. She'd thought they were pretty tight. Clearly, she was wrong. He'd been deliberately keeping things from her. Life-altering things. Not the least of which was him selling the bar. His bank accounts were nearly empty. The mortgage on the house was months behind. None of it made any sense. Where was all his money?

Not that she wanted it for herself. But it would have been a whole lot easier to refuse Alek's offer had Finn not had to vacate his home. Or walk away from their family's legacy.

She wished she could talk to her brother one last time. To find out if this was really what he intended. Or maybe to strangle him. She couldn't make up her mind. Her shoulders slumped as she cursed him again for putting all of them in this predicament. Alek was as much an innocent victim here as she and Finn.

Yet despite everything, Jamie's best friend had stepped up, no questions asked. As her brother suspected, Alek was doing the right thing for a kid he'd never met. And that should count for something. It certainly made her adore him even more. The least she could do was get over herself and do her part to make this situation work.

Sure, he'd never think of her in quite the same way she felt about him, but that wasn't his fault. And a girl could do a whole lot worse than having Alek Bergeron in her corner. Finn was the common denominator that joined Alek and her together. Possibly forever. Friends would have to be good enough for her. Resolved, she loosened the tense grip she had on the steering wheel.

"Alek even has a gym and a movie theater," Finn continued to gush.

She glanced over at him. His enthusiasm for their move continued to baffle her. It was as if he'd closed the door on the life he had with his parents and refused to think about it ever again. Her therapist didn't seem all that concerned about his attitude, however.

"Delayed grief affects twenty percent of kids Finn's age," Dr. Rose explained. "He is coping by idealizing this new relationship with Alek to recapture a lost sense of safety or love."

"It can't be that simple. Surely, he won't feel that way forever?" Sheridan had asked.

"Maybe. Maybe not. It's hard to say. Everyone is different. But rest assured his grief will manifest itself in other ways. You'll have to be ready for them."

Dr. Rose gave Sheridan the names of two grief counselors in the Milwaukee area who worked exclusively with children. Sheridan interviewed them both, choosing the therapist who had offices in the hospital where she had taken a part-time nursing job. She'd be working in the ER of a small suburban hospital near Alek's home.

Working in emergency medicine was generally not her first choice of assignments but Sheridan needed the hours to keep her license up to date. Especially since the gig in Spain would be available again next fall. Her supervisor at the travel nurse agency promised she'd have first crack at it. By then, she hoped

Finn would have had his fill of hockey goalies and would be ready for another new adventure.

Her primary reason for taking a part-time job, however, was self-preservation. There was no way she could sit around Alek's house all day. She'd go crazy. Especially on the days when the Mayhem were in town, and Alek was wandering the halls. They could be friendly roommates, but there was no reason for her to torture herself.

"Gunner Ferguson said I need to wear one of Alek's jerseys to the game tomorrow night," Finn announced. "Isn't that cool?"

"So cool."

Alek had somehow finagled to get Finn not only into a private school where some of the other Mayhem players enrolled their kids but also into the same second-grade class as the son of the Mayhem's starting forward. Gunner's mom, Claire, reached out right away, suggesting the boys video chat. Claire was a genius because the boys were instant BFFs after the call. Sheridan was begrudgingly grateful to Alek for ensuring Finn's transition to his new school would be smooth.

Claire turned out to be a godsend, too. She not only recommended a pediatrician who specialized in asthma but also offered to help carpool the boys to school. It turned out she was on staff at the same hospital where Sheridan would be working.

"Most of the other WAGs don't work," she'd confided to Sheridan during one of their video chats during the past week. "We go to Pilates together a few mornings a week as a group. Everyone is very nice. But sometimes it's good to get away from the world of hockey and do something for yourself, you know?"

"Except I'm not a wife or a girlfriend of a player," Sheridan told her. "It wouldn't be right for me to join them at Pilates or anything else."

"That's ridiculous," Claire had argued. "You're part of the Mayhem family. Granted, your situation is unusual, but you have as much right to be a part of the WAGs as anyone else. It's a non-issue. You'll see. Everyone is already excited to meet you."

That piece of information had left Sheridan more than a little intimidated. She'd never really had close friends. Growing up, the hours after school were spent doing chores at home or at the bar so her ailing mother could get some much-needed rest. Once her mother was gone, her dad and Jamie demanded all her attention. There wasn't any time for a BFF, much less a squad of girlfriends.

She'd hoped college would provide her the opportunity to flex her wings and find friends. But then Finn came along, and Madison needed her help. Night school didn't exactly provide the same interactions as living in a dorm on campus. And it wasn't like she was involved with the WAGs in Boston. That was Madison's territory. It was only a matter of time before the Mayhem WAGs would out her for the poser she was.

"I'm bringing my skates, too," Finn was saying. "Gunner said there is a mini rink in the family lounge. And sometimes they go on the ice after the game."

"We'll see," she said about more than Finn taking a few laps around the ice.

Finn's phone rang.

"I'll bet that's Alek." He pulled it from his backpack and quickly answered it. "Hello?" After a moment, he repeated himself. "Hello?" Shrugging, he hung up and put the phone back into his backpack.

"Nobody was there?" she asked.

"Nah. Dad gets a lot of calls where no one is there."

"That's odd."

Finn shrugged again. Sheridan made a mental note to check the phone and block those callers when her nephew yelled in delight.

"Yay! We are in Wisconsin. Almost there, Hattie."

The dog nuzzled his shoulder. Sheridan mentally braced herself before repeating her mantra for the next year.

I'm doing this for Finn.

ALEK TRIED NOT to squirm beneath the shrewd gaze of the Mayhem's owner. At thirty-five, Maxim Kellogg could have been a contemporary of most of the players on his team. Except for the fact the man was heir to a billion-dollar beer company, and he signed their paychecks. One-on-ones with Kellogg weren't exactly the norm.

The Mayhem were six days into the new season, and they'd already dropped their first three games. The season was long, and it wasn't unusual for any team to start out slow, especially since the Mayhem had yet to play a game on their home ice. But it was hard to ignore that Alek had allowed eleven goals to slip into the net during that time. Not a good look for a team hoping to make it to the finals.

Coach and the team's GM weren't too stressed about it. Both men told Alek to shake it off. Apparently, Kellogg preferred to address the situation head-on. Probably because the guy had signed Alek to the second-highest contract for any goalie in the league. In the year since, Alek's play hadn't exactly lived up to all the zeros in his paycheck. The whispers on sports talk radio at the end of last season were growing louder with the team's less-than-stellar start to this year.

Alek couldn't deny that the distractions of the past two weeks had played a role. Not an hour went by when he didn't question his rash decision. But then he'd hear his mother's voice reading Jamie's letter.

You're the only dude I know who will be the perfect father and role model for my son.

When he should have been focusing on his play, he'd been juggling all the details associated with Finn and Sheridan moving in with him. Including having a fence installed to contain a dog the size of a pony. Of course, the boy and his dog were attached at the hip. Foisting her off on a relative or friend wasn't an option.

Finn insisted the dog was well-mannered. Apparently, his father had trained her himself. Leave it to Jamie to have a pet that's more beast than fur-baby. Alek clenched his fists tightly.

Bottom line: His piss-poor play between the pipes was all his former best friend's fault.

Kellogg would probably think poorly of Alek for blaming a dead guy, though. Thankfully, his long-term houseguests were arriving today. He'd get them all settled in tonight, then Alek would turn things around in the Mayhem's home opener tomorrow.

Never one to mince words, Kellogg got right to the point. "Are you sure taking on a kid right now is what you want to do?" he inquired over his steepled fingers.

"Absolutely," Alek replied.

The word rolled off his tongue a lot easier than it had the week before. Kellogg wasn't the first person to ask him that over the past ten days. Since the funeral, Alek had been fielding the same question from his family, his teammates, and himself.

"If you're concerned this will impact my play, don't be." Alek tried to project as much confidence as he could, despite both men knowing there were no guarantees in life.

"Your play is the least of my worries. The season is barely a week old. And you're one of the best in the league."

The owner's reassurance had Alek's shoulders relaxing.

"Raising a child isn't something to be taken lightly," Kellogg continued. "They should always take priority. Sometimes even before hockey."

"Nothing about my work ethic is going to change. You have my word." Alek may be getting new roommates, but the goal wasn't changing. The Mayhem were winning the Cup this season, no matter what it took.

Kellogg shot him a look that clearly said "we'll see about that."

Alek was aware the man was speaking from experience. He had grown up the bastard son of the team's original owner, Norm Clarkson. Old Man Clarkson had spent three decades ignoring the existence of his "love child," only recognizing him months before his death when he gifted him his hockey team and a percentage of his beer company. According to the gossip, Kellogg almost turned his inheritance down out of spite.

The Mayhem players were glad he didn't. Kellogg was a fair and generous owner. Most of all, he wanted to win as much as Alek and his teammates did. It didn't hurt that his half-siblings owned two of Milwaukee's other professional sports teams. The competition among the family was rumored to be fierce, not to mention great fodder for the media. As a result, Kellogg spared no expense getting the talent and the facilities needed to ensure the Mayhem were always competitive within the league—and his newfound family.

"It's a responsibility I'm taking very seriously," Alek assured him.

Kellogg nodded. "In that case, he's a lucky boy to have you." The phone on his desk rang, putting an end to their discussion. "Whatever you or Finn need, we've got your back."

Alek waved his thanks as he stepped out of the owner's office. When he closed the door behind him, he heaved a big sigh of relief.

Gus, Valentine, and Picard surrounded the desk of Kellogg's executive assistant, Lori Lewis.

"Did you see the dessert menu?" Picard was saying to her.

Lori leafed through the leather-bound menu. "They look amazing. Sign me up to do a tasting with the pastry chef before you open the restaurant."

Picard winked at her. "Play your cards right, and I might name one after you."

She arched an eyebrow at him. "You should know by now your flirting doesn't work on me, Zachary. I'm not one of your adoring groupies who mail their panties to the arena."

Properly chastised, Picard carefully took the menu from her and returned it to its box.

"You've put a lot of thought into this business venture. I'm proud of you," she continued, her tone a bit softer. "Take it as seriously as you take your game, and there's no way it won't be a huge success."

Alek joined them. "As long as he's not doing the cooking. Dude can't even make a grilled cheese without burning it."

"Har, har," Picard said. "You're talking about the next big thing in steak houses. People will be driving up from Chicago for our food." He glanced at his watch. "Speaking of which, we need to get going. The first chef is interviewing tonight, and we've got food to taste, my friends. Dinner is on me."

Crap. Alek had totally forgotten that was this evening.

"Erm, I'm afraid I'm going to have to bail. Finn is arriving shortly."

Picard opened his mouth, likely to give him a hard time, before he closed it again. He nodded instead. Like the Mayhem's owner, his teammates were all quick to support his decision to bring Jamie's son to Milwaukee. Picard had played with Jamie on various US teams throughout the years. He was as shocked by Jamie's death as everyone else.

Offering up a sympathetic smile, Lori handed him a folder adorned with the Mayhem logo. "Here are your additional family passes for Finn and his caregiver."

Alek bowed slightly. "You are a queen."

She stood from her desk. "And don't you boys forget it."

That was unlikely to happen. The woman had become the Mayhem's undisputed team mom the moment she walked into the facility on her first day, anticipating the needs of the players and their families often before they did. Whenever anyone had a problem, Lori was their first—and usually last—stop to get it resolved.

"Did you say caregiver?" Valentine interjected. "Now that's what I'm talking about. The nanny just went to the top of the list of prospective"—he made air quotes with his fingers—"Brides to Melt the Ice-Berg."

"Not this again." Alek glared at his teammate.

Valentine was pushing ahead with his cockamamie scheme to find him a wife. During the team's first night on the road, he'd made a game of querying everyone associated with the Mayhem, fishing for prospective brides. He added the women's names to a spreadsheet he carried around on his phone. One of the broadcasters even added his granddaughter—who was barely sixteen.

Alek hated being at the center of such a ridiculous exercise, especially since they were supposed to be getting their shit together for the season.

"There's no nanny on top of any list because there is. No. List," he told them. "And no nanny, either. Finn's aunt is coming along to take care of him."

Valentine groaned. "One with fat ankles and sagging boobs, I presume."

Alek bit back a grin because neither described Sheridan. Her ankles were perfect, and her boobs, well, they weren't centerfield worthy, but they'd definitely felt full and perky pressed against his chest when he'd embraced her at Jamie's funeral. Not that he should be noticing his former best friend's little sister's boobs.

Or any other part of her.

Lori pressed a sticky note to the folder containing the family passes. "This is my daughter's contact info. She's thirteen and has completed all the babysitting classes. Hannah goes to the upper school where Finn will be attending. She can pitch in if you ever need afterschool care." She picked up a tablet and stylus and headed in the direction of her boss's office. "Enjoy your night off, gentleman. Try not to stuff yourselves at the tasting."

"Did you know she has a kid?" Valentine asked Picard as the two men walked away.

Picard shook his head. "Honestly, I've always pictured her as the Mary Poppins type who kept everything she owned in a satchel."

Valentine smacked Picard on the shoulder. "Who made a better Mary Poppins? Julie Andrews or Emily Blunt?"

"Not even a fair contest. Emily Blunt is *so* much hotter," Picard replied as they drifted out of earshot.

Gus bit back a chuckle before turning to Alek. "Everything okay in there with Kellogg?"

"Yeah." Alek nodded. "He wanted to make sure I know what I'm getting into."

"And do you?"

His best friend's question felt like it was coming out of left field. "You were the first person to tell me I'm doing the right thing."

"You are. With Finn. But what about with the kid's aunt?"

What the hell?

"It's not like I can take care of Finn on my own, even if Sheridan would let him out of her sight. What exactly are you implying?"

Gus sighed. "It's that Claire and Sheridan have been video chatting." He lowered his voice. "Valentine and Picard are going to want to put her on the top of their own lists once they find out she doesn't have fat ankles. Or saggy boobs."

Hell, has Gus been checking out Sheridan's rack?

"Over my dead body," he ground out through his tight jaw.

Gus's eyebrows shot up. "Ah, so it's like that, huh?"

"No!" Alek glanced around the office when he realized he was shouting. He dragged in a calming breath. "It's not like that with Sheridan. She's Jamie's kid sister, for crying out loud. I don't think of her in any other way. End of story."

It was a wonder his joggers didn't burst into flames. He'd been thinking of her in lots of other ways since seeing her again. Most of them involved her naked beneath him, her hair spread out on his pillow and her legs wrapped around his waist. It was an insane fantasy, though. They may have parted as enemies, but Alek would never take advantage of his former best friend's sister.

Because that would be a crime as bad as Jamie's.

"Hmm." Gus did that thing where he practically made his lips disappear as he nodded in approval. "You're sticking to your principles. That's good to know. Of course, that's a whole lot easier said than done once she's living under your roof." He patted Alek on the back. "I wish you luck, my friend."

"I don't need any luck," Alek replied to Gus's retreating back. "I have this under control."

His friend had the nerve to bark out a laugh as he turned the corner.

Alek remained where he was, hands on his hips. He didn't need any damn luck. He needed a willing woman to take his mind off the untouchable one who was about to move in with him. Maybe Valentine's list could be of some use after all.

SIX

"THIS PLACE IS GORGEOUS." Sheridan addressed the compliment to Peri Bergeron. There was no doubt that Alek's mother had a hand in choosing the décor of his sprawling home.

"Thank you," Alek and Peri said at the same time.

The three of them stood around the island in the kitchen—a spacious room that could house the kitchen, dining room, and den from Sheridan's childhood home. Along with its gourmet appliances was a keeping area with a loveseat, two chairs, and a double-sided fireplace that opened to the family room on the other side. A round table with banquette seating was built into a large bay window with a view of the backyard where Hattie and Finn chased each other around, working the kinks out after the long two-day drive.

"I designed it to be comfortable." Peri picked up the bottle of wine they'd enjoyed at dinner and poured some into Sheridan's glass. "My goal was to make it a place where Alek can relax and decompress away from the rink."

"Hah!" Sheridan reached for the glass, trying hard not to chug it to calm her nerves. "Relaxing and decompressing are not usually synonymous with little boys and big dogs. I'll make sure they both stay out of your space as best I can."

She risked a glance in Alek's direction. He was hard to read this evening. When they arrived earlier, he'd welcomed them warmly. Even the dog. But he'd become more guarded as they settled in and throughout dinner. He was looking at her now as though she were a ticking time bomb he needed to deactivate.

"Regretting your offer already?" The question didn't come out sounding as light and jovial as she'd hoped.

"Of course not," Peri said. "Alek, tell her she's being ridiculous."

Alek crossed his arms over his broad chest and leaned his hips against the countertop. The black cashmere sweater he wore showed off his sculpted shoulders and arms to perfection. His narrow hips and muscled thighs were encased in the soft cotton of gray joggers.

Lord have mercy.

This would be her view every day. It was all she could do not to drool. She jerked her eyes up north only to slam into bemused blue ones.

"You're being ridiculous, Sheridan," he said.

Her face grew warm. It was as if he'd read her mind.

"My mother makes it sound like I need to hide out in a soundless chamber to recover after a game." He shot Peri a look. "I don't. Finn and Hattie are welcome to roam freely." His gaze returned to her. "Same goes for you."

Was there an invitation there?

When she took another healthy sip from her glass, the corners of his lips turned up slightly, and he gave his head a little shake.

"I'm going to have to get used to the fact that you're old enough to drink wine."

Annnd, there it is again.

There would definitely be no invitation forthcoming from Alek. She needed to stop misinterpreting his signals. Of course he didn't mean what her overactive and undersexed mind thought they did.

"Ignore him, Sheridan." Peri topped off her own wineglass. "He's the same way with his sister, Alicia. He thinks she's still twelve despite the fact they are twins. You should have seen him when she was pregnant." She gave her head a disgusted shake. "He didn't think she could handle motherhood."

"She was running a marathon while pregnant with twins!"

Peri grimaced. "Yeah, that might not have been her finest moment. But in her defense, she didn't know it was twins at the time." She shrugged. "Hard to believe but Alicia has always been the more daring of the two."

"Sounds like someone I'd like to meet." Sheridan could use some pointers on how to be more daring. She started by taking another swig from her wine to annoy Alek.

"She'd like that, too," Peri replied. "Perhaps over the holidays?" She glanced between them, wearing a hopeful look.

"Mum. They haven't even been here one night yet. Why don't we table any discussions about trips to Canada for another time?"

"Who's going to Canada?" Finn raced into the kitchen.

"The only place you are going is to the showers, little man," Sheridan said. "Please give Hattie some water first."

The dog hovered in the doorway, panting. She was trained not to venture into the kitchen without permission. Who knew Jamie had such a knack for dog whispering? Managing his money? Not so much.

Peri glanced down at her phone. "My car to the airport will be here in ten minutes."

Sheridan's stomach sank. She'd been delighted and relieved to find Peri here with dinner waiting when they arrived. Now her human buffer was deserting her. More wine was probably not a good idea. She put her glass down on the counter.

"You don't live here?" Finn asked once he'd returned from the mud room that housed Hattie's crate and her dishes.

Peri stroked her palm over Finn's hair. The tender gesture had a lump forming in Sheridan's throat. Finn needed this right now. He needed Alek to step in for Jamie. And he needed the care of a woman who actually paid attention to him.

"No, sweetheart," Peri told him. "I live in Ottawa with Alek's dad. I was visiting with clients in Chicago yesterday, which meant I could scoot up here for the day and say hello to you."

"What do I call you?" Finn asked.

Sheridan's gut clenched.

An adoring smile lit up Peri's face. "How about if you call me Peri?"

Finn grinned back at her as he nodded.

"Come on." Peri guided Finn from the kitchen. "The shower in your bathroom can be a little thorny. Alek's dad can never figure it out. I'll show you the secret trick."

Hattie fell into step behind them.

Sheridan drew in a deep breath. "Thank you," she said softly.

"For what?" Alek asked.

She spread her arms out. "For this. For everything. For taking us in despite everything that happened with . . . Jamie."

"I didn't do it for Jamie. Finn is Madison's son, too."

The harsh way he spoke the words caught her off guard.

Of course.

He would cherish Finn because he once loved the child's mother. She wrapped her arms around her waist to ward off the sudden chill in the air. There was no point in disillusioning Alek now. Madison was gone. And Jamie was right. There wasn't a better role model for her nephew. What was done was done.

"Well, regardless of the reason. Thank you."

"Sheri—"

She held up her palm to stop him. "Let's set the record straight once and for all. I'm not your little sister. Nor am I in any way your responsibility. I'm here because whether he knows it or not, Finn needs me." She cursed the boulder that had formed in her throat. "And I need him." Her fingers trembled when she reached for her abandoned glass of wine and drained it. "Now if you'll excuse me, I'm going to make sure my nephew doesn't use up all the hot water. He tends to get in the shower and stay there."

"SO? How'd it go last night?" Gus asked from his stall the following morning. Both men were getting ready for morning skate.

"Fine. In spite of everything he's been through, Finn is an easy kid," Alek replied.

Sheridan, on the other hand . . .

I'm not your little sister.

His body was beginning to get that message loud and clear. The suggestive way she'd spoken the words had him instantly hard. Finn wasn't the only one who had needed a long shower before bed. Except when Alek finally crawled beneath the sheets, visions of Sheridan sipping from her wineglass kept crashing through his mind. Then he was imagining all the other things her lips might be able to do and it was back to the shower.

Gus pulled on a pair of heavily padded shorts. "Not too much disruption to your coveted personal space, I hope."

"Nah. They travel light. Thanks to Claire already arranging

a wardrobe of school uniforms for Finn, he didn't need that much. His great-aunt is sending out some stuff he wanted from his room."

"And the other aunt? Has she already bombarded your house with scented candles and frilly throw pillows?"

Alek scoffed at his friend. "I don't think she's the type. She came with less stuff than Finn."

Something about Sheridan arriving with a backpack slung over her shoulder and a single suitcase hit Alek the wrong way. It was as if she wanted to take up as little space in the world as possible. Damn Jamie for not allowing his sister to grow and discover her own self-worth. Her own voice. Her own dreams. The asshole waited until he was dead before setting her free.

"I change jobs every six months," she'd told him with a shrug. "Most long-term rentals have everything I need."

Sure, but didn't she *want* for anything? Favorite books, keepsakes, or jewelry? His sister collected so much crap for decorating her house that they needed an extra garage to store it all. Shouldn't Sheridan want a home to nest in?

"A woman who travels light?" Gus whistled his approval. "That's a rare woman indeed. You might want to think about holding on to her."

Alek shot his friend a WTF look. "How many times do I have to tell you—"

Gus held up his hands. "I know. I know. She's practically your little sister. Got it."

"Good. See that you keep getting it."

Alek's ultimatum was as much for Gus as it was for himself. Because he was beginning to realize that the only way that he would survive having Sheridan around was to keep her firmly in the little sister lane no matter how much his libido wanted him to think otherwise.

"You've been a very naughty boy, Bergeron," Valentine said

when he entered the dressing room as if Alek had been projecting his thoughts on the jumbotron. "I just met *Auntie* Sheridan out there, and she is not as implied."

Alek swore under his breath. He knew bringing them to practice this morning would be distracting, but Finn had been so eager to meet Gunner. It was a Sunday morning, and most of the guys brought their kids to hang out and watch. Plus, he wanted Sheridan and Finn to meet some friendly faces before tonight's game.

"I didn't imply." Alek clipped on his leg guards with a little more force than was necessary. "You inferred. Learn the difference."

Gus chuckled as he reached for his glove. "And 'Auntie Sheridan' is like a sister to him, so leave her off the list." He shot Alek a smarmy grin.

"Oh, no need," Valentine replied. "I've already found the future Mrs. Bergeron. Gunner's entry has gone to the top of the polls."

"Let me guess." Gus sighed. "I'll bet he suggested his teacher, Miss Lane."

"Sure did." Valentine pulled his phone from his pocket. "And I found a pic of her on the school's website. It's no wonder all the boys in the second grade are in love with her."

He shoved the phone in front of Alek. The woman staring back at him was laughing at something in the distance, her amber eyes shining. A smattering of freckles across her nose made her look school-age herself. The action shot had a ponytail of strawberry blonde hair appearing to swing out behind her.

"She's like the princess from *Enchanted*," Valentine said, his tone reverent.

"What's with you and Disney flicks?" Alek wanted to know.

Gus laughed. "Look at him. Valentine is already under her spell. Miss Lane has that effect on people. Males in particular."

He smacked Alek on the shoulder with his glove. "You'll see tomorrow when you take Finn to school. She's his teacher, too."

Valentine placed his phone in the cubby above his stall. "Dude, that's the perfect meet cute."

"Jesus, Valentine, no wonder my daughter adores you. You speak the same girlie lingo," Gus said.

"Hey, it never hurts to know your audience. Not all women are into video games and hockey, you know." Valentine pointed at Alek. "I'll bet my left nut that Miss Lane watches Hallmark when she's home alone and hosts *Vanderpump Rules* viewing parties with her girlfriends. You should probably brush up on those before you meet her tomorrow."

"Draft me up some CliffsNotes, and I promise to look them over tonight." Alek grabbed his helmet and stick and headed to the rink.

"Seriously, dude?" Valentine gave him a fist bump. "I have a good feeling about this. Remember me when you're choosing a best man."

"Sure thing," Alek called over his shoulder before leaving the dressing room.

Gus walked beside him. "Why am I getting the feeling you weren't jerking his chain back there?"

Alek shrugged. "Maybe you guys are right. I should put myself out there more."

"Well, damn."

"What's that supposed to mean?"

"Nothing," Gus replied after a long pause that told Alek his friend was choosing his words carefully. Or holding back. "Just make sure you don't do anything to hurt Miss Lane, or Gunner will come for you."

Gus stepped out onto the ice and began to circle the rink. Alek pulled his helmet over his head. He was about to lower his face mask when the sound of Sheridan's laughter drew his attention over to the coaches' box at the end of the rink. Picard was leaning against the boards flirting with her.

Dammit.

He was hurrying across the ice to intervene when Gunner and Finn raced across the bleachers to join Sheridan. Finn waved his arms.

"Alek! Over here!"

"Ah, here he is," Picard was saying when Alek skated up. "I was asking your aunt about you, Finn." Picard reached out to shake Finn's hand. "I'm Zach Picard. I had the privilege of playing with your dad when we were on junior US teams. He was a great hockey player and one of my favorite people."

Finn curled his lips in as he pumped Picard's hand up and down. "That's cool," he managed to say.

"I'm glad you're a part of the Mayhem family. Most of the kids wear their dad's jersey on opening night."

Picard signaled to Lori, who was hovering in the background. She came forward carrying a Mayhem tote bag.

"I figured you might like one of your own," Picard continued.

Finn pulled a jersey out of the bag. Gunner helped him unfold it.

"You got number one!" Gunner yelled.

"It isn't taken this year, so I exercised my authority as team captain, and I assigned it to Finn. It even has your name on the back. Check it out."

The boys flipped it over and, sure enough, the name Cobert was there in block letters. Alek's gut squeezed. How many times had he and Jamie talked about wearing the same team's hockey sweater in the pros?

Finn regained control of his voice. "This is so dope. I was gonna spend my birthday money on one of Alek's jerseys. Now I don't have to." He shot Alek a sheepish look.

Alek waved him off. "I have several jerseys I'm happy to hand down. But that one is one of a kind."

He shoulder-checked Picard, a little ashamed he hadn't thought of the gesture himself. Yet he was grateful for his teammate's thoughtfulness. Sheridan's eyes were shiny as she mouthed a "Thank you," to Picard from where she stood behind Finn.

"What do you say?" she prompted.

"Thank you," the boy shouted. "Thank you so much. This is the best gift ever!"

Something about the way Sheridan's face softened as she watched her nephew shrug the jersey over his head sent Alek's heart racing.

"We should get you one, too." Alek motioned to Lori.

"No need." Lori smiled at Sheridan. "The WAGs have it all taken care of."

Of course Sheridan protested. "I don't need—"

She was interrupted by Merriweather showing off his skating skills, shooting up a spray of ice particles in his wake when he stopped short in front of her.

"Well, if it isn't Sherrie Baby all grown up," he said. "I heard a rumor you might be coming to town. Great to see you again."

Sheridan looked a bit confused before her face brightened. "It's Brad, isn't it? You played with Jamie in Boston."

"Ayup. We were both rookies together. Although I was drafted at a younger age than your brother."

The arrogance of the little shit.

Sheridan's smile grew more brittle the more Merriweather yammered on.

"As I recall, we were the only two underage drinkers at the hotel bar that night. But we still managed to have a good time, you and I, didn't we?"

It was all Alek could do not to gag.

"There were a lot of people at the bar that night," Sheridan replied diplomatically.

"Sorry to hear about Jamie. He was a solid guy." He gestured to the two boys, oblivious to the conversation as they leaned along the rails watching Gus shoot slapshots into the empty net.

"Too bad about you getting stuck with the kid."

Alek dropped his gloves onto the ice. Picard bristled beside him. Lori's soft gasp was hard to miss.

Sheridan's eyes grew hard. "I wouldn't have it any other way."

Merriweather was either an idiot or a masochist because he wasn't picking up any of the signals around him.

"Well, everyone knows Bergeron is a hermit." He actually had the nerve to wink at Sheridan. "If you need someone to show you around town, I'm happy to offer my services."

"You already leave your wife home alone with two little kids half the week. Do you think you should be offering up your 'services' to someone else?" Picard threw out.

"You're married?" The astonishment in Sheridan's voice was hard to miss.

Merriweather glared at Picard before turning to Sheridan with an "aw shucks" look. "We have an understanding."

"I need the defensemen to the line," Coach called out. "That includes you, Merriweather."

"Think about it," Merriweather called as he saluted her with his gloved hand before skating off.

Sheridan shook her shoulders. "Why do I feel like I need a shower?"

"The better question is why didn't any of the scuttlebutt surrounding that guy mention he was such a creep?" Lori's knuckles were white where she was gripping the boards. "I'd better have a word with the GM. He could be trouble on the road." She turned to Sheridan. "It was nice to meet you. Look for me at the arena tonight. Mr. Kellogg would like to say hello to you and Finn."

Picard bent down to retrieve Alek's gloves. "Let's get this done. We've got a game tonight."

He skated toward center ice as Alek pulled on his gloves.

"I'm taking Finn and Hattie for a walk in the park this afternoon. I know you guys like to grab a nap before games. If we're gone, the house will be quiet for you."

Alek stared at her.

"What?"

"Thanks." He was lucky to manage that one word because the moment the word "nap" slipped past her lips all Alek could think about was crawling into bed. With her.

He was so screwed.

SEVEN

"THIS IS SO AWESOME," Finn announced as they took in the arena from the bird's-eye vantage point of the owner's suite.

Sheridan had to admit to being a little in awe herself. She'd been to several of Jamie's games when he played in Boston. The players always had decent seats to gift out to family, but she'd never once been invited to watch the game from a suite. Much less one belonging to the team's owner.

And then there was the Mayhem's owner, a man much younger than Sheridan expected. Wearing an Armani suit and a Jacob and Co watch that probably cost more than Alek's house, Max Kellogg looked like he'd stepped out of a meeting on Wall Street rather than a man about to attend a weekend hockey game. He greeted her and Finn with genuine interest, but she got the sense that he was also taking in the nuances of the conversations all around while he was talking to them.

"You are welcome to watch the game from up here," he offered.

Finn's smile faded before he remembered his manners. "Thank you."

Kellogg's lips twitched. "But something tells me that sitting among a bunch of stuffy grownups"—he gave Sheridan a little bow— "present company excluded, doesn't compare to watching the game from along the boards. Even with unlimited free food."

"I kinda wanted to sit with Gunner," Finn replied.

"Smart young man." He winked at him and lowered his voice conspiratorially. "I wouldn't stay up here either if I had the choice. But someone has to entertain the sponsors." He gave them a "what are you going to do shrug" before breaking out a sincere smile. "Enjoy the game, both of you. And welcome to the Mayhem family."

"Thank you, sir." Finn was already bouncing on the balls of his feet, ready to make his escape.

Lori materialized at Kellogg's shoulder. "I'll take you down to the family room."

"Thank you both," Sheridan said. "But we can go find our seats."

"Nonsense." Kellogg said. "Our family room is one of the nicest in the league. Most of the entertainers who perform at the arena use it, too, and they give it high marks."

There was no mistaking the pride in the man's voice. This was a guy who liked the best of everything but who was generous enough not to keep it all to himself. Sheridan instantly admired that about him.

Lori ushered them to the elevator. "You'll want to grab something to eat before the face-off. There's an extensive buffet, but if you don't see anything you want, one of the team's personal chefs will whip you up something." She grinned at Sheridan. "Within reason."

"Wow," Sheridan replied. She'd never been invited to the family room in Boston. That was Madison's domain. Her sister-in-law had always insisted that Sheridan and Finn spend game nights at home to avoid messing up the baby's schedule.

"And you'll get to meet all the WAGs and their families," Lori added.

That was the part Sheridan dreaded.

They took the elevator down to the lowest level. It opened to a large, airy room despite being below ground. They were greeted by the chatter of women and children seated around several tables, eating, drinking, and seeming to enjoy themselves.

"Did you bring your skates, Finn?" Lori asked. "The kids' rink is right through that door."

Sure enough, on the other side of the glass wall was a scaled-down hockey rink, complete with a regulation goal. Several boys and girls were racing around it. They were all trying to shoot a soft puck into the net.

"Gunner has my skates." Finn aimed a pleading look at Sheridan. "Please can I skate for a few minutes before the game? I promise to eat something at intermission."

"Something more than popcorn?" she asked as though she was even considering denying the kid anything.

He held up his pinkie. Sheridan wrapped hers around it, and they shook. "Don't forget a helmet," she called after him.

"Looks like he's adjusting well," Lori said.

Sheridan sighed. "As long as he doesn't get used to all of this. Our stay in Milwaukee is only for the season."

"I see," the other woman said. "Well, it will make for some great memories."

For one of them, perhaps.

"Oh, you're finally here!" a woman cried out from the far end of the room. "Yay-uh!"

Everyone turned to look at Sheridan as the tall blonde woman navigated around the tables to join her.

"That's Sloane," Lori murmured. "She's with Valentine."

Claire sidled up to Sheridan's elbow. "She's a lot to take at first," Claire said with a soft laugh. "But she's harmless."

Sheridan suddenly found herself wrapped in Sloane's arms. After getting over her confusion and embarrassment, her first thought was to ask the other woman what scent she was wearing because she smelled *ah-mazing*.

"Oh, I hate everything that you have been through." Sloane took a step back but left her hands braced on Sheridan's shoulders.

The woman was tall. At least five foot ten. The platform sneakers she wore made her appear even taller. She was also stunning. And vaguely familiar.

Holy snot.

Sheridan suddenly realized where she knew Sloane from. The woman standing before her was a social media sensation, advising millions of women on what to wear, and how to do their hair and makeup, among other things. None of which Sheridan could master.

"But you're here now, and that's all that matters." Sloane shimmied her shoulders up and down as she let out a little squeal. "And you're going to have so much fun with us. But first, let's get you dressed."

"Dressed?" Sheridan was so caught off guard, she allowed Sloane to drag her by the hand to one of the tables in the back.

A petite woman with short red hair and glasses smiled as they went past. "Don't fight it, honey," she said, her accent distinctly Nordic. "She's a force of nature."

"See how gorgeous Ingrid is in her jersey?" Sloane gestured to the woman.

Ingrid stood and did a little pirouette. Her jersey was more like a dress that she'd paired with cute purple boots. Her glasses were embellished with the Mayhem M.

All the WAGs were sporting their significant other's jersey,

Sheridan realized. Not only the kids. Claire had paired her husband's with cream-colored skinny jeans and open-toed wedge sandals. Another WAG had cropped her jersey and added contrasting fringe. She wore it with wide-leg jeans and platform sneakers.

Sheridan looked down at the Mayhem sweatshirt she'd picked up at the big box store earlier that day when she and Finn were out grabbing dog food. On closer inspection, the purple wasn't even the same shade as the color the Mayhem wore.

"Don't worry," Sloane said. "I have something that is going to look great on you."

She reached for a duffel bag and pulled out a jersey that looked like it had been lengthened to mid-thigh, similar to the one Ingrid had on.

"I brought options, but I think this would look so cute with your tennis shoes." Sloane held it out to her. "There's a bathroom over there. Go try it on. We'll zhuzh up your hair when you get back."

Sheridan froze. The dress was made from one of Alek's jerseys.

"I can't wear that."

Sloane snapped her fingers. "I see the problem." She reached back into her duffel and pulled out a baggie containing a razor and some shaving cream. "My sponsors keep me well stocked, and I love it when I get to share. The sink is pretty large in there."

"It's not that," Sheridan protested. Although, she couldn't remember whether she had shaved her legs that morning. Or the day before. "I can't wear Alek's jersey."

"You have to. All the other guys are taken. Well, except for Zach." Sloane rolled her eyes. "But everyone knows he doesn't date women here in town."

Sheridan could feel the cheap sweatshirt beginning to stick to her back. "That's my point. If I wear this out there, everyone will think Alek and I are together. And we're not."

The chatter in the room quieted. A short, heavy-set woman who looked out of place among the chic WAGS flicked her long blonde braid over her shoulder as she wandered over. Three little girls ranging in age waddled in a line behind her.

"Maybe not together like that." Her accent was more pronounced than Ingrid's. "But you are a little family now, yes? And that's all that matters. Who cares what anyone else thinks?" She gestured to the jersey that hung to the knees of the black girlfriend jeans she wore with black booties. "Just like us, you are here to support the team. A sister cheering on her brother."

Way to bring me back to the earth.

Did everyone see her as Alek's little sister?

Claire looked like she was going to interject. Sheridan shook her head with a smile. There was no point. These women were only being nice. And this was Alek's world. Given everything he was doing for her and Finn, the least she could do was try to fit in.

Resigned, she pasted on a smile and took the jersey from Sloane, grabbing the razor just in case.

Sloane wiggled her shoulders again as she clapped her hands. "I knew you wouldn't say no." She winked at Sheridan. "And think how jealous all the other women are going to be. There's never been a WAG who has worn his jersey before."

Great. Just great.

Forty-five minutes later, the WAGs had taken their seats in the stadium. Sheridan managed to talk Sloane out of a full-face makeover, but the trade-off was a bright lipstick shade that she hadn't dared to wear since high school. Finn had taken one look at her and announced she looked "fresh."

"What does that even mean?" she'd asked Claire.

Claire laughed. "It's the word du jour in the second grade. From what I gather, it's a good thing, though."

The crowd cheered as the skaters took the ice for their introductions. Sitting along the boards three rows below Sheridan, Finn and Gunner yelled to get Alek's attention. He turned in their direction and gave the boys a wave. Then his eyes scanned the crowd. He did a double take when they landed on Sheridan. She hiked one shoulder up in an awkward shrug. The soft smile he sent her way looked a lot like approval. It had her stomach doing weird things.

Beside her, Claire chuckled. "Alek isn't used to having anyone in this section other than when his family is in town."

That surprised her. "Really? He hasn't dated anyone in the six years he's been with the Mayhem?"

"There was one woman the summer before last. London Headley. He seemed pretty serious about her, but my gut told me he was simply going through the motions. It felt to me like he was trying to check 'start a family' off a list."

"What happened to her?"

"Turns out she and Trey Van Horn, the quarterback of the Growlers, had a relationship when they were teenagers. Someone meddled and they each got their heart broken. It was very romantic when they found each other again."

"Poor Alek." First Madison and now this London woman. No wonder he was still single. He was probably gun-shy. "And there's been no one else?"

"Oh, I'm sure there have been other women over the years." Claire wiggled her eyebrows. "But Alek is very discreet. And he's not the sort of guy who needs a piece of arm candy to stoke his ego. He's the type that when he finds the one to commit to, he'll be all in. You and Finn are the perfect example."

Sheridan choked on the wine she'd just taken a sip of.

Claire patted her on the back. "I only meant that he saw a need to make a commitment to both you and Finn and he quickly took it on, without hesitation. I'm not implying anything is going on." She arched an eyebrow. "Unless something *is* going on?"

"No," Sheridan managed to croak.

"Glad I got confirmation, then," Claire said. "Timothée Valentine is determined to play matchmaker for Alek this season."

"Oh." Sheridan was too stunned to come up with anything more intelligible.

"I told Timothée it might be awkward if Alek gets into a relationship while you're living there, but once Valentine gets something in that adorable head of his, it's hard for him to dial it back." She chuckled. "He's even got a detailed list of candidates."

Sheridan had no time to dwell on the other woman's bombshell because the horn sounded and the puck dropped, ending their conversation. The crowd roared when Claire's husband scored a goal in the opening three minutes. Alek seemed to be fighting for his life in front of the goal as the Dallas players peppered him with shots. He managed to keep them all out of the net until less than a minute was left in the first period. Merriweather checked one of his opponents into the boards when he should have been helping defend the net. The puck slipped in beneath Alek's outstretched leg.

During the first intermission, Sheridan went back down to the family room with Claire, who wanted to check on her daughter. The Mayhem provided childcare for the kids who were too young to sit still for the duration of the game. Grace was playing an animated game of Candyland with the three young girls who belonged to the woman Sheridan had met earlier. It turned out Freya was the wife of one of the assistant coaches who was once a goalie in the league.

"I don't go upstairs to watch them play," Freya had explained to Sheridan before the game. "Henrik says I try to coach over him." She laughed. "He claims he can hear me all the way over on the bench."

Freya paced around the room, holding a fussy baby on her shoulder. One of the WAGs Sheridan hadn't met before was seated at a table holding a screaming toddler on her lap. The mom looked spent.

"Everything okay here, Brooke?" Claire asked.

Brooke blinked as if she were holding back tears. "It's fine. This is the evening meltdown. Brad said it would be a mistake coming tonight. I should have known neither kid would let me out of their sight. But I get tired of sitting at home."

Claire knelt next to her so she could rub the little boy's back. "Why is it that little ones always know when the season starts, and they try to test their mom's limits?" She smiled at Brooke. "You're not alone. We've all been there. The guys are home tomorrow. Why don't you leave the kids with Brad and come by my place in the afternoon? I have a list of vetted child-care pros who will come to the house and watch the kids so you can enjoy a night out at the games."

"Oh." Brooke looked even more dejected. "I don't know. Brad spends the off days playing video games with some of the guys. He says it's important to build camaraderie with his team-mates. And I know it's good for his mental health to check out and think about something other than hockey."

"What about your mental health?" Sheridan surprised herself by interjecting. But really, Merriweather was all kinds of a douche.

"Sheridan's right," Claire said in a much softer tone. "You can't do this all on your own. This team is your family while you're away from home. If it helps, I can have Zach or my husband talk to Brad?"

Brooke's eyes went round. "No! Please. I-I'm going to ask my mom to come out for a few weeks to help get us settled into the season. You don't need to worry about me. I'll get everything together. Brad will play at his peak. It's all good."

Claire drew in a slow breath. "Okay. Grandma to the rescue is always a good plan. And I know you can handle this. I want you to know you can always reach out, though, okay? How about I email you those names so you have them in your back pocket?"

It looked as if Brooke was going to say more, but all she did was nod. She shifted the still crying toddler to her other shoulder. Claire got to her feet. Freya joined them with the now quiet baby.

"He cried himself out," Freya whispered. "I'll put him in the nursery."

"We should go back up," Claire said after checking on Grace.

When Sheridan looked back at Brooke, her chest squeezed. The little boy was beginning to peter out, but he still had a death grip on the jersey his mother wore. His anguish reminded her of Finn at that age. Except it wasn't his mother he wouldn't let go of. It had been Sheridan.

EIGHT

ALEK PRESSED the garage door button on the visor of his Range Rover. The game had ended a little under an hour ago, and he was finally getting home after dropping Gus off. Because it was a school night, Claire left immediately at the buzzer, bringing Sheridan and Finn back to his place.

It's their place now, too, he reminded himself.

"You never answered my question about how you're feeling," he asked his dad. It was their practice to chat by phone after each game. Not that Kirk Bergeron was one of those hockey dads who had to dissect his son's play. He wasn't. His dad was a mild-mannered history professor who preferred to talk game strategy.

"I'm feeling fine, Son," his father replied. "I appreciate how much you care, but there's no need for every conversation to circle back to my health."

"Yeah, sorry." Alek's sister had warned him their dad was getting a little testy about the constant questions concerning his Parkinson's. He loved his dad, though, and couldn't imagine life without him. It was only natural that Alek worried.

He was also profoundly grateful for the thirty years he'd

already had with his father. Finn wouldn't know that for either of his parents. Neither would Sheridan.

"How did Finn enjoy the game?" his dad asked.

Alek pulled the car into one of the three bays in the garage. "He looked like he was soaking up every minute."

Luckily, the Mayhem were able to pull out a win despite Alek's mistakes that allowed three goals. Gus tore up the defense, scoring two goals and two assists. Valentine and Picard each added goals to put the Mayhem on top.

"Glad to hear it," his dad said. "He needs a little joy in his life right now."

"Agreed." He cut the car's engine.

"I'm proud of you, Alek," his father said. "Proud of you for a great many things. But taking in Jamie's son is a very magnanimous act on your part. Especially during hockey season."

"It's not like I had a choice."

"Of course you did. Things could have been worked out legally with Sheridan. They would have been fine."

Alek rested his head against the headrest. "Yeah, but it was like Jamie primed the kid for this. For me being a part of his life. I would have disappointed him if I kept him at arm's length."

"You would have disappointed Finn or Jamie?"

"I could give a shit about Jamie," Alek snapped. "He was on the verge of bankrupting his family. He took advantage of his sister for years. Sheridan and Finn deserved better."

"So did you."

His dad's words caught him off guard. Normally, he would have agreed. Except the betrayal and heartbreak hadn't broken Alek. It had made him stronger. He was determined to do whatever it took not to let it break Sheridan and Finn, either.

"It's getting late. Go replenish your body with some carbs and electrolytes. I'll text you the link to that book about the

Canadian railroad I mentioned. You might enjoy it on next week's road trip. Love you."

"Love you, too, Dad."

The house was quiet when Alek stepped into the mudroom. Not surprising, Hattie's crate was empty. The dog never left Finn's side, shadowing him around the house as if she were the kid's personal security detail. No doubt the dog was asleep inches from Finn.

Hattie always seemed to be keeping a wary eye on Alek, as if she knew he was only tolerating her. He was embarrassed to think the dog thought that about him, but he'd never been around that many dogs. Probably because when he and his sister were five, Alicia was bitten by a dog Alek had dared her to approach. Guilt mixed with trepidation had him keeping his distance from all canines as a kid.

He'd gotten over it as he got older, but by then, he wasn't around enough to own one. Hattie seemed to be the perfect dog to have as a long-term houseguest, though. She waited at the threshold of the kitchen until she was given permission to enter. As far as he could tell, she stayed off the furniture—with the exception of Finn's bed. And she was relatively quiet, only barking when she and Finn were chasing each other around the backyard.

He entered the kitchen and stopped short. The vision of Sheridan bending over, placing a tray into the oven, had his breath hitching.

"Perfect timing." She closed the oven door and set the timer before wiping her palms on the baggy sweatpants she'd changed into. She'd also scrubbed her face clean and pulled her hair up into a ponytail. He was surprised at how disappointed he was that she'd taken off his jersey.

When he had looked up into the stands and saw her all decked out in his number, he'd felt such a rush of pride. She looked good among the other WAGs. *Damn good.* He'd unconsciously homed in on her lush, berry-red lips and imagined what they might do to him—

"I'm sure you're hungry." She pulled the protein shake he'd made earlier from the fridge. "If I remember correctly, your go-to snack after a game was turkey avocado toast, right?"

In college, he and Jamie ate like castaways who'd recently returned home from months stranded without food rather than a hockey game where they'd played their hearts out for sixty minutes. But then, their bodies had still been growing. Nowadays, he grabbed some electrolytes and fruit before leaving the stadium. Once he arrived home, he settled for simple baked sweet potato fries and a protein shake for dessert. He'd planned it all out before he left for the arena this afternoon.

"I doubt mine will be as good as the ones you guys used to make in the ancient toaster oven in your dorm, but at least we won't have the smell of burning mac and cheese to contend with."

Alek couldn't help but laugh. Jamie nearly set the dorm on fire on a weekly basis, trying to make those stupid cups of mac and cheese.

Sheridan shoved a straw into the shake and placed it and a glass of ice water on the table she'd already set for one. "Have a seat. The toast will be ready in two more minutes."

She was making him a post-game meal? *Oh, hell no.*

"You don't have to cook for me, Sheridan. I'm not Jamie." It was an ugly dig, but Sheridan in his kitchen cooking for him felt too personal. Too intimate. He was already finding it difficult enough to keep her in the little sister zone.

She sighed. "Don't read anything into this other than a simple gesture of kindness. Roommate to roommate. Now sit and drink. Your body needs to recoup the ten pounds of fluid you lost during the game."

It was no use arguing, he realized. If Sheridan was upright and breathing, she was doing something for someone else. Alek shrugged out of his suit jacket and dropped down into the chair. He guzzled the water to cool off the parts of him that were still fantasizing about her in his jersey.

"Is Finn asleep?"

"Mm." She smiled as she wrapped the remaining avocado slices in plastic wrap, sealed them in an airtight container, and placed them in the fridge. "He zonked out midway through giving Hattie the play-by-play from the first period. To hear him tell it, it was the best night of his life. A twelve out of ten."

"What about you? Did you have fun?" He couldn't explain why her answer was so important to him.

"Sure. Everyone was beyond nice to Finn."

The woman was the queen of deflecting everything away from her. "Were they nice to you?"

She pulled the avocado toast from the oven and sprinkled some chopped tomatoes on top before transferring it to a plate. "You know they were." She set the plate in front of him. "Eat before it gets cold."

His stomach growled its approval. Sheridan loaded the dishwasher as he devoured the first piece, then the second.

"Thank you," he said. "That was delicious. But I didn't invite you here to cook and clean for me. I have a cleaning lady who comes in twice a week. And I've been cooking for myself for years."

She scoffed as she wiped the countertops. "If you expect me to sit around like a guest for the next seven months, you're out of your mind."

"Nine months. We're going all the way this year."

That earned him a smile. It smacked him squarely in the solar plexus so hard it nearly stole his breath. Late-night conversations with Sheridan were going to have to be taboo. They conjured up too many fantasies. If he was going to survive her living with him, he needed to escape upstairs and take a dunk in his cold plunge tub.

Instead, he did something stupid. He used his foot to shove the chair beside him away from the table. "Will you please sit? You're making me feel guilty."

Sighing, she picked up her water and sat in the chair he'd offered. "You should already know this about me. I like to keep busy. I get bored otherwise."

"You don't say?" he teased. "It's a good thing you've got a job to go to. I wouldn't want to come home to find you've rearranged all the closets. When do you start at the hospital, by the way?"

"I'll get my schedule tomorrow. Claire and I are going over after we drop the boys off at school. I'm going to pop in to say hello to Finn's teacher first."

"I'd like to do the drop-off with you."

Judging by her expression, his request caught her off guard.

"Finn would like that," she said with a nod. "Jamie was such a constant in his day-to-day life. You measure up more than I do."

"I wouldn't say that. At the risk of repeating myself, Finn is lucky to have you."

She looked down at her hands in her lap. The silence stretched for a long moment.

"Finn doesn't talk much about Madison." In fact, Alek realized he hadn't heard the boy mention his mother once. "Why is that?"

If he hadn't been looking so closely, he might not have noticed Sheridan's flinch. She recovered quickly however, offering up a shrug.

"Oh, you know, everyone grieves differently. Besides, Jamie was practically a big kid himself. They were two peas in a pod, father and son. Maybe it's easier for Finn to quantify the things he misses about his dad, that's all."

"Makes sense," he said, even though he had a niggling feeling there was something she was dancing around. "Maybe he hasn't come to terms with losing Madison yet."

"Mmm."

He decided to change the subject. "How did you like being one of the WAGs?"

She shot him a look. "I am most assuredly *not* one of the WAGs. I tried to explain that over and over again to anyone who would listen. It became one of those situations when it was best to go along for the ride."

Another pang of disappointment sliced through him. Did she have to be so adamant about not being one of the WAGs? Not that he wanted a line of women clamoring for the prospect. He had hockey to focus on. But still, it would be nice if not every woman ran from the opportunity.

"Sloane can be very convincing," she added with a frustrated huff.

He laughed. "Yeah. Valentine doesn't get his way all that often with her."

She scrutinized him over her glass of water. "I hear Valentine is acting as your matchmaker this season. Rumor has it, he even has a list of potential brides."

Damn Valentine and his list.

Alek got up and loaded his plate and utensils into the dishwasher. "If you're worried about me bringing home strange women, don't."

She followed him. "I'm not worried about that. I know you want to be a positive role model for Finn. But you don't have to change your life completely because we're here temporarily. In fact, it might be easier on Finn to know you are happily in a relationship when we do eventually leave."

Was she kidding right now?

She rested her palm on his biceps. "I want that too."

He glanced down at her fingers, which were burning a hole through his dress shirt. Apparently, the heat was only one-sided.

"In fact," —her lips turned up in a sly smile— "as your unofficial little sister, maybe I can help Valentine vet the women on his list? Narrow it down so the process goes a lot more smoothly?"

Now she was just pissing him off by throwing his little sister remark back into his face. Two could play at that game.

"You know, that might be helpful," he told her, returning her smile with an insincere one of his own. "You can start tomorrow morning. Apparently, Finn's teacher is a top contender."

Her lips trembled ever so slightly before she nodded. "Sure. Of course."

"You're a gem." He decided to play with fire by leaning down and brushing his lips over her forehead. "Thanks for my snack. . . sis. Night."

Alek didn't dare look back. Mostly because he was unable to douse the desire that the feel of his lips on her skin had conjured up inside him. Instead, he made a beeline to his cold plunge tub.

NINE

SHERIDAN SHIFTED her hips in the child-sized chair, crossing her legs before quickly uncrossing them. If Alek noticed her fidgeting, he ignored it. Mainly because he was too busy charming the clothes off Finn's teacher. And from the looks of it, Miss Lane was there for it.

Gah!

The woman was young. If Sheridan had to guess, she'd venture that the woman wasn't long out of a sorority meeting. A trio of gold chains, two of them displaying Greek letters, circled the porcelain skin on her neck. Despite appearing so youthful, she was conservatively dressed in black slacks and a cream-colored T-shirt that she'd paired with a simple cardigan—purple, no less. Coincidence? Sheridan thought not.

She looked down at her yoga pants and T-shirt, wishing she'd dressed in something that identified her as an adult. If only she owned something like that. Her wardrobe consisted of comfy sweats and scrubs. As a result, the recent college graduate looked more mature and worthy of Alek than Sheridan did.

Not that she wanted to impress her roommate. It was no use, anyway. She already knew exactly how he saw her. A lot differently from the way he was looking at Finn's adorable teacher.

Her bravado from last night faded quickly in the harsh light of day. She thought she was mature enough to handle seeing Alek with someone else. Turns out, she was not.

The woman blushed at something Alek said. Sheridan tried not to gag. She glanced around the room. The walls were decorated with colorful bulletin boards. On the whiteboard, it looked as if Miss Lane was charting dates on a graph. Sheridan did a double take when she noticed the word February was missing the first r. She bit back a groan.

"Does Finn have a favorite subject?" the teacher asked Alek as if she didn't know the man had only recently met Finn.

"Besides hockey?" Alek flirted.

Sheridan rolled her eyes. "He's really into spelling," she lied, tongue-in-cheek.

Miss Lane snapped her gaze over to Sheridan as if she'd realized only now that there was someone else in the room.

"That's good to know," the teacher said. "We have a spelling bee every Friday with their vocabulary words."

Of course you do.

Sheridan made a mental note to make sure she quizzed Finn extra hard on Thursday nights.

"I've heard such great things from Gunner about your class, Miss Lane. This is a big adjustment for Finn. I'm glad he'll have someone like you to help guide him." Alek was laying it on so thick, she was surprised the room didn't stink.

The teacher was blushing. "That's sweet. Gunner is a great kid. And from a wonderful family."

"You probably shouldn't let them sit together," Sheridan interjected.

Both she and Alek jerked their heads around to stare at her.

Sheridan shrugged. "You know how little boys can be.

They're already thick as thieves. I wouldn't want you to have any discipline problems."

Finn had never once been a discipline problem. And Gunner had been nothing but the picture of politeness since she'd met him. Sheridan was stirring the pot, that's all. She should be ashamed of herself. Except she wasn't.

The ringing of the bell saved her from embarrassing herself further. The three of them stood. Miss Lane extended her hand to Sheridan.

"Please don't worry about a thing. I'll take good care of your nephew," she said.

Feeling like a total jerk, Sheridan nodded as she shook the teacher's hand. "Thank you."

The other woman turned to Alek. He took her hand in both of his. "If you need to discuss anything regarding Finn, please don't hesitate to reach out. I left my number in the front office."

What the what?

"I will," Miss Lane said with a lot more moxie than Sheridan liked.

As if Alek knows the boy like I do.

Sheridan moved toward the door, but Alek seemed reluctant to release the teacher's hand.

"You should come to a hockey game sometime," he offered.

"Oh. I'd really enjoy that."

Sheridan bit back a groan.

"How about a Friday night game? We can grab dinner after," Alek said.

"It's a date," Miss Lane replied with a rapturous smile.

Alek answered her grin with one of his own. "I'll be in touch next week to set it up."

The sound of kids calling to one another filled the hallway. Alek slowly dropped the teacher's hand. He turned and gestured for Sheridan to precede him out the door. She started to, but her inner demon took over.

"By the way," she said. "February is spelled wrong. You might want to fix it. We are molding young minds here after all."

With that ugly salvo launched into the air, she marched down the hall, heading in the direction of the drop-off lane where she was meeting Claire.

"What the hell was that all about?" Alek growled quietly beside her. "I have a hard time seeing Finn as a discipline problem. And what's all that BS about *molding young minds?*"

She tried not to cringe, but it sounded as awful coming out of Alek's mouth as it had coming out of hers. Still, in for a penny . . .

"Someone needed to point out her mistake. We don't want her students picking up any bad spelling habits."

They'd reached the front of the building where the younger kids were lined up neatly, waiting to enter. She didn't dare look for Finn. Hopefully, he'd never know what a fool she'd made of herself back there.

She spotted Claire's big Suburban and trudged toward it. If only Alek didn't have longer legs and quicker reflexes, she might have made a clean getaway. He wrapped his fingers around her arm and pulled her to a stop outside Claire's SUV.

"Did you have to be so bitchy back there?" he demanded.

That depends. Did you have to be so damn attractive?

"I was looking out for Finn," she snapped. "Isn't that my role? Mama Bear to your Good Cop Best Friend?"

The hardness around his mouth eased. He sighed heavily. "Sher—"

"Don't." She yanked her arm free from his warm grasp. "I know my part in all of this. Jamie made it perfectly clear how he wanted Finn's life to play out." Her throat grew painful saying the words.

Alek opened his mouth to speak again, but she waved him off.

"Miss Lane barely registered I was in the room. You needn't worry. I doubt anything I said ruined your chances with her."

The car window lowering pressed them both into silence.

"Everything okay out here, kids?" Claire asked.

Sheridan tore her eyes away first. "Mission accomplished," she announced. "Finn is safely ensconced in his classroom, and Alek has a date with Miss Lane."

"You don't say?" Claire sounded a bit mystified.

"Mm-hmm." Sheridan pulled open the passenger door. "She's perfect for him. Young, attentive, and eager. She'll look adorable in his jersey. Purple brings out the red in her hair. I'll bet she'll even let Sloane give her a makeover. It will be so sweet. They will be social media's favorite couple in no time."

"That sounds promising." Claire shot Alek an expectant look as Sheridan climbed into the SUV and pulled the door closed behind her.

For his part, Alek kept his expression stoic, his arms crossed over his chest.

"Have a great practice," Sheridan told him.

He looked like he wanted to say something, but he pressed his lips together instead before taking a big step back and waving them on.

Sheridan focused her attention out the passenger window so Claire wouldn't see her fighting back tears.

THE TALKING heads on the sports news show were blabbering on about the Milwaukee Growlers and their record-setting quarterback. Alek tuned them out from where he sat in the canteen eating a lunch prepared by the Mayhem's chef. The team had finished morning skate and the postmortem on last night's game. Most of the guys grabbed lunch to go, hurrying home, where they jumped online to play video games with one another.

Alek wasn't much of a gamer, preferring to delve into the history book his father had recommended as a way to tune out the hockey noise for the afternoon. He was scrolling through the first page when a mention of his name caught his attention.

"The Mayhem may be having buyer's remorse after signing Alek Bergeron to one of the richest contracts for a goalie," the sportscaster on the television screen said.

"Most of us gave him a little grace period last season," the other guy added. "The Mayhem were weak in defenders, forcing Bergeron to carry all the load. But the team picked up a pair of decent defensemen during the offseason."

Alek snorted. Merriweather might be decent if he put his mind to it. So far, the hoser hadn't put in the effort, though.

"Bergeron's stats haven't improved since last year, and he's far from his record-breaking season the year before," the sportscaster droned on.

Tell me something I don't know.

Earlier today, he'd worked one-on-one with Henrik Lund, the team's assistant coach for an hour. There was nothing wrong with Alek's reflexes, Lund had declared. It was what Lund hadn't said that didn't set well with Alek, however.

I need to get my head in the damn game and stop over-thinking everything.

Easier said than done. Too many other things were living rent-free in his head including anxiety about his dad's health and several distractions wandering around his house. Hence, the reason he was eating lunch at the training facility. He didn't want to risk another chance encounter with Sheridan.

She'd been all over the place emotionally this morning. If he hadn't known better, he might have guessed she was actually jealous of the attention he'd paid to Finn's teacher. Of course, that had been his intent. To tick her off.

The night before, she'd been so cavalier about him dating someone. Encouraging it even. He'd wanted nothing more than to call her out on it. Which was cruel because there couldn't ever be anything between them. She was Jamie's little sister. The line wasn't drawn in the sand but in concrete. And no matter how tempting, Alek wouldn't cross it.

But the anguish on her face when she'd described Alek as the good cop nearly broke him. She was right. Jamie had set things up that way, damn him. Well, one way to combat that was to make sure Finn always knew that his aunt was his champion. Alek could do that for Finn.

And for Sheridan.

"Don't listen to their bullshit," Valentine said as he picked up the remote and switched the channel to a rerun of *The Big Bang Theory.* "Those guys like to hear themselves talk. Nobody in this building is thinking that. Trust me."

He sat down across from Alek.

Alek squinted at his teammate. "Are you wearing eyeliner?"

Valentine grimaced. "I promised Sloane I'd give one of her sponsors a shoutout on social media. I didn't realize she was going to turn it into a live production here at the rink."

He almost felt sorry for the guy. "Please tell me you weren't pitching makeup. Or a feminine product."

Valentine scratched his nose with his middle finger. "It's a suitcase. She's moving into the travel influencer sphere."

"Interesting."

Valentine didn't appear too enthused. "Whatever." He propped his elbows on the table. "So how did the meet cute with Finn's teacher go? Any sparks?"

Oh, there were sparks. Most of them coming from Sheridan.

Not that he was sharing that morsel of information with Valentine.

"She was nice," he said instead.

"Not exactly a ringing endorsement."

It wasn't. Miss Lane was attractive and very personable. She seemed enthusiastic about getting to know him further. He was sure he'd enjoy her company. She had a pretty laugh and was intelligent.

For fuck's sake. She sounded like a dog he was thinking of adopting—if he was into dogs. He needed to try harder.

"I invited her to our next weekend home game. I'm going to take her to dinner afterward."

"Now that's what I'm talking about." Valentine reached his fist across the table for a bump. "Too bad Picard's restaurant isn't open yet. You could really impress her. Women love the royal treatment and a good meal."

"You don't say."

Valentine rolled his eyes. "I didn't mean to imply you didn't know what to do with a woman, but well, your track record speaks for itself. And we want this one to stick, am I right?"

No. Yeah. Maybe.

He'd forgotten how invigorating it was to have someone in the stands whose express purpose for being at the game was to cheer for him. Or how much more enjoyable his post-game meal could be having someone else to unwind with. He could imagine that instead of a cold plunge, he and his *someone* would enjoy a long hot shower together. And everything else that came after.

If only the "someone" he was imagining wasn't Sheridan. He swore under his breath.

"Are you listening to me?" Valentine was saying.

Alek refocused his attention on his teammate. "Yeah, sure."

"Uh-huh. I was asking how things are with Finn."

"Good. Great even," Alek replied. At least there was one thing he could be honest with himself about. "Sheridan ended up picking up a shift at the hospital tonight. Finn's school is having a fundraiser at the pizza place downtown. Gus and I are taking the kids there for dinner."

He was surprised he was looking forward to it. For some time now, Alek felt like he was on the outside looking in at the families around him. He was beginning to realize it was nice to have a reason to be included.

"Maybe Miss Lane will be there." Valentine wiggled his eyebrows.

Hmm. He hadn't thought of that. It wouldn't hurt to get more face time with her. Without Sheridan there tossing out Howitzers, Alek could put some effort into getting to know her.

"You're brilliant." He shoved his tablet into his gym bag and stood. "I'm going to hit the showers before I pick up Finn at school. I might even drop back into the classroom."

"That's the spirit." Valentine stood too. "I have a good vibe about this."

Alek wished he could say the same. He was going to give it his best effort, though.

TEN

"IT SOUNDS like you and Finn are settling in," Aunt Eileen said.

Sheridan juggled the phone with one hand while Hattie tugged her toward a cluster of arborvitaes harboring a squirrel the dog had been tracking. "For the most part."

A little over three weeks had passed since she and Finn arrived in Milwaukee, and they had developed a routine of sorts. While the Mayhem were on the road, Sheridan took on all the responsibility for Finn, shuttling him to school and his twice-weekly therapy appointments. On the nights when Alek had an off day at home, she worked the 2 p.m. to 2 a.m. shift in the emergency room.

The hospital was a private facility located in one of the wealthier suburbs. The environment was dramatically different from the trauma centers where she was used to being assigned. The pace was much slower, which meant the hours dragged. So far, her most difficult case had been a fractured hip suffered by a grandmother who was dismayed to miss the Sadie Hawkins dance at her retirement community.

The staff was friendly enough, though. Most of the other

nurses had families at home, so they welcomed Sheridan's choice to take the afternoon and evening hours. She'd planned her schedule that way to allow Alek and Finn that precious afterschool time together. They had a "guys" dinner on those evenings that included lots of protein and a heavy dose of SportsCenter.

The best part of her schedule, however, was that it gave her an excuse to be away from the house when Alek was home. Who knew having her brother's best friend as a roommate would be so enticing. Especially when he was constantly walking around in form-fitting workout clothes. She didn't have to wonder about what was underneath because the entire world had peeped him when he posed naked in the body issue for a popular sports magazine. The less she tempted herself, the better.

"Don't forget I want to see pictures of Finn in his Halloween costume," her aunt demanded.

Sheridan yanked on Hattie's leash. The dog whined in protest before falling into a perfect heel beside her. "Of course, I won't forget. Finn hasn't stopped talking about dressing up as Alek this year."

Her nephew's hero worship of Alek still bothered her. Finn's therapist confirmed Dr. Rose's theory that having a larger-than-life stand-in for Jamie was likely a coping mechanism that allowed him to delay his grief.

"Isn't that going to make things worse down the road?" she'd asked him when they met for coffee in the hospital cafeteria the other day.

"Hard to say," he'd replied with a shrug. "Every kid is different. But this behavior isn't unusual with boys his age. All we can do is keep the lines of communication open until he's ready to talk about it. I'm encouraged that he has begun to mention his father during our last couple of sessions. He shuts down when I ask about his mother, though. From what you've told me, that's to be expected."

She felt a twinge of guilt evading Alek's question about Finn's relationship with Madison when she'd spilled all the family tea with the therapist.

But that was done in the name of helping Finn.

Alek was best left thinking whatever he wanted about his former love.

"There's been a lot of chatter about Alek's play, even down here in Florida," her aunt said, interrupting her thoughts.

"Really? I'll admit that I haven't been paying much attention to sports talk. They like to blow things out of proportion." She turned the corner and headed up the street toward Alek's house. "I know the Mayhem haven't gotten off to their best start."

That's putting it mildly.

In fact, Alek and his teammates' record was below five hundred through their first month of play. They'd only played five games in front of a home crowd so far this year, winning three of them. Based on what she'd heard from the WAGs, the fans were starting to get restless.

Sheridan hadn't made it to another game since that first one. Their home games had all been played on school nights. She was grateful that Alek had backed her up on the rule that school came first. There was less drama when she and Finn stayed home and watched the games on TV.

The WAGs, on the other hand, were a different story. Despite her not making the games, they insisted she participate in everything they did. Between Freya and Sloane, Sheridan didn't have a choice but to join them for Pilates three mornings a week. As a result, she ached in places she didn't know existed. She was counting the days until they no longer felt the need to include her.

In fairness, though, she was looking forward to tonight. Claire was hosting a Halloween party at her home. While the team was still out of town, the WAGs banded together so the kids could go trick-or-treating as a group with several of the moms acting as chaperones, followed by pizza and games. Most of Finn's experience at trick-or-treating was limited to dressing up and walking around the family bar. Not that it was a bad thing. Barn Burner's patrons showered him with enough candy to last a month. Still, he was beyond stoked to finally be able to go door-to-door.

"How is Alek taking all the criticism?" her aunt asked when Sheridan and Hattie turned into Alek's driveway.

"He's a professional who knows it's only the first month of a long season," Sheridan replied as if she and Alek had actually discussed it.

They hadn't.

The few times they had spoken over the past couple of weeks, their conversations had been cordial, most of them focused on Finn. Although, there had been one that did get a little . . . awkward. It involved Hattie and her fascination for Alek's underwear. Alek's cleaning lady caught the dog sneaking into his bedroom and helping herself to his briefs.

Sheridan's first instinct was to deny, deny, deny until she recalled all the times she'd witnessed the dog sleeping on Jamie's favorite sweatshirt. Still, she wanted Hattie to know she had her back. Sheridan decided to go down swinging.

"How do you know the woman doesn't have a side hustle, selling your unmentionables to your legions of female fans while letting the dog take the heat?"

Alek's reaction was to cross his arms over his chest and look down his God-like nose at her.

She sighed. "Fine. I'll keep an eye on the jockstrap moocher.

It would help if you stopped tempting her by leaving your clothes strewn about on the floor, though."

He scoffed because they both knew the neatnik wasn't guilty of that. They'd stared at one another for a long moment before the charged silence grew awkward, and Sheridan made some excuse about checking on Finn and hotfooted it away. That had been six days ago.

The Mayhem were wrapping up a three-game road trip in Chicago tonight. The team was expected home by midnight. They were playing their first back-to-back game tomorrow evening at home. They'd have Friday off before playing a matinee game on Saturday. Alek's parents were coming into town for that game. They'd invited her and Finn to explore the Dells in Door County on Sunday.

Sheridan had always liked Alek's mom and dad. And she was grateful they were offering her an excuse to be out of town that day. Zach Picard was hosting a private party for his teammates on Sunday to celebrate the upcoming launch of his restaurant. According to the scuttlebutt at Pilates earlier today, Alek had invited Miss Lane as his plus-one.

Claire made some noises about Sheridan tagging along with her and Gus. While Sheridan appreciated the other woman's kind gesture, she was glad to have an out. Even if she had the sneaking suspicion Alek had put his parents up to arranging their little day trip so she'd be out of the picture. Given the way she'd behaved the last time she, Alek, and Finn's teacher were together, she couldn't really blame him.

Sheridan was surprised at how quickly things were moving between Alek and Finn's teacher, though. According to Finn, on the mornings he drove Finn and Gunner to school, Alek always goes through the drive-thru to get the boys a donut.

"Alek gets a coffee for Miss Lane, too. She likes lots of whipped cream on hers," Finn told her.

The teacher had also been to two Mayhem games. Both times with several other teachers from the school. Sheridan felt a pique of satisfaction that Miss Lane hadn't been invited to the family room yet.

"This is all your fault," she chastised herself, careful to cover the microphone with her thumb. "You encouraged him. And it's not like he'll ever look at you the same way. Little sister, remember?"

Sheridan jumped when a car pulled up beside her in Alek's driveway. She said a little prayer that whoever it was hadn't heard her.

"Oh my God! Is that your dog?" Sloane said from the driver's side of a sleek Mercedes convertible.

Hattie answered for her, giving the woman a confident woof.

Sloane squealed. "You are *gorgeous*."

Sheridan looked down at her ratty leggings and well-worn sneakers. Sloane was clearly talking about the dog. "Um, Aunt Eileen. Finn and I will FaceTime you later, okay?"

"Sure, honey. Enjoy the party tonight."

"I wasn't expecting to see you until the party later," Sheridan said once she'd pocketed her phone. "Did I miss something?"

The other woman was already out of her car and kneeling in front of Hattie. "What's the dog's name?"

"Hat Trick. We call her Hattie."

"That's the perfect name for a hockey dog. My fans are going to eat you up." Sloane wrapped her arms around Hattie's neck and gave the dog a squeeze.

Hattie soaked up the love as if it was her due. Sheridan rolled her eyes.

"Does she have a social media account?" Sloane asked when she stood back up.

"I'm sorry, what? Um. In case you haven't noticed, she's a dog."

Now it was Sloane who was rolling her eyes. "She's the adorable dog of a sexy hockey player. Just think of how much money you could make with a few posts a week."

"Except she's not Alek's dog. She belongs to Finn. And Alek isn't a dog person. He tolerates her in his house for Finn."

"What?" She gave the dog a commiserating look. "Shame on Alek. Who couldn't love that adorable face?" She made some kissing noises.

Hattie's tongue lolled.

"I still say you're missing a golden opportunity to pad Finn's college fund," Sloane continued. "But to each his own. I came over to make sure you're ready for the party tonight. And it's a good thing I did because this dog has given me the most awesome idea for your Halloween costume,"

Excuse me?

"Um, I have my costume," Sheridan improvised. She hadn't planned on dressing up. "I'm going to wear some scrubs and carry a stethoscope."

Sloane sighed. "That's original. I bet you wear that every year."

She did. But the other woman didn't have to know that.

"I have a better idea." She had that determined glint her eye that Sheridan had come to know and loathe. "And I can't believe I have everything you'll need. Thank goodness for all those times my dad dragged me to German Fest."

This was ridiculous. She wasn't letting Valentine's girlfriend browbeat her into wearing a costume.

"Please don't go to any trouble on my behalf," Sheridan insisted. "No one is going to see my costume."

"Of course, they are. I'm livestreaming it. And as one of the WAGs, you need to up your game. We have a reputation to uphold among the other teams in this town. I am not letting the Growler girls show us up again this year."

Sheridan had to work hard to keep her patience in check. "You seem to keep forgetting. I'm not Alek's girlfriend. Therefore, I'm not a WAG."

"I haven't forgotten. But there are only twenty guys on this team. The Growlers have nearly fifty, which gives them twice as many of them as there are of us. If we want to outshine them on social media, we need all the bodies in costumes that we can get."

"Is 'outshining' the other wives and girlfriends that important?"

Sloane rocked back on her heels as if Sheridan had pushed her. "I'm an influencer. Getting eyes on my posts is how I make my living. I want to *outshine* everyone." She blinked rapidly a few times. "I want people to know Timothée and his teammates as human beings, too. That sort of content keeps fans in the seats. Even when things aren't going their way. You should want that also."

Crap.

She hadn't figured Sloane for being such a guilt machine. But the other woman was spot-on. Sheridan owed it to Alek to play along.

"What do you need me to do?"

"Yay-ee!" Sloane's face lit up. "Meet me at Claire's at five. I'll bring everything you'll need." She pointed at Hattie as she hurried back into her car. "And don't forget this beauty. She's part of your costume." She blew a kiss to the dog as she started up the car. "Bye-ee!"

And that was how Sheridan found herself wandering the streets of Claire's neighborhood later that evening wearing a vintage beer girl costume with thigh-high white stockings and a revealing lace-up bodice.

"I cannot believe I agreed to this." She pulled her coat more tightly around her as she and Freya escorted several of the Mayhem's kids trick-or-treating.

Hattie was in her glory with people stopping them on the sidewalk to snap pictures of the dog adorned in her little feathered hat and a wooden cask around her neck. Finn and Gunner were dressed head to toe in Mayhem gear, both boys carrying hockey sticks. Their pillowcases were growing heavy with candy.

"You agreed because you are young and haven't had three babies," Freya told her. "I'd kill to still be able to pull off such an outfit." She made a noise deep in her throat. "Henrik would be chasing me around the house."

Dear Lord.

"TMI."

Freya laughed before yelling at the boys to wait before crossing the street. "Are you aware that goalies have the most stamina of anyone on the team?" She bumped Sheridan's shoulder at the mention of stamina. "They are the only player out on the ice for the entire game. Everyone thinks they are just standing around when really they are laser focused on the puck at all times. They maintain their crouch for nearly sixty minutes. You wouldn't believe what that kind of discipline does to their thighs. Mmm."

Damn the woman. Now she was picturing Alek's thighs.

"Hadn't ever thought about it," she lied.

Freya tsked before muttering something in Swedish. She followed it up with, "The man has no sense."

Sheridan didn't have time to decipher the other woman's comments because Hattie was suddenly straining at the leash. The dog let out a low growl as voices rose ahead of them. One of them belonged to Finn.

"Whatever you do, don't let go of her," Sheridan commanded as she handed the leash to Freya and rushed ahead.

"You take that back," Finn shouted as he shoved a boy twice his size.

The bigger boy laughed. The group of tween trick-or-treaters had Gunner and Finn surrounded.

"Bergeron sucks as a goalie." The older boy got right in Finn's face. "He couldn't keep a bus out of the net if he tried. The team wasted their money on him."

Finn dropped his bag of candy to the ground, its contents scattering around his feet as he gripped the hockey stick with both hands.

"Hey!" she shouted. She reached for the hockey stick before Finn could do something foolish. "What's going on here?" Although it didn't take a rocket scientist to figure that out. Finn's aggressiveness, though, was going to take some deep thought later.

The older boy sneered. "Oh, look who needs his mommy to rescue him."

"She's not my mom!" Finn shouted.

Sheridan flinched at the ugly defiance in his voice.

"She's Bergeron's girlfriend," one of the other boys interjected. "I saw her in his jersey on opening day."

She groaned as the group of boys chorused their surprise.

"Finn, you and Gunner go with Freya," she ordered.

"Yes, ma'am," Gunner murmured while Finn gave her a contemptuous look.

"Now," she mouthed at him.

His shoulders slumped as he trailed his friend. The older boys snickered. Finn spun around and slashed his hockey stick through the air. Fortunately, Freya had the reflexes of a goalie. She was able to deflect the stick so that it smashed into a pumpkin lining the walkway instead of one of the boy's heads.

The boys charged at Finn. Hattie's growl stopped them in their tracks.

"Whoa! That dog is gonna bite me!" one of the boys cried as the entire group took a giant step back.

Sheridan stepped between the dog and the group of hoodlums. "Hattie, sit," she commanded. Unlike Finn, she complied immediately. "The dog is very protective, but she won't bite unless you give her a reason to. Let's not. Why don't you guys move along and finish your trick-or-treating?"

The boys held their ground. Sheridan sighed as she crouched down and picked up Finn's pillowcase. She was scooping up the strewn candy when a pair of large tennis shoes appeared on the sidewalk next to her. Craning her neck, she looked up to see a man holding a beer, leering at her around the cigar in his mouth.

Too late, she realized her coat was gapping open, and the man had an unobstructed view right down the meager blouse of her costume. She shot to her feet. Finn would have to sacrifice some of his candy for the cause. A crowd had gathered around them, most of them with cell phones pointed in her direction. All of them getting an eyeful of her ridiculous costume. It was no use buttoning up her coat now.

"Is there a problem here, Brett?" He directed the question at the pack of tweens while his eyes never left Sheridan's cleavage.

"Only that the kid is wearing a Bergeron jersey," Finn's main tormentor replied. "The guy sucks."

Feet shuffled behind her, presumably Finn. She prayed Freya had a firm hold on him.

"I agree," the dad said. "But he's a baby. He doesn't know any better."

"Like father, like son," Sheridan mumbled as she turned away.

"Hold on there, beautiful," the guy said. "While I don't

mind pretty young women living in our neighborhood, I need to know that Cujo here isn't going to run amok and start attacking people."

She rolled her eyes.

"Who are you staying with?" the creep asked.

"We wouldn't live here if you paid us," Finn yelled. "We live with Alek Bergeron."

Oh, Finn.

ELEVEN

THE SHIT HIT the fan as soon as the Mayhem left the ice. Merriweather had the nerve to voice his displeasure with their loss the minute they arrived in the visitor's dressing room. He snapped his stick over his knee while uttering a few choice expletives.

"We coulda had that one," he groused.

He was one to talk. If he'd been where he was supposed to be in the final minute, the puck wouldn't have slipped beneath Alek's butterfly stance and into the net. Both teams would still be out there on the ice playing overtime right now.

The stats wouldn't reflect that, of course. Alek's numbers would take the brunt of the loss. So would his reputation, which was, at present, circling the toilet. He tossed his helmet into his stall in frustration.

"Closed-door team meeting tomorrow after morning skate. Players only," Picard announced.

"No fucking way!" Merriweather complained. "Tomorrow is our first back-to-back game all season. Contract says we get the day off."

"Yeah, so you can get stoned while playing video games," Valentine mumbled beside Alek.

The air in the dressing room all but crackled as the members of the Mayhem waited to see how their captain would respond.

"I don't give a shit about the contract you signed with management." Picard kept his voice low yet lethal. "But every time you pull on a hockey sweater with the Mayhem logo on it, you're making a commitment to every guy in this room. And that extends to participating in meetings and whatever else I deem necessary."

Merriweather looked as if he was going to object. One of the PR staff poked his head into the room.

"Media in five, fellas," he announced.

"Are we good?" Picard asked the room at large. He was adamant the media did not get wind of any rifts among the team. The Mayhem's wonky start to the season already had the hockey pundits dissecting the team's every move as it was.

Most of the guys murmured in the affirmative. Merriweather ripped his sweater over his head and tossed it into one of the equipment hampers before stomping off toward the showers, his skates still on his feet. Valentine shook his head in disgust. Alek exchanged a look with Gus. They needed to do their part to help change the narrative.

"Great penalty killing out there tonight, guys," Alek told his teammates. He hated losing as much as the next guy. Still, he knew they couldn't win every game. Not that the fans would see it that way. "You saved my ass multiple times while keeping the game close right up until the end."

"I agree," Gus said. "Tonight's Balls to the Wall Award goes to Seward and the PK team. Outstanding job, all of you."

Gus pulled a thick gold link chain with a three-inch gold M hanging from it out of his bag and placed it around Seward's neck. The rest of the guys clapped, albeit with a little less enthusiasm than if they'd won the game.

"Speech," they demanded.

Seward stood. "I believe in every man in this room. All we need to do is play Mayhem hockey. Let's focus on the games ahead of us and get the job done."

"You know it!" Valentine called out.

A few of the guys barked while others banged their sticks on the floor. The dressing room door opened, and members of the media flooded in. Curiously, they all made a beeline to Alek's stall, where they began bombarding him with questions.

"Alek, can we get a comment on the incident involving your girlfriend and your ward?"

"How long have you been dating Sheridan Cobert?"

"Has your dog had all of its shots?"

"Did you pick out her Halloween costume?"

What in the ever-loving hell?

Alek was pretty sure his jaw was on the floor. Every other guy on the team stared at him in silence. Thankfully, Lori stepped in to save the day.

"The game ran late, and the charter buses are waiting to drive us all back to Milwaukee. Since we have a game tomorrow night, I'm sure the guys want to get into their own beds as soon as possible. If everyone can clear out so they can get dressed and we can get the equipment loaded on the bus, I know everyone would appreciate it."

Her request was met with some grumbling, but they had been on the road for the week, too. The members of the media were also eager to get home. They cleared out without much protest. Alek's teammates all seemed to reach for their phones at the same time.

"Holy shit," one of the guys said.

Alek felt like a deer in the headlights. He stood frozen, still trying to make sense of all the questions thrown at him. He looked over at Lori.

"Do I even want to know?"

She powered up her tablet and swiped at it. An image of Sheridan on her knees wearing what he could only describe as a cheap beer garden's server outfit filled the screen. The angle of the camera made the image look provocative. For her part, Sheridan did not look amused. Lori swiped again to a photo of Finn wielding a hockey stick at a crowd of kids. Behind him, Hattie was straining against her leash.

"What the hell?" he repeated.

Gus was murmuring into his phone. He gave Alek a sympathetic look.

"Some of the kids in the neighborhood decided to pick on Finn because he was wearing your jersey. Finn took exception to it," he explained.

Alek swore savagely.

"It gets worse. One of the asshole dads chimed in," Gus continued.

Picard was immediately by Alek's side. "Who are we having a convo with?" he demanded of Gus.

Gus sighed. "Claire says Sheridan wants to let it go."

"That's on brand." Alek held out his hand for Gus's phone. "Let me talk to her." He needed to hear her voice. To know that she and Finn were okay. Then he was going to kill everyone who dared to insult them both.

His friend shook his head. "She took Finn home already."

Alek dug into his bag for his phone and dialed her number. It went straight to voicemail. He swore again.

"Let's all take a breath and get dressed so we can get on the road," Lori reminded them. "We can get more of the facts on the way. We'll be home before midnight if you all hustle."

She quit the room just as Alek's phone chimed with a text.

> Everything is fine. Getting Finn ready for bed.
> I'll see you when you get home.

He stabbed his fingers at the phone.

> Wait up for me.

He went to put his phone back in the stall so he could shower and dress before he decided to add to his text.

> Please.

She replied with a thumbs-up emoji.

It was well past midnight by the time Alek arrived home. It had taken some evasive maneuvering to avoid the media staking out the practice facility where he'd left his car. His irritation was already off the charts after spending the hour-and-a-half bus ride scrolling through the Internet, watching the ridiculous story go viral.

It didn't help that his sister was apparently spending her evening surfing the web, sending him link after link accompanied by laughing emoji. Collin's text pissed him off even more. His agent demanded that he call ASAP and explain why he was destroying Sheridan's reputation. Alek ignored him.

Light from the big screen flickered in the dark family room. He looked in to find Sheridan asleep on the sofa, several books spread out around her. He glanced at one. It dealt with grief in children. A similar book was open beneath her hand. A half a glass of wine sat on the ottoman.

He sighed softly. Of course she was going to try to carry the burden of fixing this. When was she going to learn that she wasn't responsible for everyone and everything?

He went upstairs to check on Finn. As expected, Hattie lay

across the end of the bed, standing guard over her charge. She opened one eye at Alek's approach, watching carefully as Alek adjusted the blankets bunched up around Finn's waist.

A photo on the nightstand caught his eye. It was Finn with his father. The two of them shared identical smiles. He glanced around, checking for more pictures. The photo of Alek, Madison, and Jamie that he remembered seeing hanging in Barn Burner was propped up on the small table Sheridan had converted into a makeshift homework desk. As far as he could tell, there weren't any of Finn and Madison in the room. He recalled his mom always complaining that she was never in the pictures because she was always taking them. Likely that was also the case here.

He gently grazed his palm over Finn's soft hair before turning to leave. Hattie approved of the gesture with a single wag of her tail. It was hard to imagine her attacking anyone like the dog who bit his sister all those years ago. But if someone dared to touch Finn . . .

"Good dog," he whispered.

Hattie was already snoring when Alek closed the door. He headed back downstairs. Sheridan stirred on the couch.

"Hey," he said softly, sitting down near her feet.

"Hey." Her bedroom voice had all his nerve endings standing at attention. *Among other things.* He grabbed one of the blankets off the back of the sofa and covered his lap under the guise of warming her feet.

"Looks like you encountered more tricks than treats tonight," he said.

She covered her face with her hands and groaned. "I'm so sorry."

Her words stoked his anger. He reached over and pried her hands away from her face.

"Do not even dare to apologize," he snapped. "Not everything is your fault." He dragged in a breath. "People can be assholes. Things got out of hand, that's all."

Sheridan sat up facing him. She brushed the hair off her face before pulling her knees up in front of her and resting her chin on them. "But they shouldn't have gotten out of hand. Finn has never done anything like that before."

The anguish on her face had him reaching up and cupping her jaw. "He's an eight-year-old boy. Speaking as someone who was one once, not everything he does will make sense. Even if he wasn't dealing with the emotional trauma of losing his parents, he would still act out once in a while. It's the nature of the beast."

He released a heavy sigh as he mindlessly traced her jaw with his thumb. "I hate that this happened because Finn wanted to dress up as me. People are so quick to judge these days without ever considering that there might be factors they aren't aware of."

"Mm-hmm." She leaned into his palm.

"When you dream about being a professional athlete—a public figure—you never think about the fact that the fans suddenly think they own you. And social media has made people bolder. It's like they have no filter any longer." He shook his head. "I've developed a thick skin over the years. I can handle it. You and Finn shouldn't have to be subject to any of the fallout, though. Some role model I'm turning out to be."

She brought her hand up to cover his where it cradled her cheek. "This isn't on you, either. Finn adores you."

Her tongue darted out to moisten her bottom lip. His gaze immediately homed in on it. He bit back a tortured groan.

Alek no longer saw a little sister when he looked at Sheridan. What he saw was a vulnerable woman. One he desperately wanted to kiss.

"And you?" he whispered. "What do you think of me, Sheri?"

He felt as well as heard her sharp intake of breath. She dropped her hand and went to pull away. Alek placed his palm against her neck and gently propelled her forward until their foreheads touched.

"Sher—"

She pressed a finger to his lips.

"This isn't a good idea," she murmured.

"Give me a reason why not," he asked before grazing his bottom teeth along her finger. She shivered. His heart raced in triumph.

"How about because you have another date with Finn's teacher this weekend?"

This time, he let her pull away. Mostly because he felt like he'd been dumped face-first into his cold plunge, and his entire body felt numb. Sheridan scurried from the sofa, gathering up her textbooks and her wineglass. He managed to rake his fingers through his hair, trying to figure out how to apologize for coming on to her. She was right. They wouldn't work. She was still Jamie's little sister.

Even if she is all grown up.

"Sheridan—"

"You should definitely wear your charcoal suit with your blue shirt. It really enhances the color of your eyes," she tossed over her shoulder as she walked away. "There's no way Miss Lane will be able to resist you."

THE FOLLOWING MORNING, Alek stumbled to the kitchen to make himself some coffee. Caffeine wasn't normally on his diet, but given the erotic dreams that had kept him up most of the night, he was willing to make an exception.

"Sorry," he said when he nearly collided with the subject of those erotic dreams as she was coming out of the laundry room.

Rather than the sexy beer-wench costume she'd been wearing in his late-night fantasies, Sheridan was dressed in black leggings and a teal zippered hoodie that clung to her like a second skin. Even with much of her body covered, today's outfit failed to douse the heat still simmering beneath Alek's skin.

"Good morning," she said.

It was all he could do not to roar at her.

Or throw her down on the pile of sheets on the floor and act out his dreams of the night before.

"I told you that you're not here to do housework. The cleaning lady can change the bed linens," he scolded her.

Sheridan sighed. "Wow, both of you are in a mood today," she mumbled as she headed into the kitchen. "It won't kill me to take care of mine and Finn's laundry."

Alek didn't have the bandwidth to argue with her this morning. Instead, he fumbled through the coffee pods, looking for a Tim Horton dark roast that would hopefully blow away his brain fog. "Where is Finn?"

Her back was to him as she packed Finn's lunch. "He's rinsing off before school. There wasn't time for a shower last night."

He was still digging for a coffee pod when she reached over his shoulder and plucked out the dark roast. She held it up, arching an eyebrow at him. He nodded. She was putting the pod in the coffee maker when Finn wandered in. The boy stopped short when he caught sight of Alek.

Sheridan wandered over to him and handed him his lunchbox. A whispered conversation took place. She shook her head before bending at the waist to place a soft kiss on the top of his damp hair, almost as if she was reassuring him. Something inside Alek felt as if it cracked. Did Finn think he was angry about last night's incident?

"Hey, bud," Alek said. "How about I drive you to school today?"

Finn exchanged another look with Sheridan. She nodded. The boy's shoulders relaxed.

"Sure," he replied unenthusiastically.

Not exactly the response Alek normally got, but he'd take it. He poured the coffee into a travel mug. "I'll go grab my sneakers while you eat breakfast."

"I'm not very hungry this morning."

Now Alek was starting to worry. The kid was perpetually hungry. He met Sheridan's eyes over Finn's head. She offered him a dejected shrug.

"Yeah, cold cereal doesn't sound that appealing to me, either. Did you know the chef at the training facility makes the best chocolate chip pancakes?"

Sheridan shot him a where-are-you-going-with-this look. Alek winked at her.

"What do you say to taking a mental health day today? You can come with me to morning skate, and we'll grab some of those awesome pancakes and sausage."

Finn's face lit up. "Do you think they'll have bacon?"

Alek chuckled. "Valentine will be there, so I can guarantee it."

"Can I?" Finn asked Sheridan.

She looked from Finn to Alek. "As long as Alek squares it with Miss Lane."

"I'm sure it won't be a problem," he lobbed right back.

"Yes! I'll go get my gear." He hurried off, leaving Alek and Sheridan on opposite sides of the kitchen, each with their arms folded across their chest. A smile danced on Sheridan's lips, surprising him.

"He needed that today more than you know," she said. "Thank you."

"We have a team meeting at eleven. He can hang out in Lori's office. Hopefully, he won't be too bored."

She pushed her hips away from the counter. "I'll grab him after Pilates. There are some books he wants from the library. I'll take him this afternoon so you can have some downtime to get ready for tonight's game."

"Jordan is between the pipes tonight. I have the night off."

Sheridan looked concerned.

Alek waved her off. "That's the normal game plan when we play back-to-back games."

His explanation didn't seem to placate her. "This . . . us . . . me and Finn being here. It isn't too much, is it? We haven't thrown you off your game, have we? Because Collin said the transfer of guardianship should be finalized by the end of the year, depending on the court schedule."

He was across the kitchen in three long strides, pinning her in place with his palms pressed to the quartz countertop on either side of her waist.

"The agreement was you'd stay until the end of the season," he growled at her. "End of discussion." He lifted her chin with his finger. "Nothing about you and Finn being here is throwing me off my game. You hear me?"

She nodded slightly. Her eyes were wide, and her breathing a little fractured.

"Good," he said, talking about more than her agreement.

He could feel her body responding to his nearness. Just like last night. She wasn't as immune to him as she tried to appear.

Ah, the hell with it.

Alek tipped her chin up higher as he leaned closer. Before

his lips could make contact, however, Finn could be heard stomping down the stairs.

"Are these the sneakers you want to wear, Alek?" he called as the rubber of his own shoes squeaked on the kitchen floor.

Sheridan quickly slipped beneath Alek's arm. "Come on, Hattie," she called. "It's time for your walk. Don't forget your manners and your inhaler, Finn. I'll be by to pick you up after Pilates."

She and the dog disappeared through the mudroom door.

"I'm ready when you are," Finn was saying. "I'm suddenly really hungry."

He wasn't the only one.

TWELVE

"YOU WERE RIGHT. These are the best pancakes ever," Finn mumbled around the food in his mouth.

Valentine laughed as he transferred a piece of bacon from his plate onto Finn's. "I think you almost put away as many as I did, Finnegan Begin Again. Here. Take this as a token of my respect for your gluttony."

Finn's belly laugh echoed throughout the canteen. The sound of his unbridled joy eased the tension in Alek's chest. Given everything Jamie's son had been through this past month—losing both parents, being uprooted to a new home and a new school—Alek shouldn't have been caught off guard by Finn's demeanor this morning.

Still, he'd been scared shitless. Finn's personality was so much like his father's. Happy- go-lucky. Outgoing. Resilient. Sometimes it was easy to forget the boy was only eight years old. Seeing him so down made Alek want to move heaven and earth to bring the smile back to his face. He was relieved that Finn's funk had disappeared.

"You skating with us, Cobert?" Picard asked from the doorway. The Mayhem captain had already donned his helmet and pads.

"Can I?" Finn exclaimed.

"I don't see why not," Picard replied. He glanced at the Mayhem's head coach who was refilling his water bottle. "Any objections, Coach?"

Coach shook his head. "I'm excited to see what you've got, little man."

Valentine knocked knuckles with Finn. "Let's go get you suited up."

Alek had always considered his teammates to be his brothers and the Mayhem as an extension of his family. But their acceptance and treatment of Finn touched him in a way he couldn't articulate. Not one person had questioned why Jamie had left Alek in charge of his son. Or Alek's decision to honor his former best friend's request.

He was also sure there were those in the hockey community who knew the circumstances behind the end of Alek and Jamie's friendship. Yet if there were whispers, he never heard them. For that, he was grateful.

Fifteen minutes later, the Mayhem were on the ice. Jordan would be taking all the goalie reps today. That freed up Alek to give Finn some pointers on stick handling.

"As if a goalie knows what he's doing." Valentine shook his head. "Come let the first line show you how it's done."

Finn's infectious grin had even the normally stoic Henrik smiling. Alek stretched out his legs as he glided around the ice. Finn soaked in everything Gus, Picard, and Valentine taught him until the kid was able to slide the puck between Jordan's skates and into the net. Everyone broke out into cheers.

"His father was a hell of a natural talent. They don't come twice in a lifetime like that," Henrik said when he skated up beside Alek. "But Finn shows promise. He takes direction well."

Merriweather skated past, putting in as little effort in practice as possible.

"Which is a lot more than can be said for some of the people getting paid good money to play this game." Henrik didn't bother lowering his voice. He was as sick of Merriweather's shenanigans as the rest of the team.

Smirking, Merriweather pulled up to a stop and leaned on his stick. "Oh, I don't know. I played with Cobert. If anything, his kid skates like you, Bergeron. He's even got your legs. You sure he's not your kid? I mean, look at him. He doesn't even look like Cobert."

The rink was covered in gloves before Merriweather could finish his absurd statement.

"What the fuck, Merriweather," Picard snarled.

Henrik had Merriweather by the shoulder pad and was dragging the little prick into the corner. As he did, Alek spotted Finn behind Merriweather where he likely heard everything the jerk had said. His eyes were as round as saucers, and his face deathly pale. He dropped his stick to the ice and clutched at his chest trying in vain to draw in a panicked breath.

"Finn!" Alek raced to him and scooped him up. "Your inhaler? Where is it?" he asked as he skated off the ice.

But the only answer Finn could give was a high-pitched wheeze. One of the trainers met them in the dressing room. Gus dug around Alek's stall and found Finn's backpack. He pulled out the inhaler and handed it to the trainer.

"We may be past that. His pulse ox is dropping quickly," the trainer said as he pulled an Epipen from the emergency kit.

Alek felt his own lungs seizing up. This time, he didn't know how to help Finn. He had never felt more useless in his life.

Valentine tugged off Finn's hockey pants. "My sister has asthma. I'm a pro at this," he explained as he took the Epipen from the trainer and stuck it in Finn's thigh. After it clicked, Valentine counted to ten.

The trainer inserted Finn's inhaler into a plastic tube with a mask at one end. He placed it over Finn's mouth and nose and pressed the button on the inhaler. Similar to what Sheridan had done at the funeral, he counted out breaths for Finn.

Almost as quickly as it had begun, the asthma attack subsided. Tears were streaming down Finn's cheeks when the trainer removed the mask. Gus brought over a cup of water.

"Pulse ox is back up to ninety-five," the trainer said. "He probably should let his doc take a peek at his lungs, though."

"Uh, yeah," Alek replied. He grabbed his phone. "I'll call Sheridan."

"Already done," Lori announced as she entered the dressing room. "She's on her way. It's going to be a few minutes. Why don't we wait for her up in Mr. Kellogg's office? It's a lot more comfortable up there."

Valentine had removed Finn's skates. Alek sat on the bench in his stall and carelessly tugged his off. He shoved his feet into his sneakers before reaching for Finn's backpack. Gus took it from him.

"I've got this," he said. "You take him."

Finn sat in front of Picard's stall, looking spent. His face was streaked with dry tears. His gaze was focused somewhere off in the distance. Alek crouched in front of him.

"Hey, bud. Do you feel well enough to walk?"

He nodded, but he wobbled when he stood. Alek kept his hand on Finn's shoulder for guidance while they followed Lori to the front office. The guys all murmured a "feel better" or "hang in there" as they filed past. Finn seemed to barely notice.

Questions were ricocheting around Alek's mind like shots on goal. Could Finn be his son? Is that why Jamie had left the boy in his care?

He shook his head. *Nah.* Merriweather was being a dick because he didn't want to come to practice today. He'd pay for taking it out on an innocent kid. Alek would make sure of that.

The facts were the facts. Alek and Madison last slept together the night before he left for Team Canada camp in early May. Jamie and Madison were married in July. Finn was born the following May. There was no possible way he could be Alek's son.

The pain of that realization nearly took him out at the knees, however. It suddenly occurred to him that he'd give anything to have a son like Finn. No matter the circumstances. His father would be lost to him soon. But Alek would have someone else to carry on that father-son bond.

"I'll send Sheridan in as soon as she arrives," Lori said. "There's a mini fridge over there. Help yourself to whatever you need."

Alek needed half a bottle of whisky for the discussion he was about to have with Finn. He settled for a bottle of water instead. Finn unwrapped a lollipop he'd taken out of his backpack and stuck it in his mouth.

"Aunt Sher says these help my breathing," he explained, his voice still raspy.

"Makes sense." Alek sat down next to Finn on the leather couch. "Got any more?"

Finn nodded. He pulled out a plastic baggie filled with lollipops. Alek chose one flavored with butter rum. They sat there quietly for several long moments, enjoying the candy, until Alek couldn't stand it any longer. He needed to address the elephant in the room.

"Look, Finn," he began. "About what Merriweather said—"

"Is that why my mom and dad fought so much?" Finn interrupted. "Because she was mad that you are my dad?"

Christ. Jamie and Madison fought? Was Madison unhappy?

"My dad was my best friend. But I wouldn't be mad if you were my real dad. I know my mom was your girlfriend once," Finn continued.

Alek bit back a groan. "Who told you that?"

Finn shrugged. "Grown-ups always think kids aren't listening."

Alek was regretting poking the sleeping elephant. He draped his arm around Finn's shoulders. "Your mom and I were over before she and your dad got married." He couldn't feel guilty about the lie. Not if it protected Finn. "She loved your dad more."

It was the first time he'd admitted that part out loud.

"And they loved each other enough to make you," he told Finn. Pushing the words past his tight throat was painful, but it was important the boy know that. He gave Finn's shoulders a squeeze. "Jamie will always be your dad."

The door flew open, and Sheridan sprinted in.

"Finn!"

She dropped to her knees in front of them and cupped her nephew's face.

"Your color looks really good."

"They had to use the Epi," Finn told her.

"I heard you were very brave." She brushed the hair back from his forehead. "Can you take a few deep breaths for me?"

Finn did as she asked. Alek wasn't sure what she was listening for without a stethoscope, but she seemed to be satisfied because she gave Finn the most gorgeous smile. Alek would have done just about anything to have one of those pointed his way.

"You are a rock star. What do you say we go show off to the pediatrician?"

"Do I have to?"

She nodded. "You know the drill."

Lori poked her head in the door. "There's some leftover Halloween candy in the business office, Finn. Before you go, will you help a lady out and take some of the temptation away from me?"

Finn gave Sheridan a pleading look. She nodded. He was out the door in an instant.

"Jesus," Alek groaned. "It's like it never happened."

"Yeah. It's like that sometimes." The gorgeous smile was long gone from her face. "He's eight years old, Alek. He couldn't keep up with a group of elite professional athletes even if he had a perfect set of lungs. How could you let this happen?"

He stood and dug his hands into his hips. "Whoa. That is *not* how things went down." Although now Alek was kicking himself for not keeping a closer eye on how much Finn had been exerting himself.

She tilted her chin up in challenge. "Then what brought on his attack? A pretty serious one if they had to bring out the Epi."

Alek sighed. "If you must know, it was Merriweather." *Shit.* She was going to be furious. And hurt. "He implied that Finn might not be Jamie's son. Finn overheard him."

Sheridan opened and closed her mouth several times, but no words came out. She dropped down into the spot on the couch where Finn had just been.

"Wh-what?" she croaked.

"Yeah." Alek shoved his fingers through his hair. "The asshole suggested I was Finn's father. We both know that's impossible."

She continued to stare at him, open-mouthed.

"Right?" he demanded as a fission of doubt coursed through his body.

Her eyes narrowed. "The gestation time of a human baby is the same here as it is in Canada, you idiot. Do the math."

"I did!" he snapped. "But there were a lot of curveballs

coming out of nowhere that summer. I have no idea what really went down."

She seemed to deflate right before his eyes. "Finn isn't yours. Not biologically, at least. For the time being, though . . ." She shrugged. "You handled today well. All of it."

He let out a humorous laugh as he sat down beside her. "You make a better nurse than I do." He bumped her shoulder with his. "In fact, it's impressive watching how you interact with him."

"The important thing is not to panic. Staying calm helps keep the attack from escalating." She patted his hand where it rested on his thigh. "It's always scary. But if you can keep your cool, it helps."

Alek captured her hand when she went to pull away. He threaded his fingers through hers. "Finn knows about me and Madison."

She snorted. "Figures. Nothing is ever secret for long in a small town."

"Were they happy? Madison and Jamie?"

Her head whipped around to stare at him. Her lip quivered slightly. "What do you mean?"

"Finn mentioned Jamie and Madison fought a lot."

Sheridan sighed. "It was hard on both of them when they didn't get the life they both expected."

Alek scoffed. "Yeah well if Jamie and Madison fought, it was likely about money and the way that idiot was draining their finances for who the hell knows what."

It was the wrong thing to say given the abrupt way she yanked her hand free and stood.

"They are gone, Alek. And they're never coming back. There is no point in rehashing their life. Or the choices they made that summer and after. It's water under the bridge."

"I got you some gummy bears, Aunt Sheridan," Finn

announced when he came back into Kellogg's office. He beamed up at her. "Now you won't get hangry at the doctor's office."

Alek was immediately jealous that the gorgeous smile was back on her face.

"You are going to make the perfect husband someday," she told Finn. "Let's go get you a doctor's note for missing school today."

"GUTEN TAG, FRÄULEIN," one of the attending physicians called out loudly when Sheridan arrived for her shift the following afternoon.

"Danke schön," she replied, hoping everyone would quickly laugh it off and move on.

She'd debated calling out of work tonight. The thought of leaving them shorthanded in the ED on a Friday nearly gave her hives, however. Besides, everyone working there was a professional. No one would comment on the dumpster fire that was her personal life.

She was wrong.

Social media was still having a field day with the images from Halloween. Photos of her in the skimpy costume Sloane had picked out for her circulated all over the Internet, making Sheridan the latest thirst trap. Even worse, the pictures of her angrily confronting the creepy dad had been turned into memes poking fun at the Mayhem. It didn't help that the team dropped another game last night. Not even poor Hattie could escape the ridicule.

The trolls believed Sheridan and Hattie were the catalysts

for Alek's inconsistent play this season. One even put forth the theory that Sheridan was a Wiccan who had cast a spell over him, taking over his house, while Hattie was a demon occupying a dog's body. Others simply made lewd comments about where Alek's "head" was.

All of it was outrageous. And so demeaning.

"Shame on you, girl," the charge nurse said. "You've been holding out on us."

"Hasn't anyone ever told you not to believe everything you see online?" Sheridan quipped as she scanned the board listing all the patients.

One of the other nurses snorted. "Does that mean you aren't shacking up with that stud goalie with the bedroom eyes?"

"If by shacking up, you mean are we roommates? Then the answer is yes. Nothing more."

"Mmm, mmm, mmm." The charge nurse shook her head. "I never thought I'd say this about you, Sheridan Cobert, because you are an excellent nurse, but I am deeply disappointed you are not jumping that man's bones."

"That goes for me, too," Finn's therapist chimed in as he strode up to the nurses' station in the center of the ED.

"Trent, what are you doing here on a Friday night?" Sheridan asked him.

"I get reduced rent on my hospital office space if I"—he winked at her—"volunteer one weekend shift every other month. I'm your mental health attending with social services tonight. Buckle up. Friday nights are usually bumpy."

She rolled her eyes at him. "You forget I have a trauma center background."

"I was surprised I didn't hear from you yesterday."

She sighed. "Finn had an asthma attack. By the time I got him all sorted out, the day was over. Maybe we can take our dinner break together and I'll fill you in?"

Trent gave her a thumbs-up before following a PA into one of the bays.

The charge nurse tsked at her. "You do know you're wasting your time with that one, right? He's gay and happily married."

Sheridan smiled at her. "Which makes him the perfect confidant."

"Any idea what brought on the asthma attack?" Trent asked a few hours later when they were in line for sandwiches in the cafeteria.

"Unfortunately, I do."

There were lot of curveballs coming out of nowhere that summer. I have no idea what really went down.

The guilt Sheridan felt about "what really went down" that summer was so palpable, her hands shook. She put down her tray before her mineral water spilled everywhere. Yesterday's conversation about Finn's paternity had been like navigating a minefield. But at least she'd had the truth on her side for once. If Alek started asking more questions, she wasn't sure how she would divert him.

Except the only other person who knows the truth is gone.

Trent eyed her shrewdly. "That bad, huh?"

She paid for her sandwich and followed him to a table in the corner.

"He's wetting the bed," she said when she sat down.

He paused with the sandwich halfway to his mouth. "Finn? Or the hockey stud?"

She shot him a look. He chuckled as he put his sandwich down without taking a bite. "Believe it or not, this is good news. It means the sleeping giant of grief is finally waking up."

"I know. But how do I fix it?"

"*You* don't." He shook his head at her. "I haven't known you very long, but it's obvious you've never met a problem you haven't wanted to solve. Except Finn needs to put in the work to process his grief. You and I are here to act as the guardrails. You can't *fix it* for him." He gave her hand a squeeze. "I'm good at my job. Trust me on this. You know as well as I do that Finn is going to feel this loss for the rest of his life. You can't take it away from him and carry it yourself. Especially when you're dealing with your own baggage."

She snorted. "Baggage makes it sound small and lightweight."

"The goal is getting patients to a point where it feels that way."

"I guess I want Finn to have a less difficult path than I did. Less drama, you know?"

"I do know. But there are no short-cuts with grief." Trent smiled at her. "Finn will have some things easier, though. Because he'll have you as a sounding board."

"And to change the sheets every morning," she joked half-heartedly. She didn't mind covering for Finn, but she hated that yet another thing was going wrong in his life. Gunner had invited Finn to spend the night after the game tomorrow. Finn had declined in terror.

"The less of a big deal you make out of it, the better," Trent told her.

"Yeah that's what all the books say. My lips are sealed."

She'd promised Finn. He was distraught that Alek might find out about his bedwetting. The poor kid had visions of Alek banishing them back to New Hampshire in horror. The irony was, she was sure he would be sympathetic to Finn's predicament.

It was obvious to anyone who bothered to look that Alek adored Finn. Jamie had been correct. Alek was the best choice as guardian. Finn needed a male role model, and given her dating life, who knew when the boy would have gotten one.

She had to hand it to Alek, too. Not many men would take

in a second grader they didn't know. Especially when that kid was the son of his ex and former best friend. And he'd adapted to the role without a single qualm.

Yesterday morning was a prime example. He'd sensed Finn needed cheering up without her having to point it out. He'd rearranged his day to put Finn first. And that was before the fiasco of the asthma attack which he had handled like a pro. As upset as she was with her brother for the choices he made, she wanted what was best for Finn. And that was Alek.

Too bad he's not the best thing for me.

Sheridan was ashamed to admit that her crush on Alek Bergeron was as potent as ever, despite her best attempts to keep it buried. And the blame for its resurgence rested squarely on Alek's sturdy shoulders. He needed to stop touching her. Or acting like he was about to kiss her. The guy was giving off vibes like he thought of her as more than his best friend's kid sister.

She wasn't going to fall for it, though, because she knew it wasn't true. And her heart couldn't bear to be broken by Alek a second time.

"So there really isn't anything going on between you and the stud hockey player?" Trent asked.

Only in my dreams.

She shook her head. "We're just friends. Alek is dating Finn's teacher."

"You don't say?"

"It's still in the early stages, but I think they could be perfect together," she lied.

The very thought of Alek looking at Miss Lane the same way he'd been looking at her the other night, made her stomach roil.

"Huh. And I always got the impression Bergeron was intelligent."

Trent's phone buzzed before she could ask him what he

meant. After glancing at the screen, he began wrapping up the remains of his sandwich.

"This will have to be my midnight snack. We've got several overzealous high school football fans on their way in by ambulance."

PERI AND KIRK BERGERON arrived the following morning. Their presence in the house seemed to invigorate Finn. Sheridan hadn't found the courage to broach the subject of Merriweather's comments with him yet. Instead, she let him soak up the attention of Alek's parents. Heaven knew the boy deserved it.

Kirk jumped right into professor mode, helping Finn build a diorama of a Potawatomi Indian wigwam for his social studies project on Native Americans. From the sounds of it, Alek's dad was having as much fun with the project as Finn. Peri was cleaning up the lunch dishes while Sheridan cut up cheese and vegetables to take on their road trip the next day.

"We can stop and see the museum on our drive to the Door County tomorrow," Kirk offered. "You can snap some pictures for show and tell."

"That would be dope," Finn replied.

Peri looked at her husband curiously. "Do they even have show and tell anymore?"

Finn sobered up. "Yeah. What is that?"

Sheridan and Peri both laughed while Hattie offered her own contribution in the form of a bark.

"Hattie, come," Finn said. "I need to get a pic of you with my project so we can post it on Insta."

His words had Sheridan nearly slicing off a finger. "I'm sorry. What did you say?"

Finn gave her a meek smile. "Hattie has an Instagram account. She's got almost fifteen thousand followers after only three days."

She carefully laid down the knife thinking that holding it might be making her hear things. "Hattie doesn't have an Instagram account."

"Yeah, she does." Finn pulled his phone from his pocket. "See?"

"More importantly," she continued. "*You* don't have an Instagram account."

At least she really, really hoped some kid hadn't shown Finn how to set one up.

"I don't. Honest. But you can go on a search engine and look at people's posts."

Kirk groaned. "The Internet is a double-edged sword. You should only use it with adult supervision, Finn."

"Yes sir." Finn nodded. "I only look at Hattie's profile. I promise."

"And exactly how did Hattie get her own profile?" Sheridan asked although she had a sneaking suspicion she already knew the answer.

"Sloane set it up. She's an influencer," he said as if he knew what that meant. "Dad had lots of photos of Hattie even from when she was a puppy. Look. She made this cool video. It's got over nine thousand likes."

Peri put an arm around Finn's shoulders and leaned down to watch the video. Her face softened before she glanced back up at Sheridan.

"It's very well done."

"That doesn't matter. It's an invasion of our family's privacy. She had no right. And you should have asked me about this first, Finn."

"Alek said it was okay," he argued.

How dare he.

Sheridan wiped her hands on a dish towel trying to contain her pique. It was no use. She didn't care if he was resting before the game. They were dealing with this right now.

"Excuse me," she said to no one in particular as she stomped up the stairs.

Light was shining beneath the door to Alek's room. She hoped that meant he wasn't sleeping. Although she was furious enough that waking him seemed a justified punishment.

"How could you?" she demanded when she charged into his room.

Alek stood next to his bed neatly piling clothes into his equipment bag. Clothes he probably should be wearing. The only thing he'd bothered to put on was a pair of navy joggers slung low on his waist.

Her eyes darted from his dark nipples to the happy trail of hair stretching from his belly button to below the elastic of his pants. She jerked her gaze up only to collide with his surprised eyes. She swayed slightly before refocusing her stare to a spot on the wall a foot above his very sculpted shoulder. It was safer.

"How could I what?" he asked a bit too calmly for her.

"How could you let Sloane set up an Instagram for the dog?"

"Really? That's what got your panties all up in a wad?"

She tore her eyes from the wall and glared into his patronizing ones.

"Finn is too young to be scrolling through social media. Not before he has a good handle on what behaviors are right and which ones are wrong."

"Like not knocking before entering someone's bedroom?" he mocked.

He had her there. Except that wasn't the point. She crossed her arms beneath her breasts and soldiered on.

"I told Sloane I didn't want Hattie to have an Instagram account."

"You did?"

She picked at her sleeve. "Sort of. She might have asked if she could set one up. But I didn't say yes."

He chuckled. It made the muscles in his chest dance provocatively.

"I see. I should have consulted with you first. My bad."

"Yes, you should have." She all but stomped her foot. "It's important that we stay on the same page where it concerns Finn. Have you seen what social media does to kids?"

"Duly noted. Give me the ground rules you want followed, and I will follow them to a tee."

The easy way he folded took some of the satisfaction out of her victory.

He sighed. "In my defense, I was aggravated with all the shit people were posting about you, Finn, and Hattie. In hockey, the best defense is a good offense. Taking charge of the narrative made sense. Sloane may be a bit flakey, but she knows what she is doing. I thought you might be a little more appreciative."

Well, when he put it that way.

"I am appreciative."

So appreciative that I want to lick you from your throat to your navel right now.

She started as if she'd said the words out loud. Thankfully she hadn't. Even more maddening, Alek didn't seem to be as affected as she was. But then, what had she expected?

"Sloane's plan is working. Everyone is in love with Finn's dog." He pulled a tattered T-shirt from his laundry basket. "Me, not so much right now. I thought you said you'd keep her out of my stuff."

"I promised to keep her away from your tighty-whities. I didn't say anything about ratty old T-shirts."

He stalked across the room to where she stood admiring the view. "This was a favorite."

Up close, she recognized the logo from the Ivy League championship. She gently fingered the cotton, buttery soft after years of washing.

And years next to Alek's body.

"Jamie had one just like it," she whispered, surprised at how hard the memory was hitting her. "Hattie used to sleep on it."

She didn't realize she was crying until he reached in to brush the tear off her cheek. His bare chest was now inches from her. He smelled like soap and temptation. She gulped in a breath.

He must have mistaken it for a sob because he gently cupped her face with both hands. Her eyelids fluttered closed on their own. She felt him hesitate before he pressed his lips to her forehead. They lingered there before his palms slid back to his sides and he stepped away. She pried her lids open just in time to catch him dragging in a ragged breath. He gestured to the T-shirt.

"Keep it. Give it to the dog. It makes sense that she's taking my things because she misses Jamie."

He walked over to his equipment bag, plucked a Henley out of it, and shrugged it over his shoulders. The muscles in his back put on a show, flexing seductively before the fabric slid over them.

Feeling very much like the voyeur she was, she hurried to the door before his words stopped her.

"Sheridan. Next time knock."

Shame washed through her. She nodded before softly closing the door behind her. Caressing the shirt between her fingers, she carried it to her room and tucked it beneath her pillow.

FOURTEEN

THE MOOD in the dressing room following the game that night was tense. The Mayhem had dropped another one. The fans weren't shy about letting the players know how they felt. A chorus of boos rained down when the team exited the ice. Alek slumped down on the bench at his stall, not even bothering to remove the thick pads shielding his legs.

Coach stood with his hands on his hips staring his players down. "You guys have somewhere else to be tonight? Because it felt like you were phoning it in out there."

When no one bothered to answer, he swore savagely.

"In the six weeks since preseason," he continued. "We've gone from a well-oiled machine to a team that looks like a bunch of pee wees starring in a Disney film." He looked directly at Alek. "I've given you guys the space to work things out on your own. But if this keeps up, we'll be making some changes. No one is safe."

With that threat hanging in the air, he turned on his heel and stormed out of the dressing room. His job was on the line as much as any of the players. Except tonight's debacle rested squarely at the tip of Alek's skates. He'd let five biscuits slide past the pipes. He couldn't even blame Merriweather. For once, the guy was where he was supposed to be whenever he was on the ice.

Alek opened his mouth to offer up some sort of apology, but Picard quickly shot him down.

"Nope." He pointed his stick at Alek. "Don't even start. The second we admit to having a weak link, this whole team falls apart. And you're not a weak link. You're in a slump." He looked around the room, meeting the eyes of every teammate. "We all have 'em. But the one thing about the Mayhem is we don't let it tear us apart. The rest of us need to step up and put the puck in the net. We didn't execute tonight. Me included." He heaved a sigh. "I'll go out there and take the heat from the media. No sense letting them in here to pepper us with redundant questions." He moved toward the door. "In return for my taking one for the team, everyone better come to morning skate prepared for an extra hour of drills."

He directed that last part at Merriweather. The defensemen nodded without comment, surprising Alek and probably everyone else in the room.

"Okay, then," Picard said. "After all that extra work tomorrow, we'll reward ourselves with a nice team building exercise— dinner at my place. Be prepared to have some very grateful ladies afterward because I'm sparing no expense."

"Yeah, I'll be coming solo," Merriweather announced.

"What? Your wife doesn't want a free dinner?" Picard asked.

"She doesn't like leaving the kids." Merriweather yanked his sweater off his head and headed toward the showers.

Picard shook his head in disgust before heading out to handle the media.

"Something is off there," Gus muttered.

The rest of the team undressed in relative silence. No doubt eager to put this night behind them.

"Yeah, well, he's not the only one with something off," Alek replied.

"Captain's right. This isn't all on you." Valentine sat down on the bench next to Alek. "My wrist cooled off a few weeks ago. Picard hasn't exactly been in sync either. The first line is letting the team down."

Gus snorted. "Speak for yourself, Twos," he said, referring to Valentine's jersey number of twenty-two. "I'm leading the division in points."

Valentine bent at the waist in a mock bow. "And we thank God for your talented lumber every night." He chuckled. "Oh, wait. Maybe that's only your wife who does."

Gus tossed one of his gloves at him.

Alek sighed. "I don't know. It used to be easier to focus on the game."

"That was when you didn't have a life," Gus said. "Now you've got an insta-family and everything that comes with that messing with your mojo. It's bound to affect your game. Hell, I don't have to be a psychic to know opening a restaurant is screwing with Picard's."

"Wow. I hadn't put two and two together there," Valentine said.

Neither had Alek. It still didn't alleviate the guilt he felt at letting his teammates down. "You've got a family," he said to Gus. "How come it doesn't affect your play?"

"Years of practice," Gus said with a wink. "Give it time."

Time was one thing Alek was running out of. His father wouldn't be around forever. And judging by the way Coach was looking at him tonight, Alek might not be either.

"What do you want me to do with these?" The equipment

manager appeared in front of Alek holding a large, black trash bag jammed full of something.

"And *these* are?" Alek asked.

Valentine reached into the bag and pulled out a stuffed dog toy shaped like a slice of pizza. He squeezed it until it squeaked. "Aw, the fans brought stuffies for Hattie."

"They tossed them all over the ice before the game. There's at least four dozen." The equipment manager looked aghast at Alek. "Is this gonna be a thing now?"

Alek shrugged. "At least the fans have someone they appreciate. But I don't want those. My place is already a freaking minefield of dog toys. I can't take two steps in my own house without tripping over one of her toys." Not that the dog showed any interest in them. She'd rather tear up Alek's underwear.

"You want me to throw them away?" The equipment manager looked scandalized.

Shit.

If that got out, the talking heads would crucify him even more than they already were.

Seward leaned over the equipment manager's shoulder and plucked a toy from the bag. "My pooch loves these Lambchop toys. She shreds them up faster than I can buy them."

"Take it," Alek told him. "Anyone else need a toy for their mutt?"

Several of the guys rooted through the toys, but they didn't make a dent in the bag. He was stuck with them.

Twenty minutes later, he carried the trash bag full of dog toys through the mezzanine of the arena to meet up with his family.

His family.

Up until recently, it was a rare occasion when his parents waited for him after a game. Once or twice during the season, his sister and her family might make the trip to a home game, giving him a reason to venture into the family room. Tonight, though, his insta-family, as Gus called them, waited for him, along with his parents.

Finn rushed to him as soon as Alek entered the room. He was carrying an armful of dog toys of his own. "Check it out! Hattie has fans."

"I'll say she does." Alek gestured to the trash bag.

"She's going to think it's Christmas," Finn joked.

Alek waited for Sheridan to burst Finn's bubble and tell him Hattie wasn't keeping all the dog toys. She remained where she was, however, across the room, listening to an animated conversation between Claire and Freya, all the while watching him out of the corner of her eye.

"Actually, I was thinking we could donate these to a local dog shelter," Alek told Finn.

"That's dope! Hattie just tears the guts out of them anyway."

Good to know the dog is consistent.

"I'll reach out to one of the Growlers who works with the Humane Society. He can help us."

"Really? Will I get to meet him?"

"I think that can be arranged."

"Make sure you let someone in PR know when you're doing that," Lori said as she joined their conversation. "Maybe take Hattie along to donate them. It will make a compelling human-interest reel."

She left the part about him needing some positive PR unsaid.

"I'm going to meet one of the Growlers," Finn told Alek's dad when they joined their group.

"Aren't you a lucky guy?"

Alek turned at the sound of Marissa Lane's voice. He'd forgotten he'd even invited Finn's teacher to tonight's game.

And what the hell was he thinking having her at one his parents were attending? The woman was bound to get the wrong idea, saying nothing of his mother. He hadn't even kissed Marissa yet. Up until a few hours ago, his plan was to remedy that tomorrow night, hoping it would lead to a whole lot more.

That was before Sheridan had come bursting into his room, her cheeks glowing with annoyance and her nipples fully alert. His ego appreciated the fact she'd immediately become flustered by his half-dressed appearance. So had the rest of his body.

And that was the problem. He couldn't think of anything else but getting her naked. Not even when a six-ounce rubber disk was flying at his head at nearly one hundred miles an hour.

Gus was wrong. Finn and Hattie weren't the distractions. It was the other member of his insta-family who owned that honor.

"Are those more dog toys?" his father asked.

"We're going to donate them to a dog shelter," Finn chimed in proudly.

"That's an excellent idea." His father took the trash bag from Alek. "Let's add your toys Finn and then we can go put this in the car."

"Yes, we need to head out. We've got an early start tomorrow," his mum added.

"We are going to see some real wigwams at the Potawatomi museum," Finn told his teacher. "Alek is going to take some pictures of me there so I can show the class."

His mum placed her palm on Finn's shoulder. "Alek isn't coming with us, honey."

Finn's face fell.

"I wish I could, bud. But I have to be at practice," he told Finn.

"Oh, yeah. Right."

Gunner sidled up next to Finn.

"And then he's got a date with Miss *La-ane*," Gunner announced in a sing-song voice.

Finn looked at Marissa before shifting his gaze back to Alek. The expression on his face was subdued. Sheridan appeared behind Finn almost immediately, as if the boy had unconsciously summoned her. She wore a wide smile.

"Are we ready to go?" The perky tone she spoke with was like fingers on a chalkboard.

"Yeah," Finn murmured as he bolted in the direction of the exit.

"Good to see you," Sheridan said to Marissa before racing after her nephew.

Alek's dad cleared his throat. "I'll go put this bag in the car."

His mum extended her hand to Marissa. "It was so lovely chatting with you. Thank you for what you do for the children. I hope to see you again soon." She rose to her toes and kissed Alek on the cheek. "See you at home later."

Marissa watched them go. "Um, I need to get going, too. I have some papers to grade."

Ask her out for a drink, Valentine mimed behind her.

Alek ignored his teammate. "I get that. It's a busy weekend. I'll pick you up at five thirty tomorrow?"

She nodded. "I'm looking forward to it."

Asshole that he was, he let her slip out the door without even the courtesy of a chaste kiss on the cheek like the one his mother had just given him.

ALEK ARRIVED home a little after nine the following evening. As promised, Picard's dinner was top-notch. He had to hand it to his teammate, the ambiance of the restaurant was among the best he'd ever eaten in.

Too bad he didn't enjoy a single minute of it.

"Where is everyone?" he asked when he entered his great room to find only his mother wrapped up in a blanket, reading a book. Alek was surprised at the FOMO he felt when they'd left on their road trip early this morning. He was looking forward to Finn's retelling of the day.

"Well, hello to you, too," she said. "We didn't expect you home so early."

Alek shed his suit jacket. "We have a game tomorrow. Picard made sure dinner didn't stretch too long."

"Ah." His mother fingered the corner of her paperback. "And Marissa has an early morning tomorrow, I assume."

He knew what his mother was driving at, but he didn't want to go there with her. Marissa had more than held her own with the WAGs tonight, wearing a stunning little black dress that did wonders for her generous curves. It didn't escape his notice that all the guys had eyed her at one point or another. Alek seemed to be the only male who was ambivalent to her.

And that not only pissed him off, but it confused the hell out of him.

The dress had "do me" written all over it. Marissa had also dropped several hints that she'd finished grading her papers last night so that this evening, she'd be free. *All* evening. Too bad the only action Alek had been capable of was a good night kiss that wouldn't win him any style points.

"Yep." He didn't elaborate further, instead crouching in front of the fireplace to stoke the fire burning there. "You never answered my question. Where is everyone?"

His mother's sigh filled the room. "Your father took Hattie for a walk."

"What?" Alek got to his feet. "Should he be out walking alone? At night?"

"You are being absurd. Your father is perfectly capable of doing normal everyday things. When that changes, I will let you know." Her tone left no room for argument.

He thrust his fingers through his hair. "Sorry. It's easier on you because you see him every day. You go with him to see the doctors. I don't."

She put her book down on the ottoman, then wrapped her blanket more snuggly around herself. "I get that. Something tells me there is more than your father's illness making you so edgy, though."

"In case you haven't noticed, my life has been turned upside down."

"Having second thoughts?"

"No," he answered without hesitation. "None. In fact, I want to hear about Finn's day. He sounded really excited about the museum."

"Mmm."

His mother's evasive response didn't sit well.

"What? Did he not have fun?"

She sighed. "He looked like he was trying to, but he seemed a tad off all day."

Alek moved toward the stairs.

"He's asleep, Alek. Sheridan has gone to bed, also. Let them be." She patted the sofa next to her.

He breathed a weary sigh, then he reluctantly did as she asked.

"Finn and Sheridan have suffered a significant loss. You need to allow them time to process. It may seem like they are on an emotional roller coaster some days. Give them grace." She rubbed the back of his neck. "You need to give yourself some grace also."

"What's that supposed to mean?"

"Jamie and Madison meant something to you too, Alek. Could it be that you're struggling to come to terms with their loss as well?"

He jumped up from the couch. "Fuck no. They were lost to me years ago. By their own choice, in case you've forgotten. I'm fine with their loss, Mum. Perfectly fine." He picked up his suit coat. "It's been a long day. I have practice first thing tomorrow. I'll see you in the morning."

Alek wasn't so much of a dick that he didn't peck his mother on the cheek before storming off. He was too put out by his mother's comments to notice Sheridan standing in the shadows of the laundry room, however.

FIFTEEN

"I'VE TRIED RESTRICTING his water intake at night. That doesn't seem to do anything," Sheridan told Aunt Eileen later that week. "And forget about waking him up to go pee. Once he's out, it's like waking the dead. I certainly can't lift him any longer."

"Oh honey, I wish I had the answers," her aunt replied. "What does his therapist say?"

Sheridan tapped the speaker button on her phone so she could put it down while she switched the sheets from the washer to the dryer.

"Trent says all we can do is ride it out. The pediatrician has checked Finn for other causes, but nothing has come up. It's been three weeks now. I hate to embarrass him by suggesting he wear one of those nighttime diapers, but I'm not sure what else to do."

"Maybe the counselor is right and it's just a phase."

She sighed. "Yeah. But even though he's very cavalier about it, I know it's bothering him. He's been very withdrawn and testy with me all week."

It didn't help Finn's demeanor that Peri and Kirk left Monday morning. Even Alek could barely get more than a one-word answer from him before leaving on a three-day road trip. Finn didn't seem excited when the Mayhem's Monday night game ended in a tie. Of course, they'd lost the game in Minnesota last night. Sheridan was bracing herself for two sullen males in the house when the team arrived back in town this morning.

"Thanksgiving is only two weeks away," Aunt Eileen said. "He'll feel better when he gets to the warm Florida sunshine."

"Are you sure you still want us to come?"

"Don't be silly. Besides, your uncle is looking forward to the game in Tampa that weekend."

Sheridan had forgotten the Mayhem would be in Florida for Thanksgiving, too. Claire had invited them to stay at the hotel in Tampa with them. Finn and Gunner had been talking nonstop about the pool. She prayed Finn would be out of his funk by then.

Her phone buzzed with a text that immediately had her heart racing.

"Aunt Eileen, I'll call you back. Finn's school is texting."

She ran into the kitchen to grab her car keys and her purse as she ended the call.

"Please don't be another asthma attack."

It was only when she looked at the screen that she realized the text was from Miss Lane. And it was directed to both her and Alek.

> Finn is fine, but there is something rather
> urgent I need to discuss with you. Would either
> of you be available to meet during lunch
> today?

Alek was already typing out a reply.

Does noon work?

Really? Who did he think he was?

Noon is perfect. ☺

"Hold on a damn minute, you two love birds."

Sheridan's loud protest had Hattie waking with a start. When a pithy response wasn't forthcoming, she quickly typed in a reply.

See you then.

The teacher responded with a one-word answer: *Great.* The smiley face emoji was conspicuously absent.

By the time noon arrived, Sheridan was a bundle of nerves. What was so urgent that Finn's teacher needed to see them right away? Some specifics would have been nice because Sheridan's mind was bouncing from scenario to scenario, each of them worse than the one before.

When she arrived in the classroom, Alek was already there. He was dressed casually in a pair of dark joggers and a Mayhem quarter zip. Leaning back in his chair, his smile was in full dazzle mode behind his five o'clock shadow. Miss Lane was doing her best to resist his allure as she fingered with her necklaces. Despite the dreary rain, she looked very autumnal in a long rust-colored cashmere sweater and black leggings. Sheridan, in contrast, looked like a drowned rat. She'd forgotten to grab an umbrella or a jacket with a hood before she rushed from the house.

"Good. We can get started," the teacher said when Sheridan slipped into the chair beside Alek. "I'm glad you could both make it on such short notice. It's easier to deal with these things in person rather than over the phone."

"This sounds serious." Sheridan could feel the pulse beating on her neck. "Is Finn okay?"

Miss Lane's smile was sympathetic. "He's fine. Although perhaps a little embarrassed to be caught breaking a strict school honor code violation. One that comes with automatic after school detention."

Alek leaned forward in his chair. "What did he do?"

The teacher opened her desk drawer and pulled out a cell phone. Jamie's old cell phone to be exact. Sheridan recognized the Barn Burner's sticker on the back.

Miss Lane placed it on the center of her desk. "Cell phones are strictly prohibited in the classroom. We'd prefer they don't come to school at all, but we realize some parents have qualms about that."

"Not this parent," Alek said.

Sheridan gaped at him. He'd been a "parent" for a little over a month. And once her case was on the docket, he wouldn't be a parent any longer.

"If it helps," the teacher continued. "He was only using it to scroll on Instagram. Hattie's page, specifically."

"You don't say?" Sheridan shot a pointed glare in Alek's direction.

Alek let out an exasperated-sounding sigh while he avoided meeting her gaze.

Sheridan reached for the phone. "Thank you for bringing this to our attention. It won't happen again."

Miss Lane had the nerve to chuckle. "With all due respect, all parents say that. But these are kids. This won't be the last time Finn pushes the boundaries."

"You said he has to serve detention. When will that be?" Alek asked.

"Immediately after school today. You can pick him up at five."

Alek nodded. "I'll be here."

He began to stand but Miss Lane stopped him.

"Actually, there's more," she said. She drew in a deep breath. "Finn has been . . . not himself all week. In fact, he's been downright rude to me specifically."

"How so?" Alek demanded. "Because that is not acceptable."

Sheridan slumped back against her chair. She was mortified Finn was taking things out on not only her, but his teacher, as well.

Miss Lane held up her hand to stay Alek. "No, it is not acceptable, and he knows that. He and I had a very frank discussion about the situation when we were dealing with the cell phone issue this morning." She cleared her throat and directed her gaze at Alek. "I had an inkling about what might be troubling him. It was resolved as soon as I explained that you and I are not involved with one another. And we never will be."

Ouch.

Alek went still in his chair, his lips slightly parted before he clamped them shut again. The color was high in Miss Lane's cheeks, but Sheridan had to give her props for maintaining her composure. It's not every woman who gives a sexy professional athlete his walking papers in front of an audience. Based on Alek's response, he hadn't seen the hit coming.

"There's one last thing you both should be aware of." She pulled several sheets of paper from a folder on her desk. "I found these when Finn and I were going through his backpack."

She slid the papers forward so they both could see them. The breath froze in Sheridan's lungs as soon as she took in their meaning. They were disparaging notes and drawings. All of them about Finn. Accusing him of jinxing the Mayhem. Laying the blame for the team's poor start to their season on Finn's arrival at Alek's house.

"What the hell is this?" Alek snatched one up. "Who wrote these?" He stood swiftly, swearing violently as he towered over Finn's teacher.

Sheridan couldn't fault him for his menacing tone. She felt sick, too. But it wasn't fair to take it out on the teacher.

"Alek, Miss Lane isn't to blame for these."

"Well, someone sure the hell is!" he shouted. "I want to know who wrote these. I want them kicked out of this school. I want to speak to their parents. Do they have any idea what that little boy has been going through?"

Miss Lane stood also. "The headmaster of the upper school was made aware of the situation as soon as I found those this morning. I'm sure he'll be in contact with you both today."

Her words did nothing to pacify him. Alek swiped up the rest of the notes and headed for the door.

"Sweetheart, he's going to have contact with me right now."

"Alek!" Sheridan called after him.

Miss Lane only smiled as she sat back down. "Mr. Ellis has dealt with worse. Don't worry."

Sheridan picked up one of the notes that had floated to the floor in Alek's furious departure. "My guess is these started arriving about three weeks ago," she murmured.

"Why do you say that?"

"Just a hunch." Sheridan sighed. "I'm sorry for all of this."

"Finn is a great kid. He'll be okay. The two of you make great surrogate parents."

She chuckled. "Let's see if you are still saying the same ten years from now." Guilt made her say what came next. "You know I don't think you should give up on Alek. Finn will come around. He's getting used to having Alek in is life, and he doesn't want to share him. That's all. I know Finn adores you."

The other woman shook her head. "The issue isn't Finn. I agree he'd eventually come around."

"Then I don't understand."

And she really didn't. Sure, her jealousy might have done a happy dance when the teacher delivered her blow earlier. But Sheridan knew where she stood with Alek. And a part of her would always want him to be happy.

"Don't you?" Miss Lane cocked her head to the side. "Alek's heart is already engaged."

A cold dread shot through her. There was someone else? How had she missed that?

Finn's teacher sighed. "You two make a cute couple."

Wait, what?

"Oh, no. You're mistaken," Sheridan assured her. "It's not like that. Alek thinks of me as an annoying younger sister."

Miss Lane actually snorted. "Are you sure? Because when he looks at you, that's not the vibe I'm getting."

"He doesn't look at me," she whispered.

The other woman laughed. "Oh, girl. He looks at you every chance he gets. It's almost as if he can't help it."

Sheridan stared at her in stunned silence for several frantic heartbeats until the buzzing of the phone in her hand brought her back to earth. *Unidentified caller* scrolled across the screen. Who could be calling Finn? She remembered the call he'd received several weeks ago.

Dad gets a lot of calls where no one is there.

"Hello?"

Whoever was on the other end hesitated before a gravelly male voice asked, "Who's this?"

"Who is this?" Sheridan countered.

The line went dead. A fission of alarm raced up her spine. She bounced up from the chair.

"This"—she held up the cell phone—"is staying home from

now on. If Finn ends up in detention again, it won't be because he's scrolling through his phone."

HATTIE LET out a happy bark when Alek stormed into the house an hour later. The dog must have sensed his foul mood because she swiftly picked up the remains of the stuffed shark she was in the midst of dismembering and hightailed it up the stairs. He followed her, depositing his overnight case and his equipment bag in his room with a loud thump.

"Is that helping?" Sheridan asked from the doorway to her bedroom at the other end of the hall.

He leaned a shoulder against the doorframe. "Not really."

She mirrored his pose. "What happened with the headmaster?"

Alek scoffed. "Lots of promises and ass-kissing."

One corner of her mouth kicked up. "I guess it pays to be a professional athlete."

"Not when people use me as a weapon to harass an innocent kid."

It was the wrong thing to say, judging by the way her face crumpled.

"Maybe this wasn't the best idea," she said, her voice was barely audible from where he stood.

He closed the distance between them in six strides. His hands landed on her shoulders, and he gave her a little shake. "Don't say that. Don't ever say that."

"But what if it's true? If our being here is throwing you off?"

"Now you're just being ridiculous." It nearly killed him, knowing he'd been thinking the same thing days before. Because it was bullshit. It was a cockamamie excuse for him having an off game.

Or four.

She shook her head. "We went ahead with this situation because we both want what's best for Finn. I'm worried it might have been too drastic a change for him. He's being assigned the blame for something he has no control over. Not only is it taking an emotional toll but his health is being impacted, too."

A lick of panic coursed through him. "Is something wrong with him?"

She waved him off. "Forget I said anything."

"Hell, no I'm not going to forget it." He tightened his grip on her shoulders. "Tell me what's going on."

She swore softly. "I promised not to."

"Too bad. Tell me now, Sheridan." He towed her forward so that her body was nearly flush against his.

"He's been wetting the bed," she mumbled against his chest.

Alek took a moment to process what she'd said before his body relaxed. "Is that all?" He barked out a relieved laugh.

She slapped her palms against his chest. "It's very serious, Alek. Especially to a second-grade boy. It would kill him if he found out you knew."

He wrapped his arms around her and pressed his lips to the top of her head. "You're right. I'm sorry Finn has to deal with this."

"Yeah, well, he's not the one who has to wash his sheets every day."

Alek reluctantly took a half-step back from her so he could tilt up her chin and look into her eyes. "You are doing an amazing job with Finn, Sheridan. I hope you know that. He may not appreciate you the way he should now, but I know he will later on in life. I promise."

She sniffled a few times before she nodded. "I spoke to Collin on my way back from the school. Our case is on the docket. It should be all sorted out by the end of the month."

The announcement had his gut tightening up.

"Alek, I know we said we'd stay through the season, but I think Finn and I should go sooner."

He'd taken body checks that hurt less than her words did.

"No." He wrapped his arms around her more tightly.

"Alek—"

"No!" He pressed his mouth against her ear. "Do you hear me? That is *not* happening." He breathed in her scent—vanilla and fresh rain. "I need Finn here. In my house. I need that damn jock-thief of a dog in my house."

He repositioned his hands so that they framed her face. Her eyes were wide and luminous with unshed tears.

"And I need you," he forced himself to admit. "You have no idea how much I need you."

Once the words were out, his body took over. His lips found hers, taking advantage of the surprise that allowed his tongue to sweep in. She tasted like honey and something he couldn't quite name, but he knew he liked it. Knew he wanted more. He groaned into her mouth as his body grew tight.

His hands left her cheeks to skim over her shoulders and down her arms. He could feel her body growing warm beneath the cotton of the workout top she wore. She gasped when his thumbs homed in on her nipples.

He maneuvered her against the wall, pinning her between his thighs. She countered the move with her nails against his scalp. Their teeth scraped together as each of them battled for control. Alek let his fingers sneak beneath her top. The contact with her bare skin had his cock jumping against her belly. Her head fell back when he broke the kiss, giving him full access to the tender skin covering the throbbing pulse in her neck.

"Christ, Sheridan," he whispered against her skin.

Sheridan?

Sheridan!

What the fuck was he doing?

He jumped away from her. "Shit, shit, shit. Sheridan. I shouldn't be doing this to you. I'm sorry."

The confused anguish in her eyes was nearly his undoing. But then she narrowed them to slits as she stalked toward him. She pounded a fist into his chest. It was a lot less than he deserved.

"Don't. You. Dare," she hissed. "You better listen up, Alek Bergeron, because I'm only going to say this one last time. I. Am. Not. Your. Little. Sister." She punctuated each word with a slap to the chest. "I am a full-grown woman who deserves to be treated like one," she whispered.

She pressed her palms to his chest, sliding them north so her fingers could wrap around the back of his neck. Her eyes never left his, mesmerizing him as she tilted his head downward so his mouth was a hair's breadth away from hers.

"And I have needs, Alek," she murmured against his lips. "I'm really tired of waiting for you to notice."

The breath sawed through his lungs, and his junk was so tight he thought he might explode with want. He was filled with as much pride as desire, too. Sweet Sheridan, the most non-assertive person he knew, had finally taken control and boldly asked for what she wanted.

In doing so, she'd called him out on the excuse he'd been hiding behind ever since he'd laid eyes on her again. Of course, Sheridan Cobert was not his little sister. She was his kryptonite. When she stretched up on her toes to swipe her tongue over his lips, he was a goner. Funny thing about that? Alek didn't mind one bit.

SIXTEEN

"MY BED," Alek growled against her neck.

Sheridan wasn't about to object. The man she'd not only been dreaming about but lusting over for the past twelve years was finally—*finally*—kissing her. And he was kissing her like she was the woman he desired above all others. The last thing she wanted was for him to have another moment of clarity.

Because if he did, there was no way she would survive.

Alek groaned when she nipped at his jaw. His fingers dug into her ass as he steered her down the hallway in the direction of his bedroom. As soon as they stepped over the threshold, he kicked the door closed and pressed her back against it. His mouth joined with hers again, delivering a demanding kiss full of such urgent hunger that her stomach was twisting and turning. Meanwhile, his fingers slipped beneath her shirt to skim along her back, where they made quick work unhooking her bra. She bucked against his hips when his thumbs brushed over her bare nipples.

"Not fair," she murmured into his mouth before tugging at the hem of his quarter zip.

He stepped back and reached his fingers behind his neck to

pull the sweatshirt over his head. The T-shirt he wore beneath it came along for the ride. One of his arms got tangled, making him curse before he tossed both garments to the floor. He stood before her, his chest still heaving and his hair mussed, looking like the sexiest man alive.

Sheridan sank her teeth into her bottom lip to keep the delighted giggle that threatened from escaping. He shot her a smug look, seeming to read her mind anyway.

"I'd ask if you like what you see, but I already know you do. Your body did all the talking for you the last time you were standing in that spot."

"Mmm." She aimed for a nonchalant shrug when it was all she could do to remain upright. Her legs felt like jelly. She pressed her palms to the door to anchor herself. "Except I really didn't see all that much."

Where those flirtatious words came from, she had no idea. It was as if some other, much more confident woman had taken control of her mind.

Alek cocked an eyebrow. "Well, by all means. Let's give you the full, unobstructed view."

He was already toeing off his sneakers and socks before the full impact of his words hit her. She braced her knees to keep them from buckling when he began shoving his joggers past his hips. A breathy sigh snuck past her lips as she watched the fabric slide down his thighs. The sound brought an even bigger self-satisfied smile to his face. Her skin went from tingling to burning when he stepped out of his boxers.

The man was magnificent.

And he knew it, too. His chuckle bordered on sadistic as he watched her taking him all in.

"If looking at me is what makes you happy, I'll gladly stand here all day," he told her. "Just let me turn the fire on first."

He strutted over to the fireplace in front of the bed.

Holy moly.

Of course, Alek had a perfect set of dimples on his ass cheeks.

With the click of a button on the remote, the flames in the fireplace came to life. They were no match for the ones burning inside Sheridan. Her eyes followed him as he strolled over to the big bed and stretched out on top of the duvet. He lay on his side, propping his head up on his hand. With the other hand, he patted the space beside him.

"Come here, Sheridan."

The slight tremor in his voice told her he wasn't as in control as he wanted her to think he was. It was all the confidence boost she needed. She peeled her hands from the door and walked over to the bed, stopping beside the mattress. His nostrils flared as he watched her lift her shirt over her head before shrugging out of her bra. When she stepped out of her sheepskin slippers, her nipples pebbled painfully beneath the intensity of his stare. He groaned when she bent forward slightly to roll her leggings down her legs.

And then, standing naked before him, she froze. Memories of that night hiding outside the dorm room he'd once shared with Jamie came flooding back to her. How he'd figuratively swatted her away like a gnat.

No!

She slammed her eyes shut. That was then. Alek was here now. And he wanted her. All she had to do was look at him to know that. He'd told her with his words, too. Her teenage crush finally saw her for the woman she was. The woman who loved him. Had always loved him. Even when she shouldn't have.

"Sheridan?"

Her name was uttered with such uncertainty it had her eyelids flicking open. He reached out and gently touched his fingers to hers.

"If this isn't what you want, it's . . ." He sucked in a breath. "It's okay."

She was beside him on the bed in an instant, her lips merging with his in a heady kiss. He sighed into her mouth. Moments later, they were a tangle of limbs, their skin slick with sweat as they mapped out each other's bodies. Her fingers traced the lean muscles on his back, his arms, his abdomen. He let out a hiss when she reached between them to stroke his hard length.

Alek rolled her beneath him, then tore his mouth away. His hips pinned hers to the mattress, denying her roaming hands further access. He stretched up onto his arms and gazed down at her.

"We have all afternoon in this bed, and I have a very detailed list of things I want to do with you. No need to be in such a hurry."

She flexed her hips in protest because, *dude*, she'd been waiting half her life for this moment with this man. He chuckled but didn't give an inch. Instead, his blue eyes seemed to smolder as he took his time studying her from above.

"You're so beautiful," he whispered after the moment stretched. "Inside and out."

Hearing those words after longing for them for so many years was everything. Still, she wanted more from him. So much more.

Sheridan reached up and brushed his hair back from his brow. "You're not so bad on the eyes yourself." She traced her thumb over his bottom lip. "But I'd really like it if you'd put these to better use right now."

He chuckled as he shook his head. "I don't know where you've been hiding this version of Sheridan, but damn, she is turning me on."

She moaned when his lips wrapped around her nipple. He teased it until she was begging for more.

"More like this?" he said, moving to give the other one the same attention.

Yes!

Sheridan squirmed beneath him. She tangled her fingers in his thick hair, digging her nails into his scalp.

"Or more like this," he said when he tore his lips away and kissed his way down her stomach.

Her body bucked beneath him. She felt his laugh against her skin.

"Somebody is very impatient," he murmured into her navel.

"I want you, Alek." She surprised herself by saying it out loud. She'd never been one to ask for what she wanted in bed. Today was different, though. This was her shot. And she didn't dare blow it. "I want you now."

He moved with the grace and fluidity of a natural athlete, his lips taking hers in a searing kiss a nanosecond after the words had left her mouth. She wrapped her arms and legs around him, anchoring their bodies together as their teeth and tongues collided with wild abandon.

"Fuck the list," he said when they came up for air.

Moving as one, he rolled them over, putting her on top.

She hummed as she straddled his hips.

He reached into his nightstand and pulled out a condom. Sheridan took it from him. Her hands shook as she tore it open. She let out a little hum of appreciation when she rolled it over him. His eyes, blue as flames, followed her every movement while his face remained stoic. It was costing him to let her take charge, she could tell.

She scooched up over him, trapping his cock against her very eager, very hot core. Suddenly he wasn't the only one whose breathing hitched. Still, she managed to press her palms against his chest, before deliberately leaning down to touch her nose to his. Her hair hung around them like a curtain, pieces of it catching in the stubble of his beard. Their breath mingled.

When she swept the tip of her tongue over his bottom lip, something shifted within Alek. He let out a string of earthy curse words as he dug his fingers into her hips, guiding her down none too gently onto his pulsing erection. The sheer pleasure of him filling her brought tears to her eyes. She dropped her lids so he wouldn't misinterpret her feelings and, God forbid, stop.

Through the fringes of her lashes, she could see that he was watching her with the same heated intensity he watched the puck as it slid across the ice. The thrill of his undivided attention had her muscles contracting around him. His hips jumped beneath her. She scraped her nails over his nipples, making him groan as his eyes slid shut.

She rose to her knees and waited until his eyelids fluttered back open. Burying her teeth into her bottom lip, she sank back down on him with a satisfied gasp. His eyes never left her face as Alek gripped her waist and guided her up again, then down, until they were moving together at a more vigorous pace. Her belly grew tighter with every movement until she could feel an orgasm within reach.

"Take it, Sheridan," he commanded. "I need to see you."

One hand left her hip to skim up her side where his thumb toyed with her nipple. She cried out as she rode him harder. His other hand traced along her thigh before he reached between them, his thumb finding her sweet spot. He circled her once, then twice before she flew over the edge with a delighted shout.

When she finally caught her breath, she was sprawled across his chest, his hands stroking her ass, and his erection still buried deep inside her.

"Hold on," he said against her neck before reversing their positions.

Alek somehow still had the strength to push up on his forearms. He wiped a piece of her hair from her mouth.

"Still with me?" he asked, his voice husky.

Sheridan could only manage a nod. She felt a tear leak from one of her eyes. Alek caught it with his tongue.

"You okay?"

She was more than okay. She was floating on air and feeling invincible at the same time.

"Mm-hmm," she reassured him, adding a nod for good measure. "It's that this is so much better than I dreamed."

His body went still. "You dreamed of this? With me?" he croaked.

In for a penny . . .

She nodded. "From the moment I met you," she whispered.

Alek's eyes went wide before he quickly closed them. He sucked in a deep breath. "I've been a fool," he murmured.

Her body grew tense with dread before he snapped his lids open and met her gaze head-on. His eyes were glassy. He shook his head slightly.

"Such a fool," he repeated. "Looking past what's been right in front of me all this time." He dropped to his elbows, his mouth hovering right above hers. "But no more, Sheridan. No more. I intend to worship you for as long as you let me."

He kissed her then. A greedy kiss that felt like he was branding her. Not that she minded. She hitched her legs around his back, giving him better access. Alek drove into her with such intensity that she felt another climax beginning to overtake her. He reached between their bodies. With one flick of his finger, she shattered, her body convulsing around him. Seconds later, he roared her name when his own pleasure washed over him.

A FEW MINUTES LATER, Alek slipped back into bed after grabbing a water from the bathroom. He offered it to Sheridan. The sheet slipped down low when she took a long pull from the glass, teasing him with a peek at one of her strawberry-colored nipples. It was all he could do not to reach for it. Just like that, he was hard again, as if he hadn't had the most meaningful sex of his life moments before.

Alek had entertained more than a few women in this bed over the years, but none of them as guilelessly gorgeous as the treasure next to him. Even more amazing, Sheridan seemed oblivious to the picture of sensuality she was with her flushed skin, finger-tossed hair, and kiss-swollen lips. Perhaps it was part of her mien of invisible people-pleaser she'd adopted at a young age. He hated how much she doubted herself. And he hated himself for not seeing the real Sheridan all this time.

He leaned in and brushed his lips over her shoulder. The musky scent of sex still clinging to her was doing crazy things to his nerve endings. Not to mention his balls.

"I want to hear all the things you dreamed of me doing to you," he murmured against her skin.

She trembled beneath his touch. "I thought you had your own list." The husky timbre of her voice was making him twitch.

"Who says we can't compare notes?" He reached around and palmed her breast.

Sighing, she dropped her head back, exposing her long neck to his mouth. He dragged his tongue along her collarbone, realizing there were still parts of her he needed to taste. A groan rang out in the room. He was pretty sure it was his.

Alek pressed her onto her back and crawled on top of her. She gasped when his erection brushed against her belly. He was being a jerk for jumping her so soon after their first round, but he couldn't help it. Her passionate response had turned him into a horny teenager.

"School gets out soon," she said.

He flicked his tongue over her nipple. "Detention, remember? I don't have to pick him up until five. Until then, I plan on spending the next two hours doing things to you that might get me suspended if I were still in school."

"Are you sure you want to pick him up? I can do it."

People-pleasing Sheridan was fighting her way back into the bedroom. Alek wasn't having it. He tore his mouth away from her sultry skin and lifted his gaze to meet hers.

"I said I'd do it."

She gave him a one-shouldered shrug while her fingers toyed with the top of the sheet. "I thought that with everything that went down with Finn's teacher this morning, you might, you know, want to avoid the place."

He swore to himself.

Why the hell must women be so complicated?

"If you're insinuating my ego is damaged after Finn's teacher cut me loose this morning, you're wide of the goal pipe. In case you haven't noticed, I'm much more interested in another woman."

An adorable blush broke out on her cheeks and chest.

"Still, I'm sorry it didn't work out. I—"

Alek slapped a hand over her mouth. "Don't you dare. She wasn't what I wanted. I barely kissed the woman once, and it obviously left her with a bad impression. I never wanted to kiss her here." He pressed his lips to the underside of her breast. "Or here." He traced her navel with his tongue. "Definitely not here." He spread her thighs wide and scraped his teeth along the inside of one. "And most certainly not here."

"Oh God, yes," she cried when he blew on the tender spot between her legs, already wet for him.

"Yes what, Sheridan?" he demanded. "Bring back the assertive woman who knows what she wants and isn't afraid to ask for it. Tell me what you dreamed I'd do to you. Tell me it was this." He blew on her again.

She was panting now. Her throat moved, but no words came out except for a sound that could be described as feral. She dug her fingers into his hair and positioned his head at the apex of her thighs. Alek would have laughed, but he was nearly undone by the need to taste her.

"Oh, please, yes," she cried when his tongue delved into her.

Alek tugged her to the edge of the bed and kneeled beside it before hooking her legs over his shoulders. He tasted his fill, teasing her as he brought her to the brink not once but twice before pulling back. Sheridan writhed beneath him, her fingers tangling in the sheets as she pounded her heels into his upper back in frustration.

He took pity on her. But only because he was so riled up himself, things were becoming painful. Working his tongue against her sensitive bud, he drove her to the precipice and let her fall over its edge.

"Yaaasss," she screamed as her body convulsed around him before going completely limp.

After kissing his way along the inside of her thigh, he stood and grabbed another condom. Her breathing was still erratic. Still, she watched him with glassy eyes and a half-drunk smile on her face. He flipped her over as if she were a rag doll before positioning her on her knees in front of him. Then, without so much as a mother may I, he plowed into her.

Sheridan's lusty moan was music to his ears. Her muscles contracted around him, eliciting a strained growl from somewhere deep in his chest. He felt the tremor that coursed through her body when he pressed his chest to her back. As if he had all the patience in the world, he slowly pulled out halfway before thrusting back inside, filling her to the hilt. She made a raspy sound each time he did it, undulating her ass cheeks against his thighs with every thrust.

"Tell me this was on your list," he breathed against her ear as he continued to plunge in deeply. "Tell me you dreamed of me doing this to you."

She bobbed her head as her skin slapped against his. That's when he realized he wasn't going to make it. For the first time in forever, he was going to come first. She was too damn sexy for her own good.

He reached around to fondle her breast. "Sheridan, tell me what you need for me to make it good for you."

Sheridan looked back over her shoulder at him, wearing *an are-you-kidding-me* look before grabbing his free hand and pressing it to her clit. She held it there while he worked his finger over her. Half a minute later, her body wrapped around him like a velvet glove, drawing out his climax until his knees buckled.

"You," she gasped against the mattress. "You are all I need."

He dragged in a ragged breath, deeply humbled by her words while at the same time terrified that he wasn't worthy of her.

SEVENTEEN

DARKNESS SETTLED over the carpool lane where Alek waited for Finn that evening. He watched as one of the teachers—not Marissa, thank goodness—escorted Finn from the building. Despite what he had told Sheridan, he wasn't ready for face time with Finn's teacher yet. Mostly because he was embarrassed by the way he'd pursued her, using her as a diversion when he was unwilling to admit the woman he wanted was under his roof all along. He was relieved Marissa saw right through his charade before he did. She deserved better.

Finn's shoulders slumped, and his steps began to drag as soon as he spied Alek. The teacher pulled open the passenger door of the car, and Finn climbed in.

"It was nice to meet you, Finn," the teacher said. "Good job on your homework. Have a good evening." She waved at Alek before closing the door.

"Wow. A nice detention teacher. That was never my experience." Alek put the car in drive and pulled away from the curb.

"*You* had to do detention?"

"Don't sound so astonished. I was a rowdy boy once upon a time, too. Except when I got detention, I had to shovel the snow off the sidewalks. No doing homework in a warm classroom. Next, they'll be serving you milk and cookies."

"Mrs. Levine had chips and a juice box."

Alek turned to gape at Finn. "Seriously? And they call my generation special snowflakes."

He shook his head and focused on pulling out of the parking lot onto the main road. Finn was quiet again while Alek wrestled with how to begin the conversation they needed to have.

"Is Aunt Sheridan mad?" Finn asked quietly.

Alek scoffed. "At me, yeah."

"How come?"

"Because I let you go behind her back with the Instagram account. She knew it would be a distraction. Turns out, she was right."

Finn sighed as he slid down deeper into his seat. "I'll bet she's really mad at me, too."

Alek reached over and ruffled up Finn's hair. "Nah. I calmed her down."

He shot Alek a disbelieving look. "Really? How'd you do that?"

Multiple orgasms.

"Give me credit for having some skills," Alek said instead.

"So she's not leaving?"

Alek almost slammed into the car in front of them. Finn's bottom lip was quivering when Alek looked over at him. Swearing to himself, he drove into the nearest parking lot and pulled into a spot.

"Let's have it," he said after he killed the engine. "Sheridan isn't going anywhere. Why would you even say that?"

The little boy shrugged, keeping his face averted. Alek gently placed a hand on the boy's shoulder.

"Finn," he pleaded. "Talk to me. Where is this coming from?"

"My parents used to fight about her," he mumbled.

Alek felt as if someone had sucker punched him. Madison and Jamie fought about Sheridan? Whatever for? The two women had always been thick as thieves. Madison was a big sister and mother rolled into one. Everything Sheridan needed at the time.

"My dad said Aunt Sheridan needed to live her own life. And she couldn't do that in New Hampshire. My mom was mad that she only came home for a visit and then she left again. She said my aunt was ruining her life."

Fucking Jamie. Sending his wife's best friend away when their family was making the big adjustment away from the game of hockey. When Madison probably needed someone in her corner the most.

"Look, bud. If your aunt were going to desert you, she would have done it by now. Your dad named me as your guardian. Do you understand what that means?"

Finn nodded, but he still didn't make eye contact.

"Well, in case you haven't noticed, that didn't sit well with your aunt. You are all she has left." A painful lump formed in his throat. "And not even a stint in detention or relocating to Wisconsin in lieu of Spain is going to make her walk out of your life. She loves you, bud. Much more than you realize."

Alek dug a napkin out of the center console and handed it to Finn who was sniffling in earnest.

"And while we are on that subject," Alek continued. "I love you, too. And I'm pissed as hell that you didn't come to me and tell me the nasty things the kids in the upper school were saying."

"They said you would send me away!" Finn cried. "They want you to!"

He unclipped Finn's seat belt and pulled him into a hug. "I

can't believe I have to keep saying this. No one in our makeshift little family is going anywhere. You hear me?"

"But what if it *is* my fault?" Finn mumbled against Alek's jacket.

"What if what is your fault? The fact that my teammates and I are off our game? Shit happens. Nothing is guaranteed in sports or in life. But do you see any of us pointing fingers or giving up? No. That's not how this works. We are a team. We'll work out the kinks and move on, or we won't." He shifted Finn back into his seat and placed his hands on the boy's face. "The only thing I know for sure is that no one person or thing is jinxing us. Especially not you. You hear me?"

Finn bobbed his chin up and down slightly.

"We are only six weeks into the season. Don't you dare give up on us, Finn Cobert. All we have to do is make it to the play-offs. Didn't your dad ever tell you about the time we won the Ivy League championship?"

The boy's face brightened at the mention of his father. "He said you guys swept the other team."

"Sure did. But we had the worst record in the conference. Every team gets an invite to the championship, though. We played lights out against each opponent until we reached the finals. Then we swept 'em." He mussed Finn's hair again. "Those upper school kids don't even know they gave the Mayhem bulletin board material for the season."

"You're gonna post those notes in the dressing room?"

"Hell, yeah, bud. Unless you'd rather I didn't?"

Finn jumped across the console and wrapped his arms around Alek's neck. "That's so awesome."

Alek hugged him back, surprised with the ferocity of his feelings. This child was the product of two people who broke his heart. Yet Alek would do everything in his power to protect him, to shield him from the hurt of others, to give him a life of joy.

The growling of Finn's stomach interrupted Alek's introspection.

"What's for dinner?" Finn asked, his mind already ping-ponging to needs more important to a second-grade boy.

"Your aunt wants garlic knots and a Caesar salad from Pirelli's," Alek replied as he started the car again. "That means it's a meat lover's pizza for us guys."

"Yes!" Finn gave him a fist bump.

"Gotta keep your aunt happy." Alek smiled smugly, recalling just how happy he'd made Sheridan an hour earlier.

"Miss Lane said she isn't your girlfriend even though Gunner said she is."

Alek had hoped to avoid that particular topic of conversation. "I can see how Gunner might get the wrong impression. I took her to a party at Picard's last weekend."

"How come?"

"Everyone was bringing a date." Not a lie. "And you and Gunner said she was pretty cool. I thought it would be fun to get to know her better. That's all."

"So you're not gonna marry her?"

The ABS alarm pinged for a second time when he slammed on the brakes to avoid rear-ending a minivan. "No. Of course not. That's not happening."

"Yeah. She said never in a million years."

Well, damn.

"She said Aunt Sheridan has my phone. Do you think she'll let me have it back? It was my dad's, and I want to keep it. If I promise not to bring it to school, do you think you can convince her?"

"Sure thing, Bud. If it takes me all night, I'll work on her." Alek said with a self-satisfied laugh.

"What did you do that you had to go to detention?" Finn asked a few minutes later.

They were so not going there. "I don't remember."

Finn chuckled. "I'll ask Peri. I'm sure she remembers."

That was what Alek was afraid of.

***

"YOU WEREN'T KIDDING when you said that kid sleeps like the dead," Alek remarked when he closed the door to the Jack and Jill bathroom that joined Sheridan's bedroom with Finn's. "Mission accomplished."

"Really? He went?" She couldn't believe Alek had solved the problem that easily.

"Peed like a racehorse without so much as waking up." He pulled her against his chest, burrowing beneath her hair so he could nuzzle her neck.

"Do you think it will work?"

"We'll know in the morning." His hand traced the outline of her breast, making her shiver. "Until then, how about you let me give you something else to think about?"

"Finn is right there in the next room." Her protest lacked any real bite, given she was allowing him to back her up to the bed.

"Did we or did we not establish that the boy is a deep sleeper?" He pressed his hips to hers, and she couldn't help the moan of pleasure that slipped past her lips. "But just in case, you're going to have to be a good girl and keep quiet," he whispered against her ear. "Do you think you can do that for me, Sheridan?"

It was hard for her to think with his erection making itself known against her belly. She turned her head to the side and nipped at the corner of his mouth. His hands made quick work of her clothes. She shoved his sweats down over his ass, letting out a little gasp when she realized he wore nothing underneath.

He gave her a cocky look while he shucked his shirt. "I figured they were only coming off anyway."

The bed groaned beneath their weight when he crashed down on top of her.

"Shh," they admonished each other with a laugh.

Keeping quiet proved to be a challenge, however. Between the headboard thumping against the wall and the squeaky bedframe, they had to get creative. Not that she minded. They both ended up laughing at each other more than once. In the end, she had to bury her face into a pillow when she came.

Thirty minutes later, Alek returned from the kitchen carrying a protein shake for him and a water for her. He placed a chocolate kiss on the nightstand next to her water.

"Where did you find this?" she asked as she unwrapped it.

"It was in Finn's Halloween candy reject bucket. Not sour enough for him, I guess."

He crawled into bed beside her. She shrieked when he pressed his cold feet against hers.

"Hush, woman." He wrapped an arm around her shoulders and pulled her next to him. "Mmm. This is nice."

"You can't stay."

Alek kissed the top of her head but didn't say anything. She rolled over onto his chest to look at him.

"Finn is already confused about enough things," she told him. "I don't want him to get the wrong idea about us."

He studied her for a long minute. "About us?"

"Yes." She waved her hand over his chest. "About this. Whatever this is."

She felt the muscles in his arms tense. "Whatever *this* is?"

Sheridan pulled free of him and flopped on her back. "*We* don't even know what this is."

She knew what she wanted it to be. Except she wasn't that naive teenager anymore. A relationship with Alek would be complicated. She couldn't live with herself if they were involved while she held on to the secrets that haunted her. Telling him would almost guarantee he'd want no part of her, however.

"I don't want Finn to get the wrong idea."

Or get his hopes up like I most certainly will.

"He for sure got the wrong idea about me and his teacher." Alek chuckled. "He thought we were getting married."

"What?!" She sat up in the bed.

"Yeah, so keeping this on the down low works for me." He tugged on her arm, positioning her so she was sprawled out over his chest again. "Besides, I like the idea of having you all to myself," he murmured as he combed his fingers through her hair. "But 'whatever this is,' it's important to me, Sheridan. You and Finn are important to me. I don't want to mess it up."

Alek captured her lips in a kiss that turned feverish after only a few seconds. She straddled his hips, biting back a moan as she slid against his erection. He fumbled with the condom before she took over the task. She dug her teeth into his shoulder at the same time as she sank down onto him. And then they were moving almost as one, their rhythm already familiar and guaranteed to bring them both pleasure.

Moments later, both sated once again, Alek resumed brushing his fingers through her hair with one hand while he tucked the other hand behind his head. She reveled in the feel of his heart beating beneath her palm.

"Finn wants his phone back," he said. "He promises he won't take it to school with him. He only wants it because it belonged to Jamie."

She was surprised Finn hadn't started hounding her the minute he'd gotten home. It wasn't like him to show the kind of restraint he had this evening. Now she knew why.

"He enlisted you to be the mediator, did he?"

"What can I say? I possess an appeal that he can't offer."

She snorted.

"Hey, if that wasn't enough to convince you, give me a few minutes, and I'll do better on round three."

Sheridan pressed her lips to his pecs. "If you do any better, I won't be able to go to Pilates tomorrow."

His chuckle sounded very self-assured.

"Today was the first time Finn mentioned Madison to me," he murmured right when she was about to doze off.

The topic had her instantly alert. She spread her fingers out over the warm skin on his chest, hoping the tactile contact would calm her now racing heart.

Alek smoothed his hand over her hair. "He told me they fought about you."

Her hand stilled. She felt him suck in a breath.

"Finn said Madison used to get upset every time you left after a visit."

Only because she was the one staying.

"She must have been lonely," he continued.

"You forget that Madison grew up in the next town over. She had plenty of friends."

Some a lot friendlier than others.

"I guess," he rambled on. "But I always got the sense she was fondest of you."

Time for a new topic. There were too many landmines buried in any conversation involving Madison. It stung to hear Alek speaking about his ex with such concern. To know he was still fond of her despite everything she'd done.

Except he didn't know everything Madison had done.

"What did Finn say about the upper school boys?" she asked.

Alek hesitated a moment, as if he knew she'd changed the subject on purpose. He didn't question it, though.

"He promised to tell us if they bully him again. The teachers will be on the lookout, too."

She sighed against his chest. "Why do people have to be so cruel?"

"Mm," was all he said.

His breathing became more rhythmic, a sure sign he was drifting off to sleep. She nudged his shoulder.

"Hey. You need to go to your own room."

"Five more minutes," he mumbled.

That was the last thing she remembered until Finn called her name the following morning.

"Aunt Sheri!"

She jumped from the bed, frantically searching for her flannel sleep pants and T-shirt. Finn jiggled the handle on the bathroom door.

"The door is locked," Finn cried. "How come the door is locked?"

"I'm coming." She shoved her arms into her T-shirt before glancing back at the bed.

Alek was struggling with his sweats. A bruise was forming on his shoulder, likely from where she'd bitten him. His hair stood up on its ends and there was a line of pink scratch marks down the center of his back.

"Aunt Sheridan!" Finn tried the door again.

Unable to keep her nephew waiting any longer, she took advantage of Alek's grogginess and shoved him off the other side of the mattress before rushing to the bathroom.

"What's wrong, little man?" She unlocked the door, sliding through before closing it again behind her. "Did you have a scary dream?"

Finn wrapped his arms around her waist. "I didn't flood."

His blue eyes were shining with pride when he tilted his face up.

Relief coursed through her. She brushed the hair out of his eyes before bending down to kiss him on the forehead. "That's great news. I told you it wouldn't be forever. This calls for a special breakfast. How about some cinnamon toast?"

He shook his head as he pulled away. "It's game day. I want eggs. Just like the ones Alek eats for breakfast on game day."

"You don't like eggs."

"I do now." He raced into his room. "Come on, Hattie. Let's go check your Instagram on the computer."

The dog gave her a dopey smile before Finn popped his head back in.

"If I promise not to take it to school, can I have Dad's phone back?"

Not wanting to dim his joy, she nodded her head.

"Yes!"

He was pounding down the stairs when she remembered the strange phone calls he'd been getting. She raced into the hall.

"Hey, Finn?"

Two strong arms grabbed her around the waist and tugged her back in the direction of her room.

"You're going to pay for that little shove at naptime today," Alek growled against her ear. "I have lots of ideas of how to punish you, too."

Her body reacted with an delighted tremor. "Should I be scared?" she whispered.

"Very."

"Oh, Hattie what did you do?" Finn yelled from the vicinity of the kitchen. "Aunt Sheri!! Hattie ate another pair of Alek's underwear!"

EIGHTEEN

THE MAYHEM WON their fourth straight game behind the magic of a shut-out by Alek. Gus and Picard each buttered a biscuit while Valentine slapped in two. The visitors' dressing room was bumping when the team came off the ice.

"Way to come into someone else's house and grab the dub," Coach told them in his post-game speech. "That was some fantastic puck handling on the penalty kill, boys."

The room broke out in applause and wolf whistles.

"And Valentine, helluva goal on the power play."

"Hear, hear," the guys chanted.

"I'm proud of you boys for tuning out all the chatter and going balls to the wall to get us over five hundred in the win column. We're finally playing Mayhem hockey. Let's keep it up." Coach smacked Alek on the shoulder on his way out of the dressing room.

"Great fuckin' skating tonight, boys," Picard said once the coach left. He pulled the medallion chain out of his stall. "Twos, you played lights out tonight."

Everyone cheered for Valentine. He shoved his fists in the air and mimed a boxing match.

"But I gotta give this one to Ice-Berg for blocking eighteen effing shots on goal and keeping them all out of the crease!" Picard yelled above his teammate's catcalls.

"Speech. Speech. Speech," the guys shouted.

Alek stood, taking the chain and putting it around his neck. "Great game out there, boys. Let's go home."

The room erupted in more cheers. The players began to peel their sweaters and pads from their bodies, tossing them into the laundry baskets. Someone turned on the AUX, and Motley Crüe burst from the speakers. Soon, everyone was singing along about home sweet home.

The red-eye from Quebec would put them back in Milwaukee a little before daybreak. If everything went as planned, he'd be home in time to see Finn off to school and to spend a few glorious hours between the sheets with Sheridan. After a five-day road trip, he was ready to see his makeshift family again. He missed Finn's laugh and his incessant questions. Hell, he even missed Hattie's toys strewn all over the house. And it went without saying, he missed everything about Sheridan.

"Are we bringing these home with us?" the equipment manager asked.

"I do believe Hattie has become a bigger celebrity than Sloane," Valentine said as he eyed the bag of dog toys. "And did I hear your agent is representing her now?"

Alek scoffed. "Collin talks a lot of shit when he shouldn't." He turned to the equipment manager. "Someone from a local shelter is supposed to pick them up from Will Call. Lori reached out to them by email last night. Can you check with her?"

It seemed that in every arena the Mayhem played, fans were tossing dog toys onto the ice before the game. Under Lori's guidance, Finn established the Hat Trick Foundation as part of a class project. Miss Lane even helped Finn make a video for social media. In it, he explained the toys would be donated to local pet shelters in the cities where the Mayhem played. It was crazy how well the thing had taken off in only two weeks.

"If Hattie continues chewing up Ice-Bergs's jockstraps, she's gonna find herself at the local shelter, too," Valentine joked.

"Nah," Picard said. "Ice-Berg's been playing better since the dog became a social media sensation. Who cares if Hattie is chomping on his skivvies? Don't do anything to mess with the Mayhem mojo."

Gus snorted beside Alek. "I doubt it's the dog that got you out of your funk," he murmured.

Alek glanced around the room. Valentine and Picard were already on their way to the showers.

"What's that supposed to mean?" Alek kept his voice low.

"Just a guess here, but I'd bet my left nut Hattie wasn't the one who gave you that love bite last week. Or the scratches on your back. Don't worry," Gus said when Alek took another frantic look around the room. "The guys think you're getting some action with Finn's teacher. I know that's not true because my son gossips more than a teenage girl. Which can only mean one thing. You and Jamie's little sister have progressed from roommates to bedmates."

Letting go of a few choice words, Alek snatched a towel from the shelf.

"Hey, I'm not complaining. Especially since you seem more grounded. More focused in the net," Gus continued. "Except things were already complicated between you two before you added sex into the mix, you know? I don't want to see anyone get hurt." Gus spread his arms wide. "You're my best friend, man. No one wants to see things work out for you guys more than I do. But three hearts are in play here. And one of them has already taken quite a few body checks. Tread carefully, that's all."

With those pearls of wisdom delivered, Gus headed to the showers. Alek's phone rang before he could follow. His agent's face popped up on the screen.

"Hey, Col," Alek answered.

"That was some headline-grabbing goal keeping tonight, Bergeron. Kellogg better start counting his money because I see a performance bonus in your future if you keep this up."

A performance bonus that would net Collin fifteen percent.

"It's a long season," Alek replied. "Don't go spending it yet."

Collin chuckled. "Oh, I have no doubt we will both be hearing a little cha-ching come playoff time. But listen, I didn't call about that. An opportunity has come up for you to score some great name recognition in front of a national television audience."

"Yeah, what's that?"

Players were beginning to file back in from the showers.

"The Growlers have a game tomorrow night in front of a nationally televised Thursday night audience. Luke Kessler is doing one of his Adopt a Doggie promos before the game. I got you an invite."

"Me? Why me?"

"For fuck's sake, Bergeron, don't you even look at social media? Your dog is famous."

Alek made his way to the showers. "Finn's dog."

"Yes. And people are eating up the charity he and his cute little teacher thought up. Look, Kessler is really grateful for all the donations of dog toys you've given to the shelters he supports. He wants you, Finn, Hattie, and the teacher to join him on the field pregame so he can recognize your contributions. Here's our chance to give pro hockey its moment in front of fans who might not otherwise watch the sport."

"Wow. Finn will eat that up."

"I know, right?" Collin paused. "There's just one teensy problem."

"What's that?"

"Sheridan. She says no go because"—he pitched his voice higher—"it's a school night. And Alek and I have rules." Collin groaned. "Christ, man, you two are much stricter than Jamie and Madison ever were. Finn has spent half his life in a bar, for crying out loud."

His agent's comment had Alek halting in the middle of the hallway leading to the showers. He could hear Valentine butchering a Drake song while the Swedes tried to drown him out with their rendition of "Bohemian Rhapsody."

"Were they happy?" Alek had no idea what made him ask the question.

"Were *who* happy?"

"Madison and Jamie."

Why the hell do you even care?

Collin didn't reply right away. "I guess? I mean, I didn't see them that often after he left Boston, but they always seemed fine." The line beeped. "Hey, I have to take this call. You'll work some magic with Sheridan and convince her to say yes?"

Oh, he was planning on performing quite a lot of magic on Sheridan.

Gus arched his eyebrows and tapped his finger against his wrist with the universal sign to hurry things along.

"Consider it done. But I'll need two extra tickets," Alek told Collin. "Finn will want to bring his best friend and his dad to the Growlers game tomorrow night, too."

"Yes!" Gus mouthed as he gave Alek a fist bump.

"Deal," Collin said. "I'll text you the details in the morning."

THE WIND WHIPPED around the sidelines of the football field the following night. Sheridan gave up trying to tame her hair and snuggled deeper into her shearling coat. She was grateful they'd be watching the game from the relative comfort of the owner's suite. Not only would it be warmer, but it would also make controlling Hattie much easier. The dog had spent most of her life surrounded by a rowdy bar crowd, but that didn't compare to seventy thousand football fans after an evening of tailgating. The poor thing was already a little jumpy.

"So let me get this straight," Sheridan said, working hard to keep her teeth from chattering. "The owner of the Growlers is Max Kellogg's sister?"

"Half sister," Alek explained. "Norm Clark founded Cream City Breweries, which now belongs to his oldest, legitimate son, Norm, Junior. Mr. Clark left the Growlers to his oldest daughter, the Timber baseball team to his other daughter, and the Mayhem to Max, which was a surprise to everyone since Norm had never let on to anyone that he had a fourth child."

"Wow. That sounds like it would be a bestseller if someone wrote it."

"Right?" he replied. "Mrs. Ciaciura—that's the sister who owns the Growlers—is the only sibling who has a relationship with Kellogg. Norm Junior wants nothing to do with him. And the other sister is on husband number three or four. I don't think she even lives in the States any longer."

"Well, thank goodness for his sister. It's cold out here. Why do they have to play at night?" she muttered. "In November."

Alek stepped closer, his body providing some shelter from the cold. "Don't worry. It's only until halftime. And I'll be sure to warm you up when we get home."

"You're forgetting that I'm only going to be home for a few hours," she told him. "I'm filling in on the two a.m. to two p.m. shift tonight."

Finn hadn't "flooded" for two weeks. Still, it was a risk not being home in the morning. Based on how Alek had dealt with Finn about the issues at school, she had no doubt he would handle things without embarrassing Finn.

He made a grumbling noise. She patted him on the shoulder. "It's for a good cause. I'll have Thanksgiving weekend off. I hear the pool at the hotel in Tampa is amazing."

"Wait until you see the Jacuzzi tubs in the rooms," he murmured with a wink.

"Alek!" A boy wearing a Growlers jacket and pom-pom hat sprinted toward them.

"Kyle, my man." Alek wrapped him up in a hug. "How are you?"

"Great! Whoa! Is that Gus Ferguson?" Considering they were standing on the sidelines with most of the Growlers team milling around them, it was odd to see the boy so starstruck.

"It is." Alek motioned his friend over. Gunner, Finn, and Hattie came with him. "Kyle, this is the man, the legend, Denis Gus Ferguson. Gus, this is my pal, Kyle Prince. Don't let the football gear fool you. He's obligated to wear it because his sister is married to the QB. The kid's really a hockey fan and a genius with a puck and some lumber."

Gus shook the boy's hand. "Sounds like someone I want to know. Nice to meet you, Kyle."

Alek finished the introductions. "And this is Gus's son, Gunner, also a magician on skates. And this guy is Finn Cobert. Hockey is in his blood, too. His dad and I played together in college before he went on to play for Boston."

Sheridan looked on with gratitude when Alek's hand landed on Finn's shoulder as naturally as if he'd known the boy all his life. The way his explanation about Jamie rolled off his lips so easily made her heart swell, too. The animosity he normally displayed whenever the subject of Jamie arose was nowhere to be seen when he was around Finn. His thoughtfulness made her adore him even more.

Hattie nosed her way into the circle of boys.

"Oh my gosh. You are even cuter in person." Kyle nuzzled the dog's head. "I wish I had a dog like this. Or any dog."

A beautiful redhead all decked out in Growlers gear joined them. "I tried for years to get Mom to get me one," she said. "But maybe you'll wear her down, Kyle." Her face lit up with a stunning smile when she spotted Alek. "Hey, you."

Sheridan felt a little kick to the chest at the familiar way Alek embraced her, holding on for longer than was necessary, in her opinion. She nearly jumped at the sound of an angry snarl behind her.

"Down, boy," the woman hugging Alek said when she stepped out of his embrace. "I married you, remember?"

A very tall man in a Growlers uniform made a point to step between the woman and Alek before pulling her into a possessive side-hug.

"Bergeron," he bit out.

Alek taunted him with a cocky grin. "Van Horn. You must not be treating your wife right if she's hugging other men."

"Knock it off, both of you," Collin demanded as he slipped between them. "We recently put all that bad blood press to bed. Could you two at least act like you like each other?" He glared at Alek. "You both represent the same city. The goal is for you to share fans, remember?"

Gus snorted as he leaned in to give the Growlers quarterback a man hug. "Hey, his fans don't have a problem with me," Gus said with a laugh. "Can my boy get a pic with you?"

Van Horn dropped his arm from his wife's waist and held his hand out to Gunner and Finn. Both boys' faces lit up with appreciative grins.

"As long as I can get a pic with this beauty," Van Horn said as he knelt on his knee beside Hattie. "Once she meets Kessler, she won't have eyes for anyone else. I swear the guy keeps kibble in his pocket."

Sheridan was so busy watching the boys, she didn't notice the woman had strolled up beside her.

"You must be Sheridan." She held out her hand. "I'm London Head—uh, Van Horn. Sorry. I'm still getting used to it."

"Congratulations," Sheridan said as she shook the other woman's hand.

London's smile grew as she openly appraised Sheridan. She turned her gaze to where Alek and Gus were bantering with some of the Growlers' players before turning back to Sheridan.

"You're perfect for him," she said with a nod.

Her statement caught Sheridan completely off guard. She and Alek agreed they were not ready to go public with their relationship. Especially since neither one knew what it really meant. Were they simply scratching a ten-year-old itch? Or could it be something more?

Sheridan hadn't dared tell even Aunt Eileen. Had Alek told his ex-girlfriend about her? Her suspicions must have shown on her face because London pressed a gloved hand to Sheridan's shoulder.

"I'm sorry. I didn't mean to speak out of turn. Maybe you don't even like him that way. Alek is a great guy, though. He deserves someone to share his life with. He'll never admit to needing anyone, but I always got the sense he felt—" London shrugged as she seemed to search for the appropriate words. "Not lonely, exactly. Detached might be a better word. Like he was missing out on something, but he didn't know what. Or where to look. And then poof, here you are. Someone who shares a connection with him. Almost as if you were that piece he's been missing all along."

Sheridan stood there, dumbfounded. She already knew

Alek was *her* missing piece. But could she trust that he felt the same way? The wounds his words left on her heart all those years ago were scarred over, and she didn't dare pick at them again. It was safer to believe they were simply roommates with benefits and enjoy the ride for now.

At least that was what she kept telling herself.

She didn't have time to contemplate it further because Hattie was suddenly barking and jumping at one of the Growlers players.

"Well, hello to you, too, gorgeous." He got down on his haunches and began to wrestle with Hattie.

It wasn't hard to see why the dog had gravitated to the man she assumed was Luke Kessler. His sly smile was so similar to Jamie's it almost hurt to look at him. Hattie fell at his feet and showed off her belly.

"What a good dog," Kessler cooed. "And what a generous one, too. Thanks for sharing your toys with all my shelter pups."

"We're ready for you, Luke," one of the grounds crew shouted.

Luke jumped to his feet. "That's our cue. You ready, Finn? Bergeron?"

"Did the Mayhem send any one to do social media?" London looked around. Not seeing anyone, she let out a frustrated groan. "Whomever is handling your team's PR needs to come by my firm for a little one-on-one."

"We have a guy who posts game recaps," Gus said.

London rolled her eyes. "You really need someone embedded with the team to share more than that." She pulled her phone from her belt bag. "Tell Kellogg tonight's post is pro bono. Tomorrow, he's getting a piece of my mind."

Her husband looked on with pride as London trudged after Alek, Finn, and Hattie, who walked with Luke to the center of the field.

"Wait!" Miss Lane rushed onto the sideline. The tall boots she wore beneath her green cashmere coat with its matching beret slowed her progress. "I'm here," she huffed.

Collin nearly tripped over himself getting to the woman's side.

"No worries." He offered her his arm. "Allow me."

Miss Lane fluttered her lashes. "The traffic was awful," she explained as the pair walked toward midfield.

Van Horn snorted beside Sheridan. "You might want to warn her about Collin."

"Trust me, she can take care of herself. In fact, it might be fun to see Collin get handled."

The quarterback laughed before giving her a little side-check. "I have a feeling we are going to be great friends."

NINETEEN

SHERIDAN WAS ten hours into her shift the next day when Claire came down to the ED bearing gifts.

"It's our monthly birthday celebration in occupational therapy. I thought you could use an emotional support cupcake right about now," she said.

"You are a goddess. The oatmeal I inhaled five hours ago is starting to wear off."

"That should tide you over until you get home. By the way, I can grab Finn when I pick up my kids after school. He can hang out with us until it's time to head to the arena. That should give you time for a quick nap before the game. He's welcome to spend the night, too. If he can stand being shadowed by Grace all night. She has quite the crush on him."

A morning to sleep in sounded like heaven. Especially since the Mayhem had the next day off, and she'd be sleeping in—*or not sleeping in*—with Alek.

"I'm sure Finn loves having an adoring fan club," Sheridan said.

If he even notices.

She'd been like Grace once, gah-gah over her older brother's friend. It was cute for now, but she prayed Grace had a strong heart.

"We need help out here," one of the triage nurses shouted.

Sheridan and Claire turned to see Brooke Merriweather stumbling into the lobby, carrying both her children in her arms. The baby was wailing. The toddler, however, looked to be out cold.

"Please," she cried. "He won't wake up."

Claire was already reaching for the crying baby while Sheridan guided Brooke over to a trauma bay.

"How long has he been like this?" Sheridan asked as she tried to pry the child from Brooke's arms. She was grateful to see the toddler's chest moving, even if it was only shallow breaths.

"I thought he was sleeping late." Brooke's laugh sounded hollow. "But what toddler sleeps late? Brad's right. I'm so stupid."

Sheridan exchanged a look with Claire as the resident charged into the room. "What have we got?"

"I need you to lay him down on the gurney so we can examine him," Sheridan insisted.

Brooke relented. The doctor checked his pupils while Sheridan wrapped the pediatric blood pressure cuff around the little boy's limp arm.

"Jackson." She prodded the boy on the shoulder. "Can you open your eyes for me, honey?"

No response.

Sheridan reported Jackson's vital signs. "Heart rate is eighty-five. BP is eighty-two over fifty. Temp is ninety-seven point six. Respiratory rate is normal at fifteen."

"Pupils are normal and reactive," the doctor told her. "Grab a blood gas. We need red, purple, and green tops to the lab ASAP. And let's cath him for a urinalysis."

He fired off questions for Brooke as he examined Jackson.

"Any known medical issues? Allergies? Has he had any recent falls? Any change to his urine or stool? Slurred speech? Did he have a playdate at a friend's house yesterday? Are any other kids sick at preschool?"

Brooke shook her head. "No. None of that. He doesn't go to preschool."

Jackson barely flinched when Sheridan inserted a line into his arm.

"Any drugs in the house?" the doctor asked.

The question seemed to startle Brooke. "No."

The doctor didn't let up. "Cough medicine? Pain meds? Laundry pods? Melatonin? Alcohol? Do you keep all that stuff locked up?"

Brooke grew defensive. "All the cabinets are child-proofed," she snapped.

Sheridan placed a hand on her shoulder. "These are routine diagnostic questions. No one is accusing you of anything."

"Brad will," Brooke whispered.

A fission of worry raced down Sheridan's spine.

"Where is Brad?" Claire asked.

"Uh, still at morning skate, I guess," Brooke replied. "Please, Doctor, is Jackson going to be okay? What's wrong with him?" Her voice breaking made the baby in Claire's arms cry harder.

"I'm going to take this little guy for a walk," Claire announced. "I'll track down Brad," she murmured to Sheridan before slipping from the room.

"I'm not sure what's going on with your son yet, but our job is to figure it out," the doctor reassured Brooke. "We need to run a few tests. Then we'll talk more." The doctor motioned for Sheridan to step outside with him. "You know this family?"

She nodded.

"Anything unusual about life inside the home?"

Sheridan looked back into the trauma bay. Brooke had

crawled onto the gurney with her son. The poor woman always looked so overwhelmed.

"Not that I know for certain."

It was the truth. Sure, Brad was a colossal asshat. But she'd seen things go south quickly when people started pointing fingers based on gut feelings. And when law enforcement gets involved, it's hard to walk back those kinds of statements. The priority right now was figuring out what was wrong with Jackson and getting him better. For the time being, Sheridan would keep her opinions to herself.

The doctor sighed. "Get someone down here from peds for a consult. And call someone from social work to talk to the mom. My spidey sense says there's more to this story."

"We're waiting on the preliminary test results to come back," Sheridan told Trent twenty minutes later when he stopped by to say hello. "Jackson is still somnolent."

Trent stared into the trauma bay where Brooke seemed to be singing to her son as she rocked him against her side.

"What's her story?" he asked.

"Honestly, I don't know her well enough for her to confide in me. I do know she always seems harried and afraid—"

Trent whipped his head around to stare at her. "Do you think something is going on with the husband to make her afraid of him?"

She sighed. "I don't know. Afraid might not be an apt description."

"What's the guy like?"

"Ugh. Just between you and me, he's a creep."

Trent pursed his lips before turning back to observe Brooke. "How about I see what I can suss out from her while you wait for the social worker to break free from her other case?"

Sheridan shrugged. "Why not? You're the expert at getting people to open up."

He grabbed a bottle of water from the cooler before entering the bay. Sheridan watched as he coaxed Brooke to a sitting position and offered her the water. A few minutes later, he'd charmed her into talking to him.

The doctor came to stand beside Sheridan. "The first round of tests came back negative for any of the usual suspects. The urinalysis won't be in for another fifteen to thirty minutes. The next step is a CT scan and an LP. We should have sent Trent in with the consent form for that one. Mamas tend to get frantic when you mention tapping their babies' spines."

"I wonder why," she replied sarcastically.

"Where the hell is my son?" Brad shouted as he stormed into the ED with Lori on his heels. "What are you doing to him?"

"You've got to be kidding me," the doctor murmured. He leveled an annoyed look at Sheridan. "I take it this guy is a piece of work off the ice, too, fräulein?"

"Unfortunately."

"Thanks for the heads-up."

"Please try to calm down, Merriweather," Lori admonished Brad. "These people are the ones helping Jackson."

The doctor blocked Brad's path. "Mr. Merriweather, we are unable to wake your son from sleep. We are still running tests to determine the cause. As soon as we get a signed consent form, we'll proceed with a few more tests that will give us additional information."

Too bad Brad wasn't paying any attention to the doctor. "Huh-uh," he replied before bursting into the trauma bay. "Get your fucking hand off my wife."

Trent didn't react. He kept his palm on Brooke's jean-clad thigh. Brooke wasn't as sanguine, however. She jumped from the gurney like a scared kitten.

"Brad. Jackson won't wake up." She launched herself at his broad chest only to have her husband shove her away.

"What did you do, Brooke?" He gave Jackson a shake. "Jackson!" he shouted.

The toddler didn't stir.

Brad glared at his wife. "The kid was fine last night."

Brooke looked over at Trent, as if seeking reinforcement, before straightening her spine and staring down her husband. "How would you know? You wouldn't even help put him to bed."

"He woke up later. You were passed out with the baby in our bed, as usual."

"What time was this?" the doctor asked. "Did you notice anything different about him?"

"It was around eleven, I guess. He seemed fine. He just wanted a little daddy time."

Brooke blanched. "You were playing video games."

Brad shrugged. "Figured it was about time he learned. You're turning him into a wuss with all your crap about being in touch with his feelings."

"What did you give him?" Brooke's voice had dropped several octaves.

Lori sucked in a shocked breath. Sheridan placed her palm on the helpless boy's leg, still clad in Bluey pajamas.

"Were you using drugs at the time, Mr. Merriweather?" the doctor asked quietly.

"No!" Brad shouted. He shot an ugly look at his wife. Then at Lori.

"I have some medical marijuana from time to time to recover after a game. But that's legal within the league. I'd never light up with my kid in the room, though."

"The gummies, Brad. He would have thought they were

candy. Tell me you didn't have them out where he could see them."

Brad blinked. Once. Twice. "I took a couple, yeah. But I told him I'd get him some candy today."

Brooke was beginning to hyperventilate.

Lori asked the question that was on the tip of everyone's tongue. "Did you leave Jackson alone in the room with the gummies at any time?"

"How does this concern you?" Brad barked. "This is a family matter. It's bad enough you had to drag me out of a team meeting like a juvenile delinquent being sent to the principal's office."

"Answer the damn question, Brad!" Sheridan shouted.

He was about to turn on her too when he noticed all the eyes in the ED primed on the trauma bay, including those of a security guard positioned outside the bay door. Brad brushed both his hands over his head.

"I don't know. I got up to take a piss once or twice."

Brooke's primal scream filled the bay as she flung herself at her husband and began pummeling him with her fists. "You bastard! If my child is brain-dead because of you, I'll kill you!"

Trent waved off the security guard, pulling her off Brad and over to the other side of the gurney. The doctor was already on the phone to the lab telling them to run a tox screen on the urine sample.

"I want him out of here." Brooke pointed toward the sliding door. "I don't want him anywhere near my boys."

"They're my boys, too!" Brad looked around. "Where are you hiding August? That kid's usually attached to you in some way or another."

"That's because he's afraid of you!" Brooke shouted.

"This isn't helping Jackson right now," Sheridan intervened.

"Brad, why don't you come outside with me, and we'll get the paperwork signed for the additional testing."

He sneered at her. "Haven't you damn WAGs done enough? First, Gus's wife calls in the cavalry." He gestured at Lori. "Now you think you're all high and mighty and can start bossing me around. Well, screw you. I'm not leaving my wife in here with some handsy doctor. And I'm not leaving my son. If you want to be helpful, go find August."

Brooke shot her a desperate look. "No! I don't want Brad here. And I don't want him near August. I'm so done with you, Brad." She pleaded with Trent. "Does he have to be in here?"

The phone rang before Trent could answer.

"Got it," the doctor replied, then hung up. "No need for additional testing. Jackson is suffering from an acute THC overdose."

"Oh God!" Brooke leaned down to snuggle her son. "My sweet boy."

"That's impossible. Those things aren't that potent," Brad argued. "I would have noticed if he ate the whole bottle."

"Jackson is one-tenth your size," Sheridan clapped back. "He'd only have to eat two or three to end up here."

Brad went still. "What's going to happen to him?"

"We're going to admit him to pediatrics," the doctor explained. "They'll monitor him and continue flushing out his system with fluids until something changes."

"But he'll wake up, right?" Brad asked.

"That's the hope," the doctor replied. "We'll know in about twenty-four hours."

Brooke's voice shook. "But will he be . . . normal?"

"There haven't been any definitive studies on kids Jackson's age to know the answer to that question," Trent attempted to reassure her. "But I've seen quite a few cases where the child has recovered unscathed."

Please let that be the case here, Sheridan prayed.

The doctor motioned for the security guard to enter the room. "The law requires us to contact Child Protective Services in these cases."

"Hell, no!" Brad yelled. "This was an accident."

"Stick to the facts, and you shouldn't have any problems," the doctor replied.

"Is there a possibility law enforcement will get involved?" Lori asked him.

Brad was clenching and unclenching his fists. "What the actual fuck!"

"That's the last thing any of us wants." He looked between Brad and Brooke. "Right now, Jackson is my immediate concern. What happens from here is up to CPS. My advice? Stop being an ass, Merriweather. It will help your case." He turned to Sheridan. "I'm going to see about getting him transferred to peds."

Lori moved to follow him out. "I'll let the coach know you're taking family leave tonight," she told Brad.

"Can I get you anything, Brooke?" Trent asked.

"I'll take care of my wife."

So much for Brad behaving.

Brooke ignored him. "If you could call my mother and a divorce lawyer, I'd appreciate it," she said to Trent.

TWENTY

"PINK PONY CLUB" was blasting throughout the arena when the Mayhem left the ice for the second intermission that night. They were up over the team from Seattle three zip. Coach stopped Alek at the bench before he could join his teammates in the dressing room.

"Calvin's still got fresh legs," Coach told him. "He's doing a good job covering Merriweather's shifts. Keep an eye on the back door, though. I'm noticing he tends to get jammed up in the corners, which could leave you vulnerable to a five-hole."

"Sure thing," Alek replied. "Any update from the hospital?"

Coach had filled the team in on the situation with Brad's son during their pregame meeting. Alek and Gus were already up to speed, thanks to Claire and Sheridan. Gus had lost it when he'd discovered Brad's recklessness was behind the incident. The two men had agreed to keep the details to themselves, however. The Mayhem had finally begun to play in sync. The last thing they needed was a distraction like Brad to spoil that.

"I'm hoping to hear some good news from Lori when I get inside. Maybe Sheridan left you a message," Coach said. "It was kind of her to stay at the hospital to keep them company."

To hear Claire tell it, Sheridan had stayed to keep the peace. As the guys had surmised early in the season, there was trouble in the marriage. Not that Alek was surprised. Merriweather was a dick to his wife. No doubt she was angry with him for putting their child at risk.

"The last time I spoke with her, there was still no change," he told the coach. "She was starting to worry about Jackson being out so long."

Alek was more worried about Sheridan. She hadn't slept in nearly forty-eight hours. He cussed himself out for selfishly keeping her from napping before her shift last night. His lame excuse? After five days on the road, his body craved hers. Sheridan hadn't objected, but he couldn't help feeling like an ass for sleeping like a baby while she'd gone off to work a twelve-hour shift that was now going into hour nineteen. Luckily, Lori was picking up Merriweather's mother-in-law from the airport. Sheridan would be off peacekeeping duty any time now.

Coach shook his head. "It's a scary situation. All we can do is wait. And pray."

Alek handed his gloves to one of the equipment managers waiting outside the dressing room door. They'd place them on the coils of a drying machine, ensuring they were clean and ready by the start of the next period.

The guys were in high spirits when Alek sat down at his stall. He was glad to see the defense huddled together, hyping Calvin up for the final period. The guy hadn't seen much ice time this season. Hopefully, he'd play as well for the last twenty minutes as he had for the first forty.

The equipment managers began the choreographed routine of gathering up pads and wiping them off with sanitizing spray before putting them in front of drying fans. Alek stripped from the waist up, handing his shoulder pads and his blocker to one of the managers. He'd replace his base layer with something dry after he toweled his torso down.

First things first, though, he checked his phone.

"Anything?" Gus asked after he shed his sweater and shoulder pads.

"No change."

His friend looked stricken. "No child should ever have to go through that."

Valentine ambled up to his stall beside Alek and began to strip.

"Let's see how long it takes him this time," someone yelled. "Go, Twos, go!"

The routine was a familiar one. During the second intermission of every game, Valentine insisted on taking a cold plunge. "To freshen up the legs," he explained.

And every time, one of the boys would clock him while he peeled off his skates, pads, and uniform. They only had seventeen minutes for intermission, meaning every second was important. Valentine's record was thirty-nine seconds. Getting it all back on took him a minute or so longer, which was still astonishing to Alek.

Gus reached for his stick and headed to the lumber yard, where he would reapply fresh tape. Alek would do the same shortly, but first, he needed to rehydrate. He threw back the electrolyte drink the trainer had left on his bench for him. During the second intermission, he always ate a banana. The shot of potassium helped keep leg cramps away.

While he toweled off with a damp cloth sprinkled with peppermint oil, one of the trainers refilled the water bottle Alek kept on top of the net while he was in goal. The other guys could grab a drink when they returned to the bench between shifts on the ice, but the goalie was stuck out there for the full period, carrying over forty pounds of extra padding and equipment, no less.

"Have you heard anything?" Picard asked when he stopped in front of Alek, presumably on his way to the lounge to grab his customary PB&J sandwich.

"Still no change."

Picard shook his head. "The guy's a total douche, but that doesn't mean I want his kid to suffer."

Alek pulled on a dry compression shirt fitted with extra padding to protect his chest and kidneys from an errant puck. "Agreed."

The two men walked toward the lounge.

"Any chance I can get a favor from you?" Picard asked.

"Always."

Picard looked sheepish, which was unusual. The Mayhem captain was as self-confident as they come.

"My restaurant opening is tomorrow night. Any chance you would want to double date with London and Trey Van Horn? I saw the four of you together on the field last night. You looked chummy."

Double date? The four of them?

"Dinner would be on me, of course," Picard continued when Alek didn't answer right away. "Having a big name like Van Horn in the house would give the place the stigma we need to make a splash opening weekend. I know I'm asking a lot for you and Van Horn to make nice three nights in a row."

"Three nights in a row?"

"Well, yeah. Van Horn and his wife are out there sitting with Finn's teacher. I assumed you're all going out after the game. Although your agent is yakking her ear off. The poor woman is going to need some extra lovin' after putting up with Collin all evening." Picard nudged him. "Make it up to her with a spectacular dinner tomorrow night."

Shit.

The last thing he wanted to do was let his friend down. Picard was right. Thanks to having his mug on half a dozen products, people around the world knew who the Growlers quarterback was. It would be quite the coup to have Van Horn dine in the restaurant opening night. It would mean coming clean to his teammates about his relationship with Sheridan, though.

Alek wasn't sure he was ready to do that yet. Despite how well they fit, things still felt fragile. What they had was too important for him to risk. His teammates were like his second family, however, and misleading them made him feel like a class A jerk.

Time was ticking, and he still needed to tape his stick. "We've got a noon puck drop on Sunday. A Saturday night out might not work for me. What if I can get Dex Fletcher and his wife to go with the Van Horns?" he improvised. Alek and the Scottish placekicker became friends when they discovered they shared a fondness for Scotch whisky, especially the label they both promoted in their home countries.

"Dude! That would be huge." Picard heaved a sigh of relief. "I'll save the best table for them."

"Let me see what I can do to make it happen," Alek told him.

VALENTINE'S "FRESH LEGS" added another goal in the third period to make the final score four nothing. The reporters gathered around Alek in the room reminded him he'd defended the net for eight periods of scoreless hockey. After the start to the season he'd had, Alek was relieved to be back in the groove—and out of the media's crosshairs.

His phone pinged with a text from Sheridan.

Leaving in thirty minutes. See you at home.

He shoved his phone into the pocket of his suit jacket and navigated through the crowded room to make his escape. Finn, Gunner, and Kyle pounced on him as soon as he reached the family room.

"That was awesome!" Kyle said. "Thanks for inviting us."

"Look at all the dog toys we collected tonight!" Finn and Gunner both held up large plastic bags filled with stuffed animals.

Van Horn was taking up space behind London's little brother while his wife and Claire held an animated conversation about an upcoming WAG charity event. It would be easier to get London's buy-in on dinner at Picard's, but it didn't look like the two women were going to stop chatting anytime soon. And Alek was in a hurry to get home before Sheridan.

"I'm glad you guys could make it." He took the bags of dog toys and set them down at his feet. "Why don't you go ask the equipment crew for a puck?"

The three boys ran off as if they were in a foot race. Alek looked at London again, but no luck.

He sighed. "Hey, do you have dinner plans for tomorrow?"

Van Horn scrutinized him. "As flattered as I am by your interest, you do know I'm off the market."

Alek swore softly as he pinched the bridge of his nose. "Why do you have to be such an ass?"

The quarterback shrugged. "Only to you. And because it's fun."

"Picard's steakhouse is opening tomorrow night. I'm trying to do him a solid by putting butts in the seats."

"Why? Does the food suck or something?"

Alek glared at him.

"Oh!" Van Horn rocked back on his heels. "This is for publicity. You're conceding that football players have more cred than hockey players?"

"God, I really hate you," Alek mumbled.

Van Horn laughed loudly. His wife peeked out of the corner of her eye at him, but she didn't end her conversation.

"I could be persuaded to partake in a meal there. I might even be able to sweet-talk my beautiful wife into ginning up some social media content for the place." He leaned over toward Alek. "She claims I have magic fingers. And she likes the way I use them on her body."

For fuck's sake.

"Good for you. Picard's holding a table for four. Bring Fletcher and his wife. I told Picard to have plenty of scotch on hand."

"You're not joining us?"

"I already have plans."

Van Horn crossed his arms over his chest and smirked at Alek. "Huh. Keeping your pretty houseguest all to yourself, I see. Not that I blame you. There's something about her that is—"

He was toe-to-toe with Van Horn in an instant. "You better think carefully about the next word that comes out of your mouth."

The quarterback held up his hands. "Whoa. My wife was right." He took a step back and lowered his hands as he shook his head. "For some reason, she's determined to see you happily involved with someone. I'm sure you can imagine how that pisses me off. But from what little interaction we had last night, I liked Sheridan. My first inclination should be to warn her off."

Alek felt his fingers tightening up into fists.

"But she suits you." Van Horn had the audacity to look

amazed. "And my gut tells me she can hold her own. I hope it works out for you two."

London joined them before Alek could reply.

"Boys," she murmured. "People are watching."

Van Horn placed his palm on his wife's back. "Good news. You can wear that hot new red dress you bought. We're having dinner in Milwaukee's premiere new steak house tomorrow night."

She looked between both men. "O-kkay?"

Alek took his life in his hands when he kissed London on the cheek, his lips lingering longer than they should have. "My treat," he told her. "Be sure to try the lemon cake. It's to die for."

"Do I even want to know what's going on?" she asked.

"You tell me all the time that us Milwaukee jocks need to stick together." Van Horn reached out his hand. "Thanks for both invites. Enjoy the rest of your weekend." The asshole winked at Alek.

London seemed to hold her breath as Alek shook her husband's hand.

"Thanks," Alek told him. The truth was, he meant it. The quarterback made London happier than he ever could. And someone better had come along when he least expected it. Now all he had to do was try not to screw it up.

"We each got a puck," Finn said when the boys arrived back.

"Good because the Ferguson bus is pulling out," Claire announced.

"Are you sure you want three boys at your house?" London asked.

Van Horn shot her a WTF look.

Gus walked up with a sleepy Grace nestled on his shoulder. "Don't worry. I'm going to make them clean out the garage tomorrow if they're too loud tonight," he teased.

Finn was all smiles as he and his friends raced to the parking garage. Alek tossed the bags of dog toys into the back of his SUV before retrieving Finn's duffel bag for him.

"You have your inhaler?" he asked him.

"Of course," Finn said as he took the bag. "Tell Hattie we'll take the toys to the shelter tomorrow."

Alek ruffled his hair. "Behave. Have fun. Mind your manners."

He tried to remember all the things his parents used to say to him when they dropped him off at a friend's house. Or hockey practice. Or camp.

A knot formed in his stomach. Finn was going to Gus's house, for crying out loud. Nothing was going to happen to him there.

So why did he feel like he was going to throw up?

"Finn!"

The boy waited his turn to climb into the third row of Gus's Infinity. Alek reached him in three strides. He pulled him into a hug, brushing his lips over the top of his head. "Love you, bud."

"Love you, too," Finn replied as he returned the hug.

"You have your phone?"

Finn nodded.

"Okay. You call me if you need me."

"Sure," Finn said, starting to look a little embarrassed.

Behind him, Gus was struggling not to laugh. Alek restrained himself from flipping his friend off in front of the kids. When he turned back to his SUV, Collin was leaning against the liftgate, arms and legs crossed and a droll smile on his face.

"Don't." Alek snapped.

Collin pulled out his phone and pretended to dictate into it. "Hey Siri, send Bergeron a book of dad jokes for Christmas."

Alek did flip him off only to notice too late Finn's teacher was waiting in the shadows. She had the good grace to pretend to be looking at her phone. He turned to Collin and arched an eyebrow.

"She said there wasn't anything between you two. I wanted to make sure," Collin said softly.

"Yeah. No." Alek shook his head. He was beginning to think he'd taken a puck to the head he wasn't aware of.

"Which is it?" Collin hissed.

"There was nothing." He stepped closer to Collin in order to make himself clear. "But she's not your type."

Collin's eyes narrowed. "My type?"

"A weekend fling. That's Finn's teacher. Gunner's too. You hurt her and Gus and I will tear you limb from limb. Then we'll hand the leftover bits to the boys to take care of."

His agent looked over to where Marissa was still scrolling on her phone. A goofy smile spread over his lips. "Yeah. She's definitely not my usual type. But maybe I'm ready for something else." He smacked Alek on the chest and began to walk away. "Tell Sher I'll email the paperwork to her next week."

"Paperwork? What paperwork?"

He turned and walked backward. "The forms for the custody hearing. It's been set for the end of December. I was able to coordinate it with your road trip to Boston."

Alek's confusion must have been apparent because Collin stopped walking. "She didn't tell you? We discussed it last night."

Last night felt like an eternity ago. It seems like something they would have talked about though. Could she have mentioned it, and he forgot? He had jumped her bones the moment Finn fell asleep, so she really didn't have the chance to say too much before rushing off to the hospital. That had to be it. And with everything going on with Merriweather's kid, there wasn't the opportunity today.

"Alek?" Collin was standing in front of him again. "Hey. You're still okay with transferring the guardianship, right?"

"Yeah. Sure. Whatever Sheridan wants."

It won't change anything.

Gus honked the horn as he finally pulled away. Alek waved.

"Are you sure?" Collin gestured to the retreating SUV. "Because you seem pretty attached to Jamie's kid."

"That was the whole point of them moving here."

"Yeah." Collin sucked in a breath. "But are you going to be okay when they are somewhere else?"

"What are you talking about?"

"Sheridan said in her interview she plans to go back to being a traveling nurse. To show Finn the world."

Alek swore he felt the parking garage floor move beneath his feet. "What interview? When?"

Collin gave him a pitying look. "The interview the judge conducted when Sheridan filed her petition."

"That was nearly two months ago."

"Yee-aah. Has something changed since then?"

Damn straight something had changed.

Not that he was discussing that with his agent.

"We're all good." Alek gestured to where Marissa was still waiting. "I thought you said you were going to treat her right. Quit ignoring her."

The goofy look was back on Collin's face. He saluted Alek as he jogged over to where Finn's teacher waited. Her face lit up with a smile identical to Collin's. Alek shook his head in amazement before getting into his car and driving away.

TWENTY-ONE

HATTIE RUSHED up to greet her when Sheridan walked in from the garage. The dog looked past her, presumably for Finn. She rubbed Hattie's head.

"He's not there," she told the dog. "He'll be home tomorrow."

The dog sighed before lumbering off to the mudroom, where she plopped onto her bed with a groan.

"Right there with ya, girl. It's been a long day."

Sheridan followed the scent of bacon to the kitchen. Alek was at the stove making an omelet.

"Yum."

He laughed as he slid the omelet from the pan onto a plate. "Bacon makes everything better."

Except it wasn't the bacon that had her moaning. Alek had changed out of his game night suit into a pair of soft black joggers that fit his ass like a glove. The muscles in his back rippled beneath his blue cashmere sweater. For some reason, the dish towel draped over his shoulder made him even sexier.

"Come. Eat." He gestured for her to sit at the table.

"You didn't have to make me dinner. I'm not that hungry."

Her stomach betrayed her by growling.

"Uh-huh." He pulled out the chair for her. "Sit."

She did as he asked because she realized she was in fact, starving—not to mention too exhausted to argue with him.

Alek poured some white wine into her glass. "How is Jackson?"

She sighed. "He's still out."

He whipped up an omelet for himself. "And Brad?"

"It doesn't look like they will involve the police, thank goodness. Brad is a jerk who was incredibly careless, but it wasn't premeditated." She chomped on a piece of bacon. "Lori worked the angles all day to keep the story from getting out. More to protect the team than Brad, I think. Everyone at the hospital is obligated to keep it under wraps. Now, all we need is Jackson to open his eyes."

"He will," Alek said with more confidence than she felt. "Tomorrow morning, he'll wake up as good as new and with a raging case of the munchies."

She smiled as she sipped her wine. "Someone is feeling very confident this evening. Could it have something to do with having eight shutout periods under your belt?"

Alek shot her a wicked grin as he sat down next to her. "I have lots of things under my belt that you might be interested in."

A flush burned her cheeks. "You know you didn't have to make me dinner. You were going to get lucky anyway."

"Yeah, I know. But I need you to have the strength for all the things I want to do to you later," he teased. "Besides, this has easily become one of my favorite parts of the day."

"Bedtime?"

He chuckled. "Well, that too. But I meant this quiet time after a game. Sitting here enjoying a meal with you. Talking about the day. It feels"—he shrugged— "nice. Natural, even."

His admission had her feeling warm all over. Sheridan got up and straddled his lap. She gently pressed her palms to his cheeks before leaning in to deliver a tender kiss to his lips. As with every time their lips met, things didn't stay tender for long.

Alek moaned when she shifted forward slightly. Skin met skin when his fingers slid beneath her scrubs to trace her spine. Her hands left his cheeks to dig into his damp hair. She adjusted his head to give her better access to his mouth. He gripped her hips with his fingers, grinding her core against his erection. She jumped at the contact, pulling her mouth from his demanding one.

"I need to shower the hospital off me," she panted.

He donned another one of those wicked grins. "Good idea," he said, lifting her from his lap and circling her wrist with his fingers.

Alek handed Sheridan her wineglass, then picked up his protein shake. They were both breathing hard when they rushed up the stairs. He steered her into his bedroom and its adjacent en suite.

The bathroom was bigger than most apartments Sheridan had lived in. With a heated floor, a mini fridge, and two tubs—one a cold plunge—it even had better amenities than some of her former residences. And that was without mentioning the spacious shower with dual showerheads in addition to a rain shower element overhead. There was even a function for it to operate as a sauna.

Sheridan set her wineglass on the quartz countertop and stepped out of her sneakers. Alek picked up a remote control to turn on the water as well as heat the floor. The hiss of the shower filled the room as she lifted off the top to her scrubs. Alek's gaze made a beeline for her nipples, already puckered beneath the long-sleeved pink compression shirt she wore.

"Allow me," he murmured, reaching for the string to her

scrub bottoms and tugging on it. He rolled them down over her hips, leaving her in nothing but her clingy shirt, pink panties, and *My Little Pony* compression socks. She shivered.

"Right. Let's get you in the warm shower."

Alek got down on his haunches and peeled off one compression sock. He traced his thumb along the indentation the socks made on the skin beneath her knee, following it with his lips. She felt his smile against her skin when she sighed. The other leg was next. He dragged his tongue up the inside of her thigh. When her knees buckled, she had to prop her hips against the counter to keep from falling.

He bypassed her panties, taking her shirt with him when he stood back up. His nostrils flared at the sight of her in her bra and panties. He gave his head a little shake.

"The water's warm. Get in." He spun her around and unclasped her bra before swatting her butt and aiming her in the direction of the shower.

Sheridan dropped her bra and stepped out of her panties, then moved beneath the warm spray. Groaning, she pressed her palms and her forehead against the wet tile, allowing the water to sluice over her tired muscles.

"This feels heavenly." She sighed.

"Yes, it does," Alek replied when he pressed his hard naked body against her back, reaching his hands around to cup her breasts.

She leaned her head back against his shoulder, giving his lips access to her exposed neck. He reached for the soap instead. Once his hands were full of suds, he took his time lathering up her body, gently massaging the sore muscles in her shoulders, her back, and her hips. His actions were both erotic and nurturing.

Sheridan had never felt more treasured.

"Sit," he commanded, gesturing to the long teak bench along one wall.

She had no objection to complying, given how tired her body was. He crouched down on his haunches again, picked up one of her feet, and placed it over his rock-hard thigh. Her eyelids slid closed when he began to work his magic on the sole of her foot. She whimpered when he stopped to switch feet.

Alek stood to retrieve some bodywash, giving her an excellent view of his six-pack—and everything below it. She reached out to finger his balls. He groaned.

"Mmm." She wrapped her fingers around his hard length.

"Sheri."

She leaned forward to slide her tongue along his erection.

He swore. "This is you time, Sher."

"Good," she murmured against his skin. "Then I get to do what I want."

He slammed his hands against the tile when she took him in her mouth. "I mean it, Sher," he ground out. His protests didn't last long, and his fingers found her scalp. He dug them in, guiding her head up and down along his length.

Less than a minute later, he pulled away, yanking her up off the bench and driving into her.

"Yes!" she cried, wrapping her legs around his waist.

He braced her against the wall. The steam from the shower cast a shroud around them, and the air was filled with the sound of their wet bodies slapping against the wall. She dug her nails into his back right before the world went black. He swore against her neck as his body shook with its own release.

Sheridan clung to him like a wet noodle while he tenderly dried her off with one of the giant towels. He slipped one of his T-shirts over her head and carried her to his big bed. The sheets were cool against her damp body. She shivered. He pulled the comforter over her, tucking it beneath her chin. Through the fringe of her lashes, she watched him squat before the fireplace to click the fire on. The glow of the flames illuminated the droplets still clinging to his body.

"Alek," she mumbled.

He was beside her in an instant, placing a butterfly kiss on each of her eyes. "Shh," he told her. "Sleep."

"I want you." Exhaustion threatened to overtake her, and the words came out more garbled than she would have liked.

"I'll be right back," he told her. "I promised Finn I'd tuck in Hattie."

Could he get any more perfect?

The man tolerated having a dog in his house for the sake of another man's son. That he loved Finn was becoming increasingly apparent. She knew he desired her. And she was beginning to hope it could be something more. Sheridan fell asleep, allowing herself to dream of the future.

She woke with a start eight hours later. The sun was almost up. She was in Alek's bed. Alone. The pillows next to her were cold. So were the sheets. She felt around on the nightstand for her phone, only to realize it was probably still down in her purse.

Finn!

Scrambling from the bed, she barely managed to avoid stubbing a toe as she searched for her clothes. Of course, Alek had tidied up the bathroom after their shower. Her scrubs were likely already in the laundry. Not wanting to waste time hurrying to her own room, she reached into his dresser drawer and stole a pair of joggers. She ignored the fact that they sort of fit her and raced to the catwalk landing overlooking the two sets of staircases in the house.

A sound below had her peeking over the railing. Alek was sprawled out, asleep on the carpet, his head on one of the couch cushions he'd moved to the floor. Several of the throw blankets covered his body. But it was who was beside him that had her heart stopping. Hattie rested her head on Alek's stomach while he had his hand planted on the dog's shoulder.

Sheridan crept down the stairs. She needed to find her phone so she could grab a photo. Neither Aunt Eileen nor Peri would believe this. Before she could, however, Hattie made another one of those odd sounds.

"Hattie?" Sheridan called quietly.

The dog whimpered when she moved. Alek jerked awake at the sound.

"She okay?" he said.

"I don't know." She knelt beside them on the floor. "What happened?"

Hattie groaned when Sheridan tried to pet her. Her eyes were glassy, and her tongue lolled a bit.

Alek scratched his chin. "She was really restless when I came down to check on her. Kept asking to go out. Every time I put her in the yard, though, she just went in circles. She never did anything else. I think she's probably missing Finn. I tried to get her to go upstairs and sleep on his bed, but she wasn't having it. She seemed to calm down if I was beside her. I figured I'd sleep down here with her so you could get some rest."

Sheridan kissed him. "You are . . . amazing, do you know that?"

He grimaced. "That's not what my back is saying to me right now. I'm going to need to be worked over by a massage therapist this afternoon."

She kissed him again. "Is that what they're calling it these days? Come on, Hattie, girl. Let's go have breakfast. That always makes you feel better." When she arrived in the mud room, she was surprised to see that the dog's dish was full.

"Did you already feed her?" she asked Alek when she returned to the family room.

Alek was folding up the blankets and reassembling the couch cushions. "No. I don't think she touched her food from last night."

A lick of unease hit her. Hattie *never* left food unfinished. She looked around for the dog.

"Where'd she go?"

The words had no sooner left her mouth when they heard Hattie throwing up.

"No, no, *no!*" Alek shouted, sprinting toward the laundry room. "Not in my equipment bag, Hattie!"

The dog ignored him, continuing to spew all over Alek's practice clothes. Hattie gave them a doleful look before dropping down in a pile of laundry. Her breathing was strained.

Sheridan's own breath was coming up short. "We need to take her to the vet, Alek. Right now."

"Yeah." He was already texting someone.

AN HOUR LATER, Alek paced the small waiting room of the emergency vet that his friend, Luke Kessler from the Growlers, had recommended. Sheridan sat on the wooden bench focusing on the light snow swirling around outside the window overlooking the parking lot. She and Alek had debated whether to alert Finn, before deciding against it.

"Let's wait until we know something before we alarm him," Alek had advised. "It's probably something minor anyway."

The anxious way Alek moved about the room told her he didn't think the situation was minor any more than she did.

The door to the back opened, and the vet who'd taken Hattie back emerged. The vet was ridiculously tall—taller than Alek—and thin with curly gray hair and wire-rimmed glasses he kept having to adjust. With his mouthful of giant teeth, he gave off more cartoon character vibes than skilled surgeon. But Luke Kessler assured them he was the best.

"First, the good news," he said. "We're not dealing with any poison or parasite."

His announcement didn't exactly calm Sheridan.

"But there's bad news?" she said.

The vet motioned for them to join him at the counter, where he opened a file on his tablet. "I take it our girl enjoys snacking on her family's socks and whatnot?" he asked.

Alek groaned. "Mostly the whatnot. My whatnot, to be specific."

The vet chuckled as he brought up a detailed image of Hattie's belly. "She's got something jamming up the plumbing. Looks like it might be a sock. Whatever it is, it's knotted itself around her intestine."

"That's not coming out the normal way." Alek said.

"Nope."

Sheridan's mouth went dry. "That means you have to operate?"

Alek placed his hand on her back. "When?"

The vet checked his wrist. "We're prepping the OR right now. Once the second bag of IV fluids is done, we'll take her back. The procedure should take about two hours, depending on how tightly the object is wrapped around things. Would you like to see her first?"

"Yes! Please." Sheridan was surprised when Alek followed her back. Then again, the man had slept beside the dog on the floor all night. She was beginning to think he had a soft spot for dogs after all.

Hattie lay on her side on a movable table. Her front leg had been shaved to allow the lines to be inserted. She looked so still and lifeless that Sheridan had to bite back a gasp.

"She's sedated," the vet explained. "No need to worry. We

do this surgery at least once a week." He shrugged. "Dogs can't seem to help swallowing things they shouldn't. Hattie will be back to herself in a few weeks."

"I need your word on that," Alek demanded.

"There are no guarantees. This is major surgery," the vet replied. "Any number of things could still go wrong."

"Make sure they don't."

The fierce way Alek uttered the words caught both the vet and Sheridan off guard.

Still, the vet was patient with him. "I understand your concern, Mr. Bergeron. Our pets are like family. We'll take good care of her. Especially since this one is a minor celebrity. We need her to give us a good Yelp score."

His attempt at trying to lighten the mood fell flat.

"No!" Alek roared. "'This one' belongs to an eight-year-old boy who lost both his parents in a car accident a few months ago. He can't lose Hattie, too. That's not a scenario I'm willing to live with. You hear me?"

The vet blinked, seemingly at a loss for words. "Yeah," he said eventually. "I do hear you." He placed his hand on Alek's shoulder. "I will do everything in my power to make sure Hattie pulls through without any complications." He grazed his fingers over the dog's fur. "You're welcome to stay with her until we take her back."

Sheridan slipped her arm through Alek's and leaned her head on his shoulder when the vet left the room. "We need to tell Finn."

He nodded. "Yeah."

She pulled out her phone and dialed Claire's number. When she looked up, Alek was leaning over the dog, dropping a kiss on her head.

TWENTY-TWO

FINN PICKED at the plate of pancakes in front of him. The vet suggested they get breakfast while they waited. Not wanting to spend two hours sitting on a wooden bench, Alek herded them across the street to the Oak Creek Diner. It was familiar stomping grounds for many of the town's athletes.

"Do you want some of my cinnamon roll?" Sheridan asked Finn.

He shook his head. Finn hadn't said much since Claire dropped him off an hour earlier. His eyes were still red-rimmed and puffy from when he'd sobbed in Sheridan's arms once he arrived, but he was putting on a brave face now.

"How much longer?" He'd been asking the same question every five minutes for the past hour.

Sheridan rubbed his back. "I'm sure they'll call us soon."

She'd been repeating that answer for the last hour, also.

Alek checked the time on his phone. They were approaching the two-hour mark. The restaurant was busy with customers wanting breakfast before a busy Saturday of errands. A few waiting for tables had begun to throw pointed looks their way.

"How about if we box this up in case you want to eat it later?" Alek said to him.

"I'm not really hungry," Finn replied.

Alek was signaling to the server when Sheridan's phone pinged with a text. Finn sat forward in his chair.

Sheridan shook her head. "It's Claire. You left your phone at Gunner's house. She'll bring it by the house later today." She looked over at Alek with the first smile he'd seen from her this morning. "And good news from the hospital. Jackson is awake. All indications are good. No long-term damage."

He breathed a sigh of relief. "That's awesome." He gave her hand a squeeze. "We're going to get the same result here, too. I know it."

After stopping to take a few selfies with fans, they arrived back at the clinic as the surgeon walked into the waiting room. The confident look on his face did wonders for Alek's nerves.

"Perfect timing. Everything went as expected. We removed the offending items without having to disturb any parts Hattie needs."

Sheridan's eyebrows shot up. "Items?"

"Yes." The vet nodded. "It's quite the treasure trove. A few socks. Several hair scrunchies and, ahem, the culprit doing the damage, a pair of thong underwear."

Alek choked back a laugh. All morning, he'd been feeling guilty that Hattie might die because she'd eaten a pair of his briefs. It turned out her underwear fetish didn't discriminate. He nudged Sheridan's shoulder playfully. She buried her face in her hands.

"But she's gonna be okay, right?" Finn's lips trembled when he spoke.

The vet gave him a reassuring smile. "You must be Finn. Hattie has been asking for you. She is well on her way to making a full recovery. Believe it or not, the surgery is the easy part. The difficult part will be keeping her from opening up her wound again." He patted him on the shoulder. "Can I count on you to help with that?"

Finn nodded earnestly. "Can I see her?"

"I know she'd like that. She's still a bit groggy and the techs are finishing dressing the wound. Someone will be out shortly to bring you back." The vet looked at Alek and Sheridan. "There's only room for one person at a time, I'm afraid. You'll have to take turns sitting with her."

"No problem," Alek said. "Finn can have my turn." He extended his hand to the vet. "Thank you. We really appreciate it."

"Glad I could help. I'll see you back there in a few minutes, young man."

Finn stretched his arms around both Sheridan's and Alek's waists and hugged them. Sheridan buried her fingers in the boy's hair. Alek swallowed roughly as he pulled them both in closer. His little makeshift family was going to be okay.

She plans to go back to being a traveling nurse. To show Finn the world.

Collin's words echoed in Alek's head. With everything that had gone on last night and this morning, he'd forgotten to bring up the subject of the guardianship hearing. Or Sheridan's future plans. She'd only promised him this season. But that was before. Surely she'd changed her mind by now?

The cold rushed in when someone opened the door to the clinic.

"Hi-yee!"

The sound of Sloane's voice had Sheridan jumping away.

"Oh, this better be a happy hug and not a sad one," Sloane cried.

"I told you this was a bad idea," Valentine mumbled as he stomped the snow off his sneakers.

Finn pulled out of their embrace and raced over to Sloane. "Hattie is gonna make it!"

Sloane let out a dramatic sigh. "Oh, thank the lord."

"How did you know we were here?" It was hard to tell if Sheridan was surprised or annoyed.

The other woman unwrapped the colorful scarf from around her neck. "The WAGs had an emergency meeting for coffee this morning. We were brainstorming ways to help Brooke out with all this mess with Jackson." She lowered her voice. "And Brad." She shook her head in disgust. "Claire told us why you were unavailable. Of course I had to run over here to check on our little superstar."

"Of course." Valentine was still mumbling.

Alek shot him a quizzical look, but his teammate shook his head.

"That's very sweet of you," Sheridan told her.

"Her fans are very worried about her." Sloane pouted.

"You posted about her surgery?" Sheridan no longer sounded as if she thought Sloane was all that sweet.

"She has hundreds of thousands of followers. Who knows? It might have been their good mojo that helped her pull through," Sloane replied with a smug look.

One of the techs emerged from the back. "Hattie is ready for visitors," he announced.

"Oh, yay!" Sloane pulled out her phone. "We can update her status."

Sheridan blocked the other woman's path. "Only one visitor is allowed back at a time. And that will be Finn."

Sloane looked like she might object before donning her social media smile. "Of course. Maybe I can interview the vet who saved her life?" She arched an eyebrow at the tech. "Hattie's followers would love that."

"Uh, I'll see if he's available," he said before ushering Finn back and closing the door.

"Tell him it will be awesome publicity!" Sloane called after them.

"For you," Valentine said just loud enough for Alek to hear.

"Trouble in paradise?" Alek whispered back.

Valentine grimaced.

"So you two made quite a cozy photo op when we walked in." Sloane bounced up on her toes.

"Nothing to chirp about there. They're friends," Valentine snapped. "Sheridan and Finn are like Ice-Berg's siblings. Don't read anything into it."

A shadow fell over Sheridan's face. "Didn't you say you wanted to get in with the trainer today?" she said to Alek. "Finn and I can Uber home when they kick him out of back there."

Alek felt a little like he'd taken a body check. He knew Sheridan was simply steering the conversation away from their private life. That didn't mean he had to like the tactical way she did it. He wanted to pull her aside and remind her that he did not think of her as a little sister. She was so much more to him. Except he didn't think he could put what exactly "more" was into words. And he certainly didn't want to have that conversation in front of Valentine and his content creator girlfriend.

"Timothée and I can take you home," Sloane offered.

"Actually, I could use a good stretch of my shoulder to work out the kinks before tomorrow's game," Valentine said. "If you're headed to the practice facility, mind if I hitch a ride?"

Alek felt a little like he'd been backed into a corner. He wanted to stay with Sheridan and Finn. Hell, he wanted to stay with them forever. But not if Sloane was going to hang around, poking her nose into everything and turning it into fodder for social media. He looked over at Sheridan, willing her to read the question in his eyes. She nodded ever so slightly. He sighed.

"No problem. Text me when you leave here?" he asked because he had no right to insist that she did even though the Neanderthal within was begging him to do just that.

"Of course."

He wanted to kiss her. To bring them back to the connection they'd had last night and all morning. The guarded look in her eyes stopped him, however. She wasn't angry with him. He understood her well enough to know that. It was the situation that had her ticked. Not only Sloane's intrusiveness but also the fact that they needed to figure out where this relationship was headed.

Alek thought he knew the direction he wanted it to go. But, dammit, Collin's words had sown a tiny seed of doubt. He'd thought he'd been on the same page with women who meant something to him before. Both times, it turned out he'd been reading the wrong book.

"I'll see you at home, then." It was the only thing he could say.

He stopped at the front desk and handed over his credit card. "Whatever the dog needs, I want her to have it."

The receptionist ran it through the card reader and passed it back to him. "We'll keep this on file."

"We'll be back with a bag of dog toys tomorrow afternoon." Valentine winked at her, making the woman blush.

The snow was really coming down when they stepped outside. Valentine brushed off Alek's side mirrors with the sleeve of his jacket before climbing into the passenger seat. His groan echoed throughout the interior when Alek started the car.

"That sounds heavy." Alek remarked.

"I don't know what's wrong with me," his teammate said. "Sloane is every guy's wet dream wrapped up in a very stylish package."

Alek pulled onto the highway. "But?"

"But I can't help feeling like she's using me." Valentine slumped down into the seat.

"It comes with the territory. You're a rich professional athlete. Top of the food chain."

"Yeah. Those women are normally easy to spot. At least they used to be." He groaned again. "I thought Sloane was different. I thought we wanted the same things."

"What changed?"

"She's becoming more and more obsessed with social media. It's all she talks about. Don't get me wrong, I'm not so self-centered that I want to be with someone who is solely focused on me. I'd much rather she have other interests, just as long as it doesn't involve content creation. Can you imagine thrusting a kid into that kind of atmosphere?"

Alek jerked his head around to stare at him. "Wow. You've thought about having kids with her?"

"Well, sure. I mean, I want to have my kids chasing me around at morning skate before I'm too old. Or cheering me on from the boards. I think Sloane is only after the fame and atten-tion. If something better came along, I have this bad feeling she'd throw me over in a heartbeat."

They were quiet for a long moment before Valentine spoke up.

"I'm starting to think you've had the right approach all along, Ice-Berg. Maybe I should follow your lead and steer clear of all the complications that come with a long-term relationship and hope that someone leaves me a kid."

Alek squeezed the steering wheel until his knuckles were white. That hadn't been what he was doing. Well, not exactly, anyway. At one time in his life, he'd wanted what his teammate wanted.

Until his best friend took it away.

Except he had another chance at it now. But if he messed it

up, he'd lose Sheridan and Finn forever. And that would break him.

Their arrival at the training facility should have put an end to the conversation, but Alek wanted his friend to know he was in his corner.

"I'd say trust your gut, Twos," he said as they hurried through the snow and into the building. "But mine hasn't always been reliable where women are concerned. It might be best if you tell her how you feel. Maybe she thinks you want her to be a social media queen, and she's only doing all of this for you."

Valentine perked up. "You think?"

He didn't think so, but for his teammate's sake, he hoped so. "Hard to say for sure. That's why you need to talk to her."

"Thanks, Ice-Berg." Valentine clapped him on the back. "You picked up a few things being the son of a professor."

The training room was crowded, which was understandable given that they had a noon game the next day. None of the guys wanted to get up any earlier than they had to on a Sunday morning.

"How's the pooch?" Picard called from one of the tables where a trainer was applying ultrasound to his ankle.

Alek signed in for the next available trainer. "Vet says she's going to pull through."

"How many of your jock straps did they pull from Hattie's belly?" Henrik asked. The assistant coach was icing his back.

"None," Alek replied, feeling triumphant. "It was a pair of Sheridan's thong underwear."

Laughter and a few wolf whistles filled the room.

"Oh sure," one of the guys scoffed. "Are we supposed to believe that?"

"How do we know you're not wearing women's underwear?" another teased.

"Har, har." Alek flipped them all the bird.

"Were they the gold ones?"

A hush fell over the room at Merriweather's odd question. The guy was leaning against the wall sipping a water. Alek felt his blood begin to boil just by looking at the insolent smile on the douchebag's face.

"What did you say?" he demanded.

Merriweather had the gall to shrug. "The shiny gold ones. I doubt they are the same pair she wore back when she was trolling the bench in Boston. But those are the ones I remember."

Gus came from nowhere to stand beside Alek. "Don't listen to him. He's lying. The asshole is simply stirring the pot," he said.

His words made Merriweather chuckle. "Cobert didn't believe me, either. Thought his little sister was pure as the snow. When really she was a sl—"

Alek's fist landed on Merriweather's mouth before he could finish the word. Water arced across the room when his water bottle went flying. Gus and Picard tried to shoulder themselves between the two men.

Blood trickled from the corner of Merriweather's mouth, but that didn't quiet his maniacal laugh. "Whoa. You're awfully protective of your friend's little sister. Something going on that we don't know about?" he taunted. "I mean, it looks like you've already screwed things up with the cute little teacher. What makes you think you can hold on to a fast one like Sheridan?"

"Oh no, he didn't," Picard said as he loosened his grip on Alek's waist.

Not that Alek heard him. He had Merriweather pinned to the floor in an instant, his fists slamming into the other man's body. The roaring in his ears was slowly drowned out by the sounds of his teammates yelling at him to stop. Multiple pairs of hands reached in to tug him off the other man. Merriweather landed a punch to Alek's mouth right when Picard squeezed himself between them. Valentine and Gus yanked Alek to his feet.

Merriweather sat up and sneered. "She's not worth it, man. Sheridan is very chummy with one of the doctors at the hospital. He claims to be a therapist, but a home-wrecker is what he is, if you ask me. Don't say I didn't warn you."

"Nobody asked you." Valentine kicked him in the ribs. "You wrecked your home all by yourself. Not some doctor."

It was the first time any of them had seen Merriweather move that fast. He had his hands around Valentine's neck before anyone could stop him.

"Fuck you, man," Merriweather shouted.

The players and the trainers all scrambled to break it up. Valentine had red marks around his neck and was gasping for air when they pulled them apart. Picard was in the midst of yanking Merriweather away by his hair when Coach rushed in.

"Hey!" he yelled while one of the assistants blew his whistle.

Everyone was breathing heavy as they dropped their hands to their sides. Henrik handed Alek a towel for his bloody lip. No one made a similar gesture to Merriweather, however.

"What the hell is going on in here?" Coach demanded.

A charged silence fell over the room. No doubt one of the trainers, or even Henrik, would be pressed into recounting the events to the coaching staff and management. The players, however, kept their lips zipped.

Coach swore violently. "This is what I get for not staying home and helping put up the Christmas decorations." He stared Alek down. "Don't leave this building without having someone look at that lip." He redirected his gaze at Merriweather and sighed heavily. "You. Come with me."

He turned on his heel and stormed off without even waiting

to see if Merriweather would follow. Everyone stood still for a long moment wondering if their teammate would have the balls to disobey, until he snatched up a towel and pressed it to his mouth. He took his time, strutting from the room, shoulders back and head high as if he'd been selected to captain the team. None of his teammates bothered to make eye contact with him on his way out.

One of the trainers guided Alek over to a chair while another checked out Valentine. The rest of the guys picked up the items that ended up being collateral damage.

"He split it pretty good," the trainer said. "A squirt of Dermabond will fix it right up. Sit tight while I go grab some." He handed Alek an ice pack. "Hold this on it while you wait."

Picard and Gus made their way over to him as soon as the trainer left.

"That guy is toxic," Gus said softly. "He had no qualms about hurting Valentine."

"I'm going to coach. If he doesn't listen, I'll go over his head to the GM," Picard added. "But that guy is *not* staying in our dressing room."

Their words barely registered with Alek. He was too busy contemplating the things Merriweather said about Sheridan. They weren't true.

Were they?

The fact was, he'd known Sheridan a long time ago. And had he *truly* known her then? He couldn't imagine Sheridan two-timing him with Finn's therapist. Except he never thought in a million years that her brother would steal his girlfriend away once upon a time, either.

"Alek." Gus shook him by the shoulder. "Don't even think about believing any of that bullshit Merriweather said. The dude was gaslighting you. Trying to drive a wedge within the team. That's his MO, remember?" He lowered his voice. "You and Sheridan are good together, man. Don't let that jealous little prick ruin that for you."

The trainer returned. Alek winced when the guy pressed on his lip. "That should do it. I've put some antibacterial meds on there too. Keep icing it." He shot Alek a sheepish look. "And remember that other people's saliva can carry a lot of bacteria. So, uh, you know, no kissing tonight. Got it?"

Alek should have been bitter about that part of the prescription, but right now all he felt was confusion. He didn't want to doubt himself for choosing poorly again. Except with his track record, how could he not?

Valentine appeared by his side, looking none the worse for wear.

"You good, Twos?" Alek asked him.

His teammate nodded. "It'll take a lot more than that to take me out." He cleared his throat. "I'm going to follow your advice and talk to Sloane tonight. Do me a solid and give Sheridan the same courtesy, will ya?"

When Alek didn't respond he continued.

"It's nobody's business if something is going on with you two," Valentine said. "But Sloane was right earlier. You looked pretty cozy with your little family. Don't let that jerk-off spoil it."

Picard returned to the training room. "I didn't have to go far up the chain of command," he announced. "Coach suspended him indefinitely. They're bringing up the wunderkind, Parker Dern, to fill his spot."

"The seventeen-year-old?" Valentine looked as surprised as everyone else. "Is that even allowed?"

"He turned eighteen last week," Henrik told them. He looked over at Alek. "He's green, but he's a once-in-a-lifetime talent. This will be fun."

Alek wasn't so sure about that. Then again, he wasn't sure about anything right now.

"Looking forward to it," he mumbled around his swollen lip as he stood. "I'll see you boys in the morning."

"I thought you wanted to have your back worked on?" Valentine said.

"I'm good," he replied.

Gus followed him out. "Here," he said as he pulled something out of his equipment bag. "Finn's phone. It slipped into the cushions of the sofa. Good thing it rang when someone called him this morning, or it could have been weeks before we discovered it."

"Someone called him?"

"Yeah. Three times from an unidentified number. Every time Gunner answered, whoever was on the other end hung up."

"Probably a sales call." Alek shoved it into the pocket of his jacket.

"Most likely. I turned it off so we could get through breakfast." Gus placed a hand on his shoulder. "You've had a crazy day. Wanna get a beer and a slice of pizza?"

"Nah. But thanks. I didn't sleep well last night. I'm going home to take a nap."

Gus nodded. "Sounds like a good plan. I'll see you in the morning."

"See you at the arena."

Alek waited for his friend to drive away before he headed off in the direction of the pet shelters on the list Lori had given him. Normally, it was Finn and Sloane who dropped off the toys. It drove Lori crazy that he wouldn't go with a camera crew. This was Finn's show, he would tell her. It was easier than telling her he wasn't really a big dog person. Luke Kessler could have that slice of the charity pie, thank you very much.

Although, he'd put money on Sloane trying to dethrone him in the near future.

Right now, though, Alek didn't want to go home. He had too many things to untangle in his brain. And his heart. Driving around town and dropping off pet toys would be a welcome distraction.

Two hours later, he pulled into his last stop. It was the emergency clinic where Hattie was recovering. Sheridan had texted forty minutes ago that she and Finn were Ubering home. There wouldn't be any chance of running into them here.

The receptionist looked surprised to see him when he arrived with a trash bag full of pet toys. "Oh, your family already left," she told him.

Your family.

Her words were like a knife to the gut. A few hours ago, he'd thought of them as one. Now, doubt ate at him. He needed to follow his own advice and talk to Sheridan. And he would. Once he figured out what to say. In the meantime, he could check on Hattie.

"I was out delivering these toys that fans donate at our hockey games," he told the woman. "I thought I'd stop in and see how Hattie is doing?"

"Do you want to go back and see her?" She didn't wait for an answer, instead pressing the intercom button and announcing his presence.

"I'm sure she needs her rest," he protested. "I don't want to disturb her. An update on her condition is fine."

The vet appeared in the doorway. His toothy grin was still present even after a long day of rescuing pets. "You won't be disturbing her. In fact, she was asleep when Finn left earlier. She's been a little blue since she woke up and found him gone." He waved Alek back. "Come on."

Alek didn't bother telling him Hattie avoided him at all

costs. It was easier to let things be awkward. Except the dog surprised him when they arrived in the recovery area. Hattie hurried to her feet. She looked past him, but she didn't retreat as she normally would have when she didn't see Finn. Instead, she wagged her tail tentatively.

"You're welcome to sit with her. She's still a little woozy, but she's recovering nicely." The vet scooted a giant pillow into the run where Hattie was recuperating. "I'm going off to check on our patients in the cat room."

Hattie continued to watch Alek with a guarded expression in her big brown eyes.

He sighed. "Last night wasn't a one-night fling, then, huh, girl?"

She wagged her tail with a little more gusto. Alek shrugged out of his coat.

"Down," he commanded.

The dog lay down immediately, resting her snout on the edge of the pillow.

Alek chuckled. "How did I not know you were such a flirt?"

As soon as he was seated on the pillow, Hattie crawled forward so that her head rested on his thigh. He buried his fingers in the soft fur of her neck.

"I shouldn't be surprised. You were Jamie's dog once."

He leaned his head back against the concrete wall behind him and looked up at the ceiling.

"Damn you, Jamie," he whispered hoarsely. "If making me love them, then yanking them away is your way of screwing me over a second time, so help me, I will come up there and drag you down, right straight to hell."

TWENTY-THREE

SHERIDAN AND FINN rushed into the family room at the arena with only a few minutes to spare before the team took the ice for skate around. A noon game left little time to get packed for a flight to Florida that evening before she took Finn to sit with Hattie at the vet clinic. Alek left for the arena super early that morning. She knew because she'd lain awake waiting for the garage door to close before venturing downstairs.

She'd managed to avoid Alek all afternoon and evening yesterday. Finn, who'd been exhausted from the sleepover the night before, coupled with worry over Hattie, had passed out as soon as they arrived home from the vet. He'd been restless, though, and calling out for his parents in his sleep. It was easier to hide out in Finn's room under the guise of taking care of him than to face Alek.

Valentine's reminder that Alek only thought of her as a sister was a wake-up call of sorts. As much as she didn't want to admit it, Jamie—and Madison—still cast a long shadow over her relationship with Alek. At least, the relationship she wanted to have with him. The closer she grew to him, the harder it was to live with herself for the role she played in the whole sordid affair of nearly a decade before.

She'd slipped back to her high school self, once again letting herself dream about a life with Alek. Only now, that fantasy was for the three of them to be a family. Hattie, too. Except she had no idea if he wanted that. He certainly acted like he did. Yet he hadn't corrected Valentine when he misspoke yesterday. It would have been the perfect time to set the record straight. The fact that he didn't left her feeling unsure of everything.

"Can I go up to my seat?" Finn asked. "I want to tell Alek that Hattie is much better this morning."

"Sure. Go ahead." Sheridan took his coat and draped it over the back of a chair as he raced out.

Freya carried two cups of coffee over and handed one to Sheridan.

"Bless you." Sheridan took a resurrecting sip.

"I figured with the past few days you've had that caffeine was likely needed. Although there are mimosas if you want something stronger. How's Hattie?"

"Improving. Finn is a little hesitant to head out for Thanksgiving break tonight, but this actually works out better," Sheridan told her. "She can board at the vet while she heals. The staff agreed to FaceTime Finn so he can see her twice a day. Which reminds me, I need to get Finn's phone from Claire before we fly out. He left it at their house the other night."

"Claire's not here yet. She's still dealing with the police."

Sheridan rocked back on her heels. "The police?"

"Yeah. Someone broke into their house while she and the kids were at church this morning. Likely the same crew who robbed Trey Van Horn and Dex Fletcher from the Growlers last night."

"What?!" Sheridan noticed as she glanced around the room that the mood was more muted than usual.

"There's been a rash of burglaries at the homes of pro athletes lately. The Growlers players had precautions in place and not much was taken."

She felt a fission of fear crawl down her spine.

"What about at Claire and Gus's? Did they lose a lot?"

Freya shook her head. "Claire's parents are in town for an early Thanksgiving. Her dad skipped church. Luckily, he's a retired cop and was able to scare them off before they got their hands on anything."

"Very lucky." Sheridan heaved a sigh. "And very scary."

An image on the monitor caught her attention. Alek was warming up on the ice. When he shoved his mask on top of his head to grab a drink of water, she gasped.

"What happened to Alek? He looks like he's been in a fight."

Freya gave her an odd look. "You don't know?"

Sheridan felt a little guilty for hiding away last night. "Uh, no. I was busy dealing with Hattie. I haven't seen Alek since we took her to the vet."

"He got in a fight with Brad Merriweather yesterday," Freya announced.

"Oh my gosh! What were they fighting about?"

Freya scrutinized her for a drawn-out moment before replying. "Henrik didn't say. He was busy getting the new kid into town for tonight's game. Brad has been suspended indefinitely." She lowered her voice. "The team is negotiating with his agent to admit him to inpatient counseling. They're citing his temper. He tried to strangle Timothée." She leaned in closer. "If you ask me, I wouldn't be surprised if the guy doesn't have a concussion disorder. And self-medicating with drugs, even if they are legal, doesn't help."

Sheridan plopped down into the nearest chair. "Wow. I

missed a lot while I was distracted with Hattie. How are Brooke and the boys?"

"She took them home to her parents. For good."

"That was a smart move," Sheridan said with a nod.

She was proud of the other woman for standing up for herself. It wasn't always the easiest thing to do. There were so many times in her life when Sheridan had gone with the flow, toughing it out and not rocking the boat for the sake of her family. Mostly for the sake of Jamie.

The one time she had decided to take the reins in her life, she'd imploded a friendship. And crushed her heart in the process. Her hands shook just thinking about it. She could right that wrong. But at what cost to her future with Alek?

The WAGs began to file out of the room and into the arena to find their seats before the horn blew at the start of the first period. Freya and Sheridan followed.

"How is Valentine?" Sheridan scoured the group of WAGs, looking for Sloane. It was odd not to have the woman filming content before the game. "I hope Brad didn't injure him, too."

"The only thing hurting on that boy is his heart," Freya said. "He and Sloane broke up last night."

Her announcement had Sheridan nearly tripping over her own feet. "What?! I swear. I feel like an entire lifetime happened in the past forty-eight hours. Do you have any more tea to spill?"

"Only that Zack Picard is pouting because Sloane made a scene at his restaurant when she walked out on Timothée. Of course, a video of it landed on social media. Not only that but both the Growlers were being robbed while they were enjoying dinner there."

Sheridan slapped her hand over her mouth and shook her head from side to side.

"I know," Freya said. "You can't make this stuff up."

The Mayhem were already down two goals, and they weren't even through the first period when Claire slipped into her seat next to Sheridan.

"How *are* you?" Sheridan squeezed her friend's hand.

"Grateful my dad was home and that he didn't shoot anyone," Claire replied with a humorless laugh.

They jumped from their seats and cheered when Alek blocked a shot on goal after it slipped past the stick of the new defenseman.

Claire groaned. "A big day for that kid. He looks frenzied, though."

"Truth be told, they are all playing out of sync today."

"Not surprising. There's been lots of drama in and out of the dressing room."

"So I heard. Do you know what was behind the fight with Brad?" Sheridan knew Alek was disgusted with the situation with Jackson. Still, she was surprised he'd confront his teammate about it. Especially if it might upset the team's cohesive play. In Alek's eyes, winning the Cup was the only thing that mattered.

Claire donned a critical look similar to the one Freya wore when Sheridan asked her the same question. "You really don't know?"

She shook her head. "Freya said Henrik didn't tell her."

The other woman scoffed. "Freya is lying. They fought about you, Sheridan."

The horn sounded to end the first period.

THE MAYHEM LOST THREE ZIP. Alek's streak of eight scoreless periods ended two minutes and thirty-nine seconds into the game. And he couldn't even blame Merriweather's replacement. Once the kid got past his first-period jitters, he'd played up to his potential. Too bad none of the team's points leaders—Valentine, Gus, and Picard—did the same. They all seemed to be going through the motions out on the ice.

Alek included.

As a result, the dressing room was subdued when Coach walked in.

"There were some good moments out there. Unfortunately, there were some stupid ones, too. Valentine, that was a cheap shot you took. If you're going to drop gloves and land in the sin bin, make it worth it next time. Lucky for you, Jensen and his line carried us on the penalty kill." He looked at the new kid, Parker Dern, who'd been touted by many in the league as hockey's next big thing. "Solid job tonight, Dern. Keep it up." Coach handed him a puck.

The guys broke out in applause.

"Let's put this one behind us, boys," he continued. "We've got a three-game road trip that ends in sunny Florida and a full day off with our families on Thanksgiving. Pack up your gear, and let's be on our way to Dallas for tomorrow night's game."

As soon as the coaching staff exited, Alek stood.

"Look, boys, we are going to have an off game here and there. The important thing is for us to pull together on this road trip so we don't have a string of them." He pulled the chain with the medallion out of his stall. "Without a doubt, the guy who deserves this tonight is Dern. Welcome to the show, Junior. Great game."

His teammates all stood and applauded. "Speech. Speech," several of them chanted.

Dern pulled the medallion over his head. "Man, what a great night. I'm stoked to be here."

Alek bit back a chuckle when the kid's voice squeaked.

Gus guffawed beside Alek. "Jesus, he's still a baby."

"The rookie needs a nickname," someone called out.

"The way he parked his ass in the corner and kept the other guys out of the crease, I think we should dub him Park-His-Ass," Picard called out.

They all started shouting "Park-His-Ass" at the top of their lungs, and the kid's nickname was born. The mood grew a little lighter as everyone packed up their gear in preparation for the trip to Dallas.

"You good?" Alek asked Gus.

His friend sighed. "I can't say I'm thrilled leaving my wife and kids at home after today. At least my in-laws will be around until Claire and the kids fly out later this week."

"Do the cops have any leads?"

"Not that they've said." Gus shouldered his equipment bag. "Everyone in my neighborhood has cameras. Van Horn and Kessler likely have the same setup where they live. It's only a matter of time until they catch these guys. I'm sure it's a relief knowing Sheridan and Finn are headed to Florida tonight, though."

"Yeah." Alek was grateful Sheridan and Finn wouldn't be home alone, especially since Hattie would be at the vet for a few more days.

"What gives?" Gus narrowed his eyes as he studied Alek carefully when he didn't elaborate more.

"Nothing." Alek stowed his headphones in the side pocket of his equipment bag.

"I call bullshit. Dammit, you let the lies Merriweather spewed yesterday get in your head, didn't you? Never mind, it's all over your face. Now you're bent on ruining the best thing that ever happened to you." Gus swore as he grabbed the strap of Alek's equipment bag and shoved it to him. "Come with me."

"You're way off base. That's not what's happening," Alek

protested even though it was exactly what was happening. "Everything is fine."

"Good. Then you won't mind coming with me to meet some friends of Claire's." Gus gestured for Alek to lead the way out of the dressing room.

They maneuvered past the reporters still lobbing questions at Dern and exited into the hallway.

"I'm telling you, Gus," Alek grumbled. "It's not what you think."

He stopped short at the sound of Sheridan's laugh. She stood outside the family room, chatting up a tall, sandy-haired man who looked at her as if she was his next meal.

"Alek!" Finn ran up, dragging two bags full of dog toys. News of Hattie's surgery had twice as many fans tossing toys onto the ice. "Guess what? Dr. Trent is going to deliver these to some shelters in Michigan when he goes home for Thanksgiving. Isn't that cool?"

"Real cool," Alek replied, his eyes still focused on the exchange between Sheridan and the other man. It was obvious by the relaxed way she interacted with him that they knew each other well. That didn't sit well with him. His chest grew tight as he imagined Sheridan and this guy together. He hadn't wanted to believe Merriweather, but it was hard not to, judging by how their bodies leaned into one another with familiarity.

Sheridan's smile was wary when she first noticed Alek before she donned the chipper people-pleasing one he was starting to despise.

"Here he is," she told the guy next to her. "Alek, I'd like you to meet Dr. Trent Adams. Trent and I work together at the hospital."

"He was my friend first," Finn interjected.

A low roar sounded in Alek's ears when Trent smiled down at Finn before ruffling his hair.

"Yes, I was," he told the boy before aiming his pearly whites at Alek. "What a treat to get to see this part of Finn's life."

"Uh-huh." Alek sounded like a Neanderthal, but he didn't trust himself enough to say more.

"Of course, my husband is more of a sports fan than I am," Trent continued. He shot Sheridan a guilty look. "He'll kill me when he finds out Trey Van Horn was at the game we were supposed to come to Friday night. So let's keep that on the down low, okay?" He nudged her shoulder with his.

"His wife's little brother is a friend of mine." Finn puffed out his chest with pride. "I can probably get you an autographed football."

"That would be an awesome Christmas gift for me to give him." Trent high-fived Finn.

Alek was having trouble keeping up with the conversation, however. Relief, guilt, and annoyance all flooded through his veins. Jesus, he'd been a fool for believing anything out of Brad Merriweather's deceitful mouth. Even more so, he was disappointed in himself for not trusting Sheridan. Damn Madison and Jamie for making him constantly mistrust his judgment.

"I'm sorry. Did you say, 'your husband'?" he croaked out. The relief he felt was clogging his throat.

Sheridan must have misunderstood his distress because she shot him an astonished look.

"Yes. Gary." Trent's tone became clipped. "Claire took him out on the ice to get a picture."

"Told you Merriweather was baiting you, dumb-ass," Gus muttered beside Alek.

It was a toss-up between punching his friend or kissing him. He had no doubt Gus arranged this "meeting."

"Uh, we can do better than a picture on the ice," Alek offered. "How would Gary like to meet some of the guys?"

Trent's eyes went wide. "He'd probably talk about it for the rest of his life."

"Better than having him talk about Van Horn and the Growlers forever and ever." Alek signaled to one of the equipment managers. "And a hockey stick trumps a football any day. Finn, why don't you take Trent into the lumber yard and help him pick out a stick for Gary? We'll get the guys to sign it."

Finn grabbed the doctor's hand. "Let's go shopping, Dr. Trent."

Sheridan wore an indulgent smile as she watched the exchange. Alek shifted his gaze to meet hers. He wanted to say so much to her, starting with how he'd been a colossal fool for putting her in the same box as the other women who had jilted him before. The woman standing before him wasn't like any other woman he knew. And he was damn glad for another shot.

Gus slapped him on the back. "I think I'll go find Claire and Gary."

"Hey," Alek said when they were alone.

"Hi." She cleared her throat. "Sorry for disappearing last night. I guess Finn wasn't the only one overwhelmed by the possibility of almost losing Hattie."

"No worries. You were still catching up on sleep from your shift at the hospital. I did the same. Hattie was pretty restless the night before."

Her lips twitched. "Lucky for you, you managed to eke out a nap with her at the clinic yesterday afternoon."

He rubbed his fingers through his hair. "I guy can't do anything around town without someone ratting him out."

"At least it didn't make it to social media. Your cover as a *dog tolerator* would be blown."

"Kessler would have a field day with that."

She moved closer and reached up to gently trace his bottom

lip. He managed not to wince when her finger drew close to his wound.

"Does it hurt?" she whispered.

The only thing he felt was the pounding of his heart brought on by her delicate touch.

"Nah." He let his equipment bag slide from his shoulder and dropped it on the floor by his feet. Placing his hands on either side of her waist, he tugged her body in close to his.

"Liar." She rested one hand against his chest while the other fiddled with the lapel of his suit jacket. "According to the rumor mill, you two fought about me."

Alek sighed. Sheridan never liked to be the center of attention, much less to cause any controversy. The idea that she was the catalyst of any sort of conflict within the team had to have wounded her. Merriweather was lucky he was out of Alek's reach at the moment.

He leaned his forehead against hers. "He said some unforgivable things. All of them untrue. None of the guys believed him." *Except for the idiot in front of you.* "I straightened him out."

"Brad was always jealous of Jamie. It's so silly. My brother is gone and never coming back."

"And so many of us still harbor some ire toward the guy."

It was the wrong thing to say, given how stiff her body grew beneath his fingertips. She dropped her hands and stepped out of his hold. Her eyes were shiny when she brushed the hair out of her face.

Dammit.

"We need to talk." She looked around the hallway, where anyone could happen upon them at any moment. "I-I need to straighten out some misconceptions you have about Jamie."

Alek didn't want to talk about Jamie. He wanted to talk

about her and him. And their future together. A future that didn't involve his former best friend.

He gripped her elbows, pulling her back against his body. "You just said Jamie isn't coming back. There's no point in dredging up the past and all the pain that went with it. I want us to start fresh and new. Do you hear me? I. Want. Us."

Her mouth dropped open, and her eyes went round. He gave her a little shake.

"I want our little makeshift family, Sheridan. For keeps. And if my lip didn't hurt so freaking bad right now, I'd prove it by kissing you senseless."

She gasped in a breath before burying her face into his chest. He wrapped his arms around her, brushing soft kisses against her hair.

"Bus is leaving in ten, chumps!" Picard called out from somewhere down the hallway.

Alek swore. There was so much more he needed to say to her. To do to her. Not here, though. They'd have the entire day on Thursday. Enough people would be around to entertain Finn so they could carve out some alone time where he could tell her and show her exactly how he felt.

He shifted her away from his body, then lifted her chin with his finger. Her wet face nearly made his heart stop. "Please tell me those are happy tears?"

Her lips wobbled as she nodded. He blew out a sigh of relief, dropping his hand when Finn came bounding down the hall.

"I got a puck for Uncle Alan." He waved it in the air. "Aunt Sher, you promised we could stop by and say goodbye to Hattie before we left for the airport. Can we go right now?"

"Go," Alek said. "And make sure you tell her I said hello."

Finn gave him a hug. "We'll see you in Florida."

"Yes." Alek winked at Sheridan over the boy's head. "Yes, you will."

TWENTY-FOUR

AUNT EILEEN THUMPED the rolling pin against the counter. "That's the dumbest idea I've ever heard."

Sheridan stirred the simmering apples with a wooden spoon, taking a moment to savor the sweet scent of cinnamon and cardamom. It did wonders to soothe her frayed nerves. She and her aunt had been having the same argument for three days, ever since Sheridan had revealed that she and Alek were involved as more than Finn's guardians. Always a sucker for a happily ever after, her aunt was delighted.

"Alek deserves to know the truth," she asserted.

Thump!

"The truth isn't germane to your relationship with him," Aunt Eileen protested. "Jamie and Madison are gone. Besides, even if they were alive, you can't go back and rewrite history. Does it really matter now?"

"It matters to me." Sheridan threw down the spoon. "Jamie will always be my brother. No matter the stupid things he's done. Alek blames him for stealing Madison away. We both know nothing could be further from the truth. He should know that, too."

Her aunt put down the rolling pin and wiped the flour from her hands with a dish towel. "Or is this about finally extinguishing any flame he might still have for Madison?"

The softly worded question had guilt washing over Sheridan like a tidal wave. She steadied herself against the countertop. Was she that petty? She had been once. Petty enough to destroy her brother's friendship.

Tears burned the back of her eyes. Alek still said Madison's name with such reverence even though she was as duplicitous as Jamie. More so, even. Much more so.

"Oh, sweetie." Her aunt hugged her. "No one is being hurt by keeping this one truth buried. But you stand to lose so much by opening an old wound. Here is your chance to finally get what *you* want after spending your entire life giving to everyone else." She stretched out her arms to look at Sheridan. "You deserve this. Don't sabotage your happiness because you think you need to do what's honorable."

Was that what she was doing? *Sabotaging* her happiness? She could hear her therapist yelling "*yes!*" The woman had been accusing Sheridan of that for years. Of being scared to commit. Of feeling as if she didn't deserve the same joy others had.

She dragged in a deep breath. Maybe her therapist and her aunt were right. But did Sheridan have the strength to take that leap of faith? Alek had unwittingly broken her heart before. She didn't think she could survive it twice in a lifetime.

Except this wasn't like before, she reasoned with herself. Alek finally saw her much differently. Things were good between them. He'd been telling her repeatedly these past few days how much he wanted her and Finn to be a part of his life for more than the season. Sure, he hadn't said the three magic words yet, but he suggested they come out to Finn as a couple this weekend. She knew Alek well enough to know he wouldn't do that unless he felt something deeper for her.

Aunt Eileen dropped her arms and stepped back. "Obviously, you need to do what you need to do to live with yourself. Whatever you decide, I'll support you."

Sheridan took both her aunt's hands in hers. "I couldn't have gotten through the past eighteen years without you. Thank you for being my second mom and for keeping me on track."

Her aunt laughed out a sob. "It's been a pretty topsy-turvy track, but I'm awfully glad to have been along for the ride."

Finn burst into the kitchen. "I need your phone," he said. "It's time for me to check in on Hattie. Alek is going to Face-Time with us."

She hadn't been surprised to learn that Finn wasn't the only one checking on Hattie multiple times each day. The clinic staff were quick to share that Alek FaceTimed the dog even without Finn being on the call. He could deny it all he wanted, but Alek didn't tolerate Hattie for Finn's sake. He had a real soft spot for the dog.

Sheridan smiled to herself as she handed Finn her phone. "Not too long. Alek needs to get his nap in before the puck drops. And we should get on the road to Tampa if we want to be at the hotel in time to watch the game with the rest of the families."

"Are we taking the pies?"

Aunt Eileen laughed at him. "Uncle Alan wouldn't have it any other way."

The Mayhem owner had rented out an entire resort in Tampa. The families were arriving this afternoon. The team would travel there after their game in Nashville tonight. There was a watch party this evening with crafts for the kids. Thanksgiving Day would be spent beside the heated indoor-outdoor pool while a team of chefs cooked dinner for the Mayhem family. Aunt Eileen had been preparing a variety of pies all week. She'd bake them in the resort's kitchen tonight.

Sheridan was looking forward to catching up with the WAGs. It had only been a few days since the last home game, but she'd gotten used to seeing Claire and some of the others practically every day. For the first time in her life, she knew what the companionship of a circle of friends felt like, and she liked it. She liked it a lot.

DERN WORE THE MEDALLION AGAIN, thanks to earning his first assist as a pro that night. The kid danced in the aisles during the two-hour flight from Nashville to Tampa. The Mayhem had won the second game of the road trip, a hard-fought shutout against one of the league's leading franchises. After getting over the speed bump they had suffered at their last home game, Alek and his teammates had a lot to be thankful for on American Thanksgiving.

Valentine followed Dern up the aisle, referring to the rookie as his assistant since he'd scored the goal from Dern's assist.

"Dern is going to *park his ass* at my house," Valentine announced. "We can't have my assistant living in some long-term-stay place. Not when I need him to keep feeding me apples for the rest of the season."

"More like Valentine is lonely now that Sloane is gone," Gus murmured to Alek.

"She's already moved out?" He was a little surprised the influencer hadn't fought harder for a relationship with one of the league's most recognizable stars. "That explains him dropping gloves tonight."

"Yep. Sloane moved out and moved on," Gus replied. "She's back in California with some pasty white dot.com type." He pulled up a picture on his phone and showed it to Alek.

"Damn. Two's instincts about her were spot-on."

"Sad but true." Gus eyed Valentine. "I suspect his bonhomie is simply a front."

"Having Dern to babysit will be a good distraction."

Gus shot him a look. "The kid is barely old enough to vote. Valentine has at least eight years on him. And Junior is already following him around like a puppy dog." He gestured to the aisle with his chin. Dern was shotgunning a beer with Valentine while some of the guys cheered them on. "I only hope we haven't replaced one problem with another."

Alek hoped so, too, but that was tomorrow's worry. Right now, the only thing on his mind was Sheridan. He was eager to see her. Thanks to several long phone conversations, they'd gotten back to where they were before the incident with Merriweather had shell-shocked him. Now all he needed was to ensure her body remembered what page they were on. He shifted uncomfortably in his seat, contemplating the ways he was going to reacquaint himself with every part of her.

"This is your captain speaking—"

Cheers and jeers went up among the players as they all sang out "Not my captain" before chanting Picard's name. Fortunately, the charter pilot was familiar with the routine enough to pause until they settled back down.

"We are beginning our approach into Tampa International Airport. Please take your seats, gentlemen, and fasten your seat belts," he continued.

The two male flight attendants made their way up the aisle to corral everyone back to their assigned spots.

"Hey, Ice-Berg!" Valentine shouted from six rows up. "You're on my team for beer pong tomorrow morning. We are going to teach Park-His-Ass here how the pros do it."

Gus scoffed. "See what I mean?"

Alek sighed. "Yeah. Let's rope in Picard tomorrow."

"Odds are he'll be locked in his room with one of his puck bunnies all day."

"Lori, then," Alek replied. "She'll have some ideas."

It was close to one thirty in the morning when the Mayhem arrived at the resort. Thankfully, the bar was already buttoned up tight. Gus herded Valentine and the rookie in the direction of their rooms while Alek pretended to search for his. Once everyone was out of sight, he circled back to the front desk and asked for the envelope Sheridan had left for him. In it was the key to her room. Finn was staying with her aunt and uncle in a suite next door. Alek made a mental note to buy the couple a very big Christmas gift.

A soft light glowed in the bar area when he entered the room. He left his roller bag at the door, stripping out of his suit jacket and stepping out of his shoes as he headed for the bedroom. Moonlight filtered in through a crack in the drapes, illuminating the bare skin on Sheridan's shoulder. A primitive sound escaped the back of his throat.

He wanted this woman. Physically. Spiritually. In every way possible. It was like nothing he'd ever felt before. At first, it was simply to protect her. To safeguard her from the mess Jamie continued to make of her life. To allow her the opportunity of being near Finn.

Now, though, his desire for her was boundless. She was the first thing he thought of when he opened his eyes in the morning and the last thing he thought of when he closed them at night. He couldn't imagine life without her.

He loved her.

Sheridan and Finn were his everything.

He'd thought he had known love before, but he realized he

was wrong. *So wrong.* What he'd felt for Madison was desire. Plain and simple teenage horniness.

As for London, she had been his ticket to companionship, respectability, and safety. He'd desired her, sure, but his pursuit of her was more about gaining a partner and a family. Achieving a rite of passage in life.

With Sheridan, he'd get all of that, along with someone who understood him. Who made him complete. Who made him want to be a better man. To be worthy of her love.

"Are you planning to stand there all night staring at me like some pervert? Or will you please come to bed and warm me up?" She watched him from behind her lashes.

A low growl of excitement escaped his throat. Alek hurried out of his clothes, stepping over them where they landed. The bed groaned when he dove onto the mattress next to her.

Her arms were around him instantly. "How's your lip? Are you sure you're up for this?"

Alek huffed in disdain. "Woman, I'm a professional athlete. Playing in pain is my superpower."

He proved his point not once but twice.

SHERIDAN AVERTED her face when she and Alek strolled into the breakfast room hand in hand with Finn the following morning. She wasn't sure why she felt so shy about taking their relationship public. Everyone in the hotel was part of the Mayhem family or her family.

Finn had taken the news as if it was the natural course of things. There had been no questions about the future, thank goodness. She and Alek didn't offer up any either. Mostly because the two of them hadn't discussed it.

Living in the here and now was just fine with Sheridan. A

commitment meant making a promise. And she wasn't sure she could do that yet. Not without absolving herself for her actions of a decade earlier.

"Well, well, well, Finnegan Begin Again. What have we here?" Valentine stopped them in their tracks. He spoke so loudly that the room quieted around them, all eyes now focused in their direction.

"I win," Finn announced with a toothy smile.

"Yes, you do." Freya winked at Sheridan as everyone cheered.

Sheridan was confused. "Won what?"

"No fair," Jensen called out from behind the buffet. "He had insider knowledge!"

She gave Alek a questioning look. "What are they talking about?"

He leaned over and pressed a kiss to her mouth. Wolf whistles and catcalls sounded throughout the room. Finn pulled free of both their hands with a disgusted groan.

"The list," he told her when he pulled his lips away. "If I know these clowns, some wagering was going on."

"You guessed it," Valentine said. "Finn just won himself two hundred and fifty bucks. Minus the ten I spotted him." He fist-bumped Finn. "Send me your handle, and I'll Venmo you."

Finn's smile faded. He looked back at Sheridan. "I don't have Venmo."

"Don't worry, bud." Alek rubbed the top of Finn's head. "I'll collect from Twos and put it in your piggy bank."

"I get to count it first, right?"

Everyone laughed.

"By the way," Alek said to Finn. "Your phone was in my coat pocket. It's charging upstairs. You'll be able to FaceTime Hattie whenever you want today."

"Cool!"

Finn made a beeline to the kids' table while Alek pressed his hand to Sheridan's lower back and guided her to where Aunt Eileen and Uncle Alan were having breakfast.

"Is that Senator Jack Dern?" Aunt Eileen jerked her chin in the direction of a table in the corner. "I thought the resort was closed to the public?"

Alek pulled out a chair for Sheridan. "He's part of the Mayhem family now. His son, Parker, just got called up."

The words were no sooner out of Alek's mouth when the rookie appeared in the dining room. He started toward the table where Valentine and some of the single guys were sitting when the senator called out to him.

"Parker! Over here."

His father's tone implied he wouldn't take no for an answer. Parker's shoulders slumped somewhat before he changed course and headed to the table where his father waited. They were far enough away that it was difficult to overhear their conversation. Their body language spoke volumes, however.

Parker's father motioned at his son's shoulder-length dish-water-blond hair before shaking his head. Sheridan thought the wavy locks suited Parker. Along with his hair, his faded brown eyes and the dimple in his chin reminded her of one of the surfers she'd met while working at a small hospital in a beach town in Southern California. Not only had the guy been easy on the eyes but he'd also been easygoing and laid back. Too bad Parker didn't look as relaxed right now.

Aunt Eileen tsked. "I never liked that man. Watching him browbeat his son only validates that feeling."

The senator gestured as if he were shooting the puck with a hockey stick.

"Tell me that guy isn't giving Junior instructions on how to handle the puck? Does he not know his kid's a virtuoso with a damn hockey stick?" Alek stood from his chair.

Max Kellogg appeared behind him, staying Alek with a hand on his shoulder. The Mayhem's owner was dressed in black slacks and a dark purple cashmere quarter-zip with the Mayhem emblem on the chest in gold. He had on a pair of those "dress" sneakers. Apparently, that was as casual as the guy got.

"Happy Thanksgiving, all." He smiled broadly at Aunt Eileen. "I hear I have you to thank for most of our dessert this afternoon."

Aunt Eileen blushed. "It's my pleasure."

"Well, I'm sure it will be all our pleasures." He gestured for Alek to retake his seat. "If you'll excuse me, I'm going to catch up with the senator. Enjoy your breakfast."

They watched as the Mayhem owner dazzled his way into a chair at the senator's table. A minute later, Parker was practically jogging over to sit with Valentine. Beside her, Alek sighed.

Sheridan arched an eyebrow at him.

Alek shook his head. "I'm not sure if that scenario is any better for the kid."

She squeezed his hand. "He's got you and the rest of the guys watching over him. He'll be fine."

He scoffed.

"Finn tells us you'll be spending Christmas in Canada," Uncle Alan said.

"You're welcome to join us," Alek offered. "My parents would love it." He took Sheridan's hand. "It would be fun to celebrate with all the family in one place."

Her heart skipped a beat at his use of the word family. This was really happening. She and Alek were going to have the life she'd been dreaming of since she was sixteen.

But not without her coming clean. It would be wrong to build a life together with a lie between them. Even if it meant she risked losing him all over again. She chanced a glance at her aunt, who shot her a warning look as if she knew exactly what Sheridan was thinking.

"Alek!" Finn called before she could say anything. "Can we go swimming now?"

"Not until you've wiped all that chocolate off your face," Alek teased. "Did you leave any chocolate chip pancakes for me?"

Uncle Alan rose from his seat. "I'll take you, Finn."

"Hurry up, Ice-Berg." Valentine and Gus were herding all the kids in the direction of the pool. "We're playing water polo. Lori's daughter is talking smack. She says you won't be able to keep the beach ball out of the net."

Alek was out of his chair in an instant. "Challenge accepted." He leaned down and kissed Sheridan thoroughly. "I hope you're coming to cheer for me."

"As long as you're on the same team as Finn," she teased.

"Always," he whispered against her lips. "You, Finn, and Hattie *are* my team."

Sheridan chewed on her bottom lip as she watched him walk off with Finn and Uncle Alan.

She said a silent prayer that he'd still feel that way once she came clean.

TWENTY-FIVE

THE REST of Thanksgiving passed by in a blur of pleasant moments. Sheridan was glad to have the distraction of Alek and the Mayhem family to help her through the first holiday she'd spent without Jamie. Rationally, she knew they would have spent the day apart anyway had she been in Spain as planned. But he would have been only a phone call away and not being together wouldn't have hurt so badly.

Today, of all days, she wished she could speak with him one last time. As things progressed with Alek, the guilt she felt about her role in blowing up their friendship weighed even more heavily. Jamie had been an injured party, too. He just never knew it.

A giant television had been rolled out beside the pool after dinner. The kids were going to watch *Elf* under the stars. The WAGs spread out on chaise lounges along the pool deck, strategically placed to keep an eye on their children. Sheridan watched little Grace hang on every word Finn said, while Alek shared a joke with Gunner.

Freya sighed as she slid onto the chaise next to Sheridan's. "We are going to have to go to Pilates every day next week after your aunt's pies."

Sheridan patted her belly. "I know. I might have indulged in too many helpings of stuffing."

"You weren't fooling anyone, you know."

"About what?"

The other woman laughed. "Everyone but the two of you knew there was something there."

Sheridan turned to stare at her aghast.

"It was always here." Freya gestured to her eyes. "Whenever you looked at each other." She mimed a chef's kiss. "Desire."

Freya reached over and patted Sheridan's arm. "You are good for him. And I think he is exactly what you needed, too."

"Grace wants to FaceTime with Hattie." Finn dug through Sheridan's pool bag.

"Finn, that's the fourth time today. You're going to drive the staff nuts."

"Shelby is the only one working today, and she said to call as often as I want because she's bored," Finn replied. "Come on, Grace. Let's go over there where it's quiet."

"Aw, man. We're really going to go inside to break down film?" Valentine whined. "*Elf* is my favorite movie."

Gus wrapped an arm around Valentine's shoulders. "Come on, Twos. It's only for an hour. You can watch the movie after the kids go to bed."

Valentine was still grumbling when Grace screamed.

"Hey!" Finn yelled. "Leave her alone! Give that back!"

A sea of athletes swarmed in the direction Grace and Finn had gone. Sheridan scrambled from the chaise lounge and ran after them. "Finn!"

By the time she arrived, Gus had scooped up a terrorized Grace and was doing his best to soothe her. Valentine, Jensen, and one of the defensemen had someone pinned to the ground. Alek was squatting in front of Finn, counting breaths with him. Aunt Eileen arrived with his inhaler, but Finn waved it away.

"My phone," he gasped. "That man has my phone."

"What in the hell?" Henrik shouted as he and several of the defensemen arrived on the scene. They surrounded their teammates on the ground who were trying to subdue a very large man who was shouting something in another language. One of the defensemen yelled something in Russian, and the big man on the ground stopped struggling long enough for Valentine to free Finn's phone from the guy's grasp. He slid it across the concrete toward Finn.

"FBI. Freeze!"

Sheridan gasped when Finn stilled in the act of retrieving his phone. Alek stepped between him and two other men with their guns trained toward the man on the ground. Henrik swore colorfully in Swedish while positioning his large body in front of Gus and Grace. The big guy at the bottom of the pile ceased his struggling.

"What in the Sam Hill is going on here?" Senator Dern marched right into the middle of the fray as though he were bulletproof.

"Dad!" His son reached for him, but the senator shrugged him off.

"Who's in charge here?" the senator demanded.

One of the guys holding a gun on them actually blinked long and hard before motioning with his head to several men and women who had surrounded them. They slipped between the defensemen and the pile on the ground and began carefully extracting Mayhem players until the burly man was in handcuffs. His face was bloodied when they hefted him upright. He scanned the ground, and spying the phone, he lunged for it.

Parker was quicker, however. He kicked the phone up into the air with his foot, juggling it with his thigh before it landed in his hand. The rookie started to pass it to Finn, but one of the men holding a gun cleared his throat and held out his palm. The senator grabbed it before his son could hand it over.

"Identify yourselves," he commanded.

Several of the Mayhem players looked at him in awe. His son rolled his eyes, however. With the big man secured, the men and women surrounding them put away their guns.

"I'm Special Agent in Charge Matt Kovaluk, Senator," the one who asked for the phone announced.

"The senator's son. I thought you looked familiar," the senator replied. "Your mother's office is a few doors down from mine."

Agent Kovaluk donned a chagrined look as he nodded. "With all due respect, sir—"

Senator Dern cut him off. "My son is a member of this team. I demand to know who this man is and why you are apprehending him. Since no other guests are staying at the hotel tonight, I can only assume someone associated with the Mayhem is the target. You're in the Organized Crime Unit out of Manhattan. Don't tell me one of my son's teammates is involved with organized crime?"

Sheridan yanked Finn's back against her chest. Aunt Eileen mumbled something unintelligible.

"Only my friend Sergi here is associated with a group of Russian moneylenders who operate out of Upstate New York." The FBI agent looked around. "I'm not here for your son's teammates."

Sergi grumbled something in Russian before spitting in the direction of Agent Kovaluk.

Alek's teammate's reply in Russian sounded more like a taunt. Sergi spit again. Henrik put his arm out to keep the player from retaliating.

The senator persisted. "So what's he doing here?"

"That's a good question. We've been following him for

months, hoping to connect him to the gang. We were very surprised when he ventured to Milwaukee last week. And now here to sunny Florida." Agent Kovaluk's gaze landed on Sheridan. "Miss Cobert, may I have your permission to speak with your nephew?"

She was momentarily mesmerized by the man's beautiful eyes before she realized he knew her name.

"How do you know who I am? Or that Finn is my nephew?"

The FBI agent drew in a deep breath. "It's possible that Finn's parents may have been tangentially involved in this case."

The ground felt like it was shifting beneath her feet. "Wh-what?"

Alek wrapped his arms around both her and Finn. "Do we have to do whatever this is in front of an audience?" he snapped.

Agent Kovaluk locked eyes with Alek for a long moment before nodding and giving some indiscernible signal that had his team standing aside. Claire raced forward and grabbed Grace from her husband's arms. The rest of the Mayhem looked at Alek for direction.

"We're good here," he told them. "Thanks for your help."

No one moved.

"Coach is waiting for you inside," Alek said firmly.

Gus moved closer. "You sure?" He looked at Alek, then at Sheridan.

Alek gave her a gentle squeeze. "We're sure. Thanks, man."

It was another moment before Gus signaled to the rest of the team, and they reluctantly trudged away. All except the senator and his son.

"Senator, if you could give me that phone, we can get this resolved and let everyone get back to their evening. I assure you, your son isn't in any danger." Agent Kovaluk held his hand out again.

"Dad. Give him the phone. This doesn't concern us," Parker urged.

It looked as if the senator might not agree. He handed the phone off to the FBI agent several tense heartbeats later, however.

"I can get one of my staff on the Judiciary Committee to provide all the intel for me," he said with a shrug. "Come on, Parker. You need to watch those films before tomorrow's game."

He walked away. Parker rolled his eyes again before looking between the guy in handcuffs and Alek, then down at Finn.

"You sure you don't need anyone?"

She felt Alek's body relax slightly where it was pressed against her back.

"Thanks, man," he said. "We're good."

Parker nodded. He gave Finn an empathetic look before stepping away.

Agent Kovaluk knelt in front of Finn. "That was a very brave thing you did protecting your friend."

Finn remained silent. His shoulders were stiff beneath her fingers. His breathing didn't seem labored, a fact for which she was extremely grateful.

The FBI agent looked over his shoulder at Sergi. "What's on the phone?"

Sergi spit again.

"Finn?" Agent Kovaluk handed him the phone. "I need you to be brave again and open the phone so I can see why Sergi tried to take it from you. Can you please do that for me?"

"Don't you need a warrant?" Aunt Eileen interjected.

The agent stilled briefly before aiming a pleasant smile at her aunt. "We don't need one. But I can get one. If I do, I have to seize the phone and take it into evidence. If Finn voluntarily opens the phone and scrolls through its content with me, all I'll need is to take a screenshot of whatever we find, and Finn can email it to me." He looked at Finn. "Your phone wouldn't have to leave your hand."

Finn looked up in question at Sheridan. She had no idea what to do.

Aunt Eileen wrung her hands. "What could Jamie possibly have on his phone?"

Perhaps the reason behind him selling the bar.

Sheridan turned to Alek. His face was drawn, and his eyes narrowed as if he'd been thinking the same thing. Had Jamie gotten mixed up in something he shouldn't have? She wasn't sure she wanted to know. Except she and Finn couldn't live the rest of their lives looking over their shoulder wondering.

She nodded at Alek before giving Finn's shoulders a gentle squeeze. "Go ahead, Finn."

Her nephew didn't hesitate, punching in the code—double O seven twice for Jamie's jersey number, seven. The burly Russian would have likely figured it out with a few tries.

"Thank you," Agent Kovaluk said softly.

Sergi growled.

"Let's start with the photos," the agent suggested.

"Which album?" Finn turned the phone so the agent could see it.

"Your dad was organized. I like that."

Sheridan stared at the screen over Finn's shoulder, shocked at how Jamie, the messiest person she knew, had meticulously organized his pictures. Every photo was sorted into folders by categories: the bar, hockey, Finn, Hattie. There was even a folder with her name on it. Then there were folders for places he'd visited, friends, even his collection of hockey skates. She smiled as she shook her head at that one.

"Do you see anything unusual?" The agent directed the question to her.

"Not really. It's all typical Jamie."

Finn scrolled down to the bottom of the page.

"Wait!" Sheridan leaned in closer. "Does that say *Monk?*"

Beside her, Alek chuckled in surprise. "He loved that show."

"We both did," she said. "If he met the stars from that show and never told me, I'm going to—" She stopped herself before voicing the words that spontaneously came to mind. "Can I see that, Finn?"

Sheridan took the phone and swiped the folder open, hoping for a picture of Jamie and their favorite television private eye. What she saw instead had her knees buckling. It was a carousel of photos featuring Madison. In all of them, she was with other men. The brute currently in handcuffs behind her appeared in a few of the shots with another man and Madison.

Snippets of past conversations with Jamie began to filter through her mind.

I'm not sure what's going on with Madison. She seems so withdrawn.

I don't think I can make her happy.

Madison won't even consider marriage counseling.

I need to do what's best for Finn.

Judging by the photos on his phone, Jamie had been playing private eye. He'd been spying on his wife. Sheridan shuddered with dismay, nearly dropping the phone.

Her brother had been sending out clues for months that his marriage was in trouble. Except Sheridan hadn't listened. A tidal wave of shame washed over her. She'd tuned him out because she needed Jamie and Madison's marriage to work to absolve her of the guilt she carried. Guilt for destroying her brother's relationship with Alek. And now Jamie was gone, and she could never ask his forgiveness.

"Sher?" Alek steadied her with a hand on her elbow. "What is it?"

She looked into his beautiful eyes and felt a jolt of pain so savage it stole her breath. Jamie wasn't the only one she needed absolution from.

"I believe this is what your friend was looking for." She handed the phone to Agent Kovaluk.

The FBI agent whistled through his teeth as he swiped through the images. He placed his palm on Finn's head.

"Your dad was as good a detective as he was a hockey player. You should be very proud of him. I'm going to have your aunt email me this folder and then the phone is all yours again."

Sheridan didn't want Finn hanging around that long. "Aunt Eileen? Can you take Finn over to the pool? I think the movie is starting."

Her aunt looked confused and perhaps a little miffed. It couldn't be helped, though. Right now, keeping Finn from getting hurt was Sheridan's highest priority. No matter how much the FBI agent sugarcoated things for Finn, she didn't want her nephew to know the truth about his parents' marriage.

"Save me some popcorn." She traced her fingers over Finn's cheek and gave him a reassuring smile.

Typical of an eight-year-old, he seemed unfazed by the events of the past few minutes. "Okay. But hurry. You don't want to miss the part when he yells at the fake Santa."

Alek shifted closer as Aunt Eileen hurried Finn away.

"Now, what the hell is on that phone?" he demanded as soon as they were out of earshot.

"Some very incriminating photos of a certain Russian crime boss watching our friend here loading stacks of money into a suitcase." He turned to the big Russian. "And you swore up and down you didn't work for the guy. This is the last piece we needed to connect you to a string of ugly crimes against people who owe this group money."

Sergi let out a string of Russian words, all of them sounding vicious and vulgar.

Agent Kovaluk tsked at him.

"Stupid hockey player," Sergi barked out. "He thinks he can pay off debt by blackmailing." More Russian words flew through the air.

Alek choked out a sound of disbelief. "Are you kidding me? Jamie was *gambling*? With the Russian mob no less?" He slapped his palms on top of his head angrily. "Well, isn't that a great way to provide for your family? Not to mention keeping them safe. I guess now we know the reason he sold off his family's legacy. What a dumbass."

Sheridan gnawed on her bottom lip. One look at Agent Kovaluk's merciful expression and she knew the real story. He sighed before opening his mouth to correct Alek. Sergi beat him to it, though.

"Hockey player no gambling. He a sucker for his wifey." He shook his head. "She good gambler. Until she got greedy."

His words weren't exactly a surprise to Sheridan. Her heart ached for her brother. Selling the bar to cover Madison's losses had to have been like selling a piece of him. But he'd always had a soft spot for his wife. Madison had no qualms about taking advantage of his love.

"I'm sorry? Wh-what?" Alek stammered in his shock. "*Madison* had the gambling problem?"

She held her breath, waiting for Alek to deny it. To defend his former lover. It would crush her.

Even if she deserved it.

His hands were in his hair again. "Holy shit."

"Blondie a terrible driver," Sergi said.

Every muscle in Sheridan's body tensed.

Alek took several steps toward the Russian before the agents intercepted him.

"What did you say?" he demanded of Sergi.

"I only trying to give them a warning." The Russian shook his head. "But she drive too fast."

The sound of Alek swearing violently echoed in Sheridan's ears before everything faded to black.

TWENTY-SIX

THE TEAM DOCTOR exited Sheridan's bedroom in the hotel suite, softly closing the door behind him.

"How is she?" Alek demanded at the same time as the irritating FBI agent.

Alek glared at the agent. He should be thanking him for catching Sheridan when she fainted, but the image of the guy's hands all over her was etched onto his brain. It still had him seeing red.

"Her heart rate and BP are stable now. I gave her something that will help her sleep. Several of the WAGs have agreed to take turns staying with her tonight, although I'm sure she'll sleep right through," the doctor told them.

The only one who would be staying the night with her was Alek. He'd chase the coven of WAGs away as soon as he got rid of the cavalry.

The doctor clapped him on the shoulder. "If something changes, you know how to reach me."

Aunt Eileen slipped in as the doctor was leaving. "Finn is asleep in our room. How is Sheridan?"

"Asleep," Alek replied. He looked over at Agent Kovaluk. "So I guess that's it?"

He should be ashamed of his tone toward the agent. But, hell, the man had rained down drama ever since he showed up. Not the least of which was drawing his gun on the two people he cared about most in this world. His stomach cramped up thinking about anything happening to Sheridan or Finn.

"We've got everything we need for now. My superiors and the district attorney may have further questions. I'll try to keep Finn out of the proceedings as best I can." He pulled a card out of his wallet. "Sheridan can call me if she has questions." His lips twitched when he extended his hand holding the card. "Or if she just wants to talk."

An ugly sound escaped the back of Alek's throat. Aunt Eileen saved him by plucking the card from the agent's fingers.

"Thank you," she told him. "Will you have enough to make a conviction?"

"We've been accumulating evidence on Sergi for a while now. I have to warn you, though, he may take a deal by handing over some intel on his employer."

Eileen gasped.

The agent placed his hand on her forearm. "But I will go the distance with the state and local authorities to make sure he stands trial for what he did to your nephew and his wife. That I promise you." His gaze hardened as it locked with Alek's. "Make sure Miss Cobert is aware of that." He handed Finn's phone to Aunt Eileen. "No kid should have to lose their parents."

He signaled for the other two agents and the three of them left the suite. Heaving a relieved sigh, Alek headed for the mini-bar. He pulled out a tiny bottle of Canadian whisky and twisted off the top. Had Sheridan's aunt not been watching, he would have downed it straight from the doll-sized container. Instead, he reached for a glass.

"Can I get you something?" he asked.

"No. Thank you."

Thanks to the mirrored backsplash, he could see her wringing her hands furiously behind him.

"Jamie was always such an optimist. Just like his dad. Ed couldn't accept that his love wasn't enough to save his wife." Her sigh sounded painful. "Something tells me Jamie felt the same way. I only wish he'd confided in one of us. In anyone."

The whisky burned going down as it mingled with something that felt a lot like remorse. Jamie had been his closest friend for three years, during the most formative period of their young lives. He'd never had a brother, but he imagined his bond with Jamie was just as strong. Had Alek been a bigger man, perhaps he wouldn't have tanked the friendship. Maybe Jamie would have reached out, and all of this could have been avoided.

Or perhaps not. It turned out the woman he thought he once loved wasn't who either of them believed her to be. Had he been naive, thinking only of the sex? Probably. Hindsight is twenty-twenty.

Alek slumped down onto the sofa, his bones heavy with regret. He'd missed Jamie. All these years later, this was the first time he'd admitted it to himself. He couldn't help but feel cheated. Jamie had still loved and trusted Alek enough to leave him his most precious gift: Finn. In spite of everything, his best friend still believed in their friendship.

And what had Alek done? Ignored him. Jamie's father was gone. His friend didn't want to burden Sheridan any more than he had for years. Instead, he'd faced the problem of Madison alone. Without Alek by his side.

Fuck.

He tossed the whisky bottle across the room, belatedly realizing Sheridan's aunt was with him. When he glanced around, though, the older woman was nowhere to be seen.

"Good," he mumbled as he crossed the room to retrieve the other two midgets of whisky from the fridge. Remembering he had a game the next night, he pulled out a bottle of water also. He'd drink it before he joined Sheridan in bed.

The next morning, he awoke on the couch with the little whisky bottles scattered around him. Somehow, two others had joined them. The water bottle remained unopened on the table in front of him. His head pounded as he reached for it. Every time he stretched his arm out, however, the water seemed to move farther away.

Alek unleashed a string of obscenities.

Someone across the room grunted in disgust. The sun behind the guy's head blinded Alek, obscuring his face.

"You missed morning skate." Gus used his sneaker-clad foot to scooch the bottle closer.

"First time for everything," Alek managed to grind out through the cotton lining his mouth.

The contents of his stomach roiled when he sat up. Slamming his eyes shut, he counted to ten before wrestling the cap off the bottle and downing its contents in one long swallow. He leaned his head back against the couch cushion and waited for the water to take effect. His eyes slipped closed again.

"How's Grace?" he managed to ask.

"No nightmares, thank goodness. And she's having the best time lording it over her brother that he missed an adventure with cops and robbers."

Alek chuckled before realizing his head wasn't feeling all that jovial this morning. He groaned. "I should go check on Finn."

"He's fine. The boys came over to the arena with me. Junior

is teaching them both how to play hacky sack right now. Finn seems to be a bit of a natural."

"That tracks. His father was, too. At Dartmouth, we played as a team before every game."

The memories came flooding back, the same as they had last night. A painful lump formed in Alek's throat. He'd share them with Finn. Every single remembrance.

Until now, every time Finn brought up Jamie, Alek found a way to redirect the conversation. No more. In Finn, he had a piece of his best friend. And he'd make sure the boy knew his father. He'd do right by Jamie that way.

Sure, the guy had stolen his girlfriend. Married her, even. But something told him there was more to the story. Alek realized he'd been a stubborn fool by never giving his friend the chance to explain. And now, he'd never have that opportunity.

"The Fed said Sergi was the guy who tried to break into our house. He'd pinged Finn's phone to that location."

Alek immediately became more alert. "Are you kidding me? Jesus, man, I'm sorry."

Gus waved his apology off. "You sound like Sheridan, apologizing for something that's not your fault. She seems to think if she and Finn hadn't come to Milwaukee, none of this would have happened."

"That's ridiculous." His heart began to pound in his chest. "If she hadn't come to Milwaukee, she and Finn would be sitting ducks for Sergi and his friends. God knows what would have happened."

"But she did come to Milwaukee. And they are both safe." Gus leaned forward in his chair, seeming to be carefully choosing his words. "Still, Claire is concerned. She said Sheridan was talking nonsense this morning about taking Finn to Spain as soon as the custody hearing is finalized."

Alek's head spun as he shot from the couch. He braced a

hand on the armrest to steady himself. "She can't do that. She promised she'd stay through the end of the season. Longer even. I was planning on forever, dammit." Too late, he realized he'd said that last bit out loud.

"Does she know that?"

He'd never wanted to punch his friend so badly. But when he started to tell Gus that of course she knew it, he had to bite the words back. Had he said them to her? Had he said *all* the words to her?

Alek swore again.

He staggered in the direction of the adjoining room, where he could hear the shower running. His shoulders relaxed a bit. He knew exactly how he could make her realize she didn't want to go anywhere.

"Don't even think about it, man," Gus said.

"What?"

Gus sighed. "I know exactly where your head is right now. At least the one that shouldn't be driving today. Take it from a man who's been in a serious relationship with the same woman for twelve years. Shower sex isn't the answer to everything." He shook his head. "Sheridan is in a vulnerable place right now. Your best play is to hear her out. Tell her you love her. Any other move and you'll go down in flames. Trust me on this."

Alek's hand hesitated on the door handle. He was a man of action who desperately wanted to show Sheridan how he felt. Gus was right, though. Last night's findings hurt her as much as they had him. Crashing the net was probably not the best idea.

He gave his friend an acquiescent nod.

"Ice-Berg," Gus said when Alek reached for the door handle again. "Rehydrate while you wait." He tossed a sports drink at Alek. "We have a game in six hours. The bus back to the arena leaves at four thirty. You need to be on it."

Alek took a seat on the corner of the freshly made bed and

waited for Sheridan to finish her shower. Soft rock music played from the television, making him both restless and sleepy. He got up and paced around the room while he sipped from the bottle of electrolytes Gus had given him. The sight of Sheridan's luggage open and half packed didn't do much to calm his nerves.

It reminded him of when she arrived with everything she owned in one bag. Did she still think of herself as temporary or replaceable? How could he make her believe in herself? In them. He was fingering a silk camisole inside her suitcase when he realized the shower had stopped running.

Sheridan emerged from the bathroom wearing the fluffy white robe provided by the resort. Her face was flushed from the steam, but her eyes were red-rimmed and puffy as if she'd been ugly crying while in the shower. His heart shuddered.

He hustled across the room to stand in front of her. His hands bracketed her face. "None of this is on you," he said, trying to make her see reason. "Jamie made the choice to run off with Madison."

His words were meant to calm her. Unfortunately, they had the opposite effect. Tears began to stream down her face. She shook her head emphatically.

"But if it weren't for me, he wouldn't have made that choice," she cried. "He would still be here today."

"That's crazy talk. Do you even hear yourself? You had nothing to do with it."

She pulled out of his embrace and wiped her face on the sleeve of her robe. When she turned back around to face him, an expression that looked a lot like dread had settled in her eyes. "There's something I need to confess."

His chest constricted. "Confess?" He didn't like the ominous sound of that word.

Sheridan pulled in a deep breath as though it was her last.

"All this time, you've blamed Jamie for taking Madison away from you."

"Yeah. Because he did."

"No. Jamie didn't do that to you. I did."

———

SHERIDAN'S HEART cracked a little more seeing the way Alek's face hardened at her disclosure. They'd grown so close in the past month, moving past their previous roles of brother's best friend and best friend's little sister. Yesterday, he'd been talking about the future. She'd be lucky if he was even talking to her once she said her piece.

"That doesn't even make sense. What are you talking about?"

He looked ragged from spending the night on the sofa. When she woke to find him there, she knew yesterday's revelations had knocked him off kilter, too. He'd made Jamie out to be the bad guy in this scenario for so long. Finding out Madison was flawed must have been a huge paradigm shift. It was easier to blame Jamie for taking something away rather than to believe Madison hadn't chosen him.

And that had to hurt.

It was impossible to avoid the truth now that it was out there in the open. He tossed a plastic bottle between his shaky hands, trying to appear more composed than he was. She bit back a sob. This was going to be even harder than she imagined.

She sank down on the corner of the bed. "You might want to sit."

He crossed his arms over his chest, practically anchoring himself to the floor. "Just tell me what's going on."

Nodding, she drew in another deep, calming breath, only to have it sound fractured. "It was the summer you were in

Europe, and Jamie was in New Hampshire waiting for the draft."

Alek made an annoyed sound.

"I'm sorry. Of course you know when it was." She picked at a piece of fuzz on the robe. "Madison hung around our house a lot. I assumed it was because she missed you and wanted to be around familiar faces. I was taking on every shift I could get at the bar to earn money for school. She and Jamie spent most of their time together. Then, all of a sudden, she was sitting in on the meetings with his agent. Even the contract negotiations. The next thing I know, Jamie is telling me they are in love and he's taking her with him to Las Vegas for the draft."

Alek gave his head a little shake. He held his palms out. "Yeah? That's on Jamie. I don't see how you are to blame for anything."

Sheridan jumped up from the bed. She *was* to blame. And Jamie was gone because of her silence.

"Jamie thought you'd broken up with Madison!"

He shot her a confused look. "What?"

She huffed a frustrated sigh. "Madison told him she'd given you an ultimatum. She wanted to know if you two had a future together. According to her, you told her no and then broke things off. Jamie was furious at you for stomping on her heart like that."

"That's a bunch of bullshit. I never broke up with her. I was going to propose to her when I got back. You know that. I showed you the ring. What did he say when you told him that?"

Her throat grew so tight she couldn't get any words out. At least that was the excuse she was hiding behind for not answering him. Time stretched painfully until she could see the exact moment the truth dawned on him.

"You told him, didn't you?"

God bless him. He doesn't want to acknowledge the truth. After everything I've told him, he still wants to believe in me.

She didn't think she could love him more. At the same time, she could feel the pieces of her heart skittering around her chest, where it was slowly disintegrating.

Alek slammed his fists against the wall he was leaning on. "Are you kidding me? All this time, Jamie believed that about *me*? My best friend hated me for something I didn't do?" He barked out an ugly laugh. "Hell, I hated him right back. What the fuck, Sheridan?"

There was no excuse she could give that would make him understand.

He tossed the half-drunk sports drink onto the bed so he could work his fingers through his hair as he paced around the room. His face was pained when he turned on her.

"You let this lie go on for ten years! And now Jamie is gone, and we can't get those years back."

Something inside her snapped. "Don't you think I know that! My brother is dead because of *me*!" She stabbed her finger into her chest. "If I had spoken up, he never would have married that gold digger!" she choked out. "Even though he claimed to have loved her first. He said he only stepped aside because she appeared to prefer you. And he thought you made her happy."

Alek slammed his eyes shut as he leaned against the wall again for support. She swiped her tears away with her fingers. Seeing him more clearly didn't change anything, however. The truth was written all over his face.

He hated her.

Not as much as she hated herself, though.

"Why?" he croaked. "Why didn't you say something?"

Who knew it could be so physically painful to bare one's soul? There was no turning back now, though. Her defense wasn't going to make him despise her any less. She might as well rip the bandage off.

"Because I was a stupid teenage girl." She gulped in a breath. "A misguided seventeen-year-old who was in love with her brother's best friend."

There.

She'd said it.

"I guess I thought with Madison out of the way, you'd finally see me." She shrugged. "I didn't think my idiot brother would marry her while they were in Las Vegas." She shook her head. "By then, it was too late."

Alek remained quiet. Sheridan didn't dare look at him. Seeing anger or, worse, pity on his face would likely destroy what was left of her.

"The joke was on me, though," she continued. "I went up to Dartmouth the night you got back. I was going to explain, I guess. I don't know what I would have said." She sniffled. "I do know I was desperate not to lose you—even if it was only as a friend. You were so important to me." She took a moment to steady herself. "When I arrived, I overheard you talking to one of the guys, though." She swallowed roughly. "I hung out in the hall eavesdropping. You sounded so angry. And hurt, I imagine. You said some pretty brutal things about Jamie. I was sick to my stomach about the mess I'd caused. I was going to come in and tell you the truth. But then"— she drew in another deep breath —"then you started on me. You said at least you wouldn't have me hanging around twenty-four seven making moon eyes at you any longer. Then you laughed and said I was a fool for not understanding there was no way you'd ever think of me as anything more than an annoying little sister."

Alek made an anguished sound, but Sheridan avoided looking that way and instead soldiered on.

"I know I have no excuse. I should have spoken up that

night regardless of my hurt feelings. That was wrong of me. And I'm sorry." She cleared her throat. "Forgive me. Don't forgive me. It doesn't matter. Because the one person whose mercy means the most isn't around anymore for me to apologize to. And now I know for sure the blame for that rests with me. I'll never, *ever* be able to forgive myself for Jamie's death."

"Sher—"

"Don't." She held up a hand to block him. "Nothing you can say will make this better. I totally understand if you never want to see me again, but please, *please,* don't hold this against Finn. Jamie was right. He needs you in his life. I already took his father away from him." She gulped a sob and headed for the bathroom. "We can figure out the logistics later. Right now, I need some time to process where I go from here. And that's something I need to do alone."

THE KIDS WERE SPLASHING in the resort pool when Sheridan ventured downstairs that afternoon. She wasn't particularly feeling social, but she needed to check on Finn. The fact that he didn't have an asthma attack with all that went down last night was a minor miracle. Aunt Eileen told her he'd even slept through the night without incident. It looked as if her sweet nephew had turned a corner dealing with the death of his parents.

Too bad she was beginning to doubt she ever would.

She hesitated by the pool deck. Avoiding Alek would be easy. The team was in meetings in the ballroom. They would be climbing aboard a charter bus and heading to the arena shortly. Evading the WAGs was a different story.

"There she is!" two of the wives chorused. "Sheridan! Over here. We saved you a seat."

Claire shot her an empathetic look. The women were only trying to be nice. After all, they thought she'd be one of them for the foreseeable future.

If they only knew.

Pasting on a wane smile, she chose the chaise closest to

Claire. Grace was bundled up in a bright beach towel, asleep against Claire's legs.

"Chasing her brother and his best friend has taken its toll on her," Claire said quietly.

Any other time, Sheridan would have laughed at the irony. Not today.

"I can relate," she murmured.

Finn came scampering out of the pool, the soles of his feet slapping against the concrete as he hurried toward her. He threw his arms around her neck, drenching her with pool water in the process.

"You're okay," he said.

The sound of relief in his voice made her chest feel slightly lighter. Their relationship had been forever altered when his parents died. She was no longer the zany aunt who spoiled him rotten when she visited. Now she was his primary caregiver who doled out discipline. It seemed he was coming around to the new order of things.

Sheridan gave him a big squeeze. There would likely be more bumps in the road—especially where Alek was concerned. They'd get through them together, though. She'd gotten the Cobert men through rough patches like this before.

"I'm fine," she reassured him. "Better now that I've had a hug from you."

Finn's teeth chattered. "It-it's colder out h-here than in the w-water."

"You boys have another half hour to play," Claire said. "But when it's time to go up and shower, I don't want to hear any arguing."

"Yes, ma'am," both boys shouted right before Finn splashed them with a cannonball.

Grace whimpered.

"Why don't you take her up? I'll keep an eye on the Junior Mayhem," Sheridan offered.

Claire glanced back warily at the other WAGs, several of whom were gathering up their stuff and heading inside. "Are you sure?"

"Of course. You've had them all morning. I can handle the boys. And everyone else. Go."

The other woman didn't need to be asked twice. She slipped her feet into her flip-flops and gathered up her pool bag. "Their towels are here. Oh, and Finn's phone is underneath them. They've already FaceTimed Hattie." She lowered her voice. "Between you and me, I think the staff is going to be sad to lose their fifteen minutes of fame when that dog goes home."

"Sloane is still posting Finn's videos?" Sheridan had really hoped that nonsense would die down.

Claire scooped up Grace. "The woman hasn't met an algorithm she can't master. And right now, Finn's dog is her gravy train. I overheard Lori talking to the publicity staff earlier. They would love to replicate even a smidge of Sloane's success with the Mayhem's account."

A groggy Grace wrapped her arms around her mother's neck.

"You're sure you're good keeping an eye on them?" Claire asked again.

Sheridan reached for Finn's phone. "No worries. I'm going to catch up on the videos Sloane has been posting about our Hattie."

Dog videos are the perfect prescription for battling despair, aren't they?

The other WAGs were all hurrying upstairs, too, leaving Sheridan and the boys with the pool to themselves. She settled in the chaise, letting the sun's rays warm her skin while she scrolled through Finn's phone. As she swiped over the icons, her finger was drawn to the long list of photo albums. The one labeled "Monk" had been deleted, thank goodness. Curiosity got the better of her, and she clicked on the album bearing her name.

She was surprised that among the photos there were also several videos.

"Huh."

She tapped on one. It was dated six months ago. Her breath caught when Jamie's smiling face popped up on the screen.

"Hey, Sheri," he said as if he was standing right in front of her.

Joy exploded in her lungs.

"You're always razzing me that I don't communicate with you enough. Or that my penmanship sucks. So I've come up with the best solution."

He spread his arms wide, and she recognized his small office at the bar.

"Ta-da! It's an hour after closing. The one time of day when I have a few minutes to myself. It takes me a while to come down from being on all night, which is why I'm still here working. Payroll is a bitch with half the servers trading off shifts." He groaned. "I don't know how Dad made this look so easy."

His big smile was back. Sheridan grinned along with him.

"Who knew our dad was a magician, right?" He swiped at his face. "I miss the big guy. Shit. Now I'm getting maudlin. This is a stupid idea."

"No!" she cried when the screen went black.

Tears spilled from her eyes as she frantically pressed her lips to the phone.

"Oh, Jamie, please don't go."

Oblivious to her distress, the boys were still splashing in the pool. Around her, the birds chirped, and someone whistled as they passed through the breezeway connecting the restaurant to the pool area as though it was a normal day and her brother hadn't just been resurrected on his cell phone. Sheridan was grateful not to have an audience while she sucked in huge gulps of air, trying to regain her composure.

"It's not stupid, Jamie. It's priceless," she whispered when she dove back into the phone again.

There were five videos in all. Most of them lasting a minute or two. In one, Jamie was trying to recount the evening's escapade with Phil, the bar's resident drunk. Her brother was giggling so hard that he couldn't get through the story. Her own smile was filled with gratitude, knowing that she and Finn would forever have the sound of Jamie's laughter to listen to whenever they needed it.

The final video was a bit longer. It had been recorded three weeks before his death. She traced her tongue over her bottom lip to stop it from trembling.

Jamie was sitting out on the bar's patio overlooking the river right as twilight was beginning to land. That had always been his favorite time of day. He was twirling an unlit cigar between the fingers of one hand.

"Guess where I just came from?" he began. "Oh, you won't be able to guess, so I'll just tell you. The Dartmouth team's ten-year reunion."

He popped the stogie between his teeth.

"Damn, it was great to see the boys," he mumbled around the cigar. "Of course, Ice-Berg was a no-show." He sighed as he pulled the cigar back out of his mouth. "He's got an excuse, seeing as he's in training camp." Her brother chuckled. "I'm not gonna lie, every guy on the team is as surprised that Alek even made it to the pros, much less is still starting in goal."

Jamie shook his head with a smile. Sheridan did the same.

"I'm proud of him," he said with a sigh. "So fucking proud. He deserves it."

She pressed her hand to her heart.

Something shifted in his countenance causing him to sober up.

"Lots of secrets were unleashed over the weekend. I mean, *lots.*" He looked directly into the camera. "Imagine my surprise when one of them involved you." He flicked the cigar at her.

She glanced around, making sure the boys were still where they were supposed to be and not listening.

"You lied to me, Sheridan Leigh," he said. "Sure, it was a lie of omission, but a lie is a lie."

Sheridan's pulse beat hard against her neck. What was he talking about?

"Alek didn't break up with Madison. In fact, he was going to propose to her. And Smiley says you even approved of the ring."

He couldn't have shocked her more if he walked out of the pool right now. Her hands were shaking so hard, she nearly dropped the phone.

"I should be mad at you. Especially with the way things turned out with Madison." Jamie sighed. "But I'm as much at fault as you. I saw what I wanted to see. I let her manipulate me." He pointed the cigar at her again. "And you, sly sister o' mine, have always been in love with Alek. Oh, don't think I didn't notice. I did."

She slunk back against the chaise in astonishment.

He knew!

"Believe it or not," he continued. "I'm proud of you for taking a risk and going for something. I wish you'd do that more often. You are always so busy trying to make everyone around you happy that I think you forget that you are worthy of your own joy, Sheridan. Always chase your happiness."

Jamie cleared his throat.

"Things with Madison and I aren't going to work out." He twisted the wedding band on his finger. "Not for lack of trying on my part. She's got some things going on that I can't help her with." He looked away for a long moment before dragging his gaze back. "But I wouldn't call the relationship a mistake. It gave me Finn. And we'll be okay. We've got each other. And we've got you.

"If I could change something, though, I'd move heaven and earth for you and Alek to be together. You are two of my very favorite people in the whole world." He winked. "Well, besides my son. You are the perfect person to soften Alek's icy-sharp edges and keep him balanced. He's way too hard on himself. And he is a true romance hero. He would worship the hell out of you, all while he gave you the confidence to be your best self."

Sheridan was back to gulping in air again as Jamie leaned toward the camera.

"Promise me if you ever get the chance again, you'll take it. I mean it," he demanded. "Nothing would make my life more complete than seeing you both happy."

A mumbled voice behind the camera had Jamie looking away.

"Be right there," he said to someone before he focused his attention back to the camera. "You know, I should send you this one." He shook his head and waved his hand. "Ah, you're coming home for a visit before you leave for Spain. We are going to talk about this in person, young lady." He jabbed the cigar in the direction of the camera again. "Because it's your turn now. One of us needs a great love like Mom and Dad had. It may as well be you." He groaned. "Will you take a breath! I'm coming!"

Sheridan lunged forward when the camera went black.

"He knew," she whispered before practically shouting it. "He knew!"

"Are you calling us?" Finn asked from the side of the pool. "Is it time to get out?"

She checked the phone. They still had ten minutes left.

"Yes," she lied.

If she hurried, she might be able to catch Alek. She leaped up from the chaise and tossed each boy his towel.

"He knew, and he forgave me," she muttered.

The two boys exchanged a bewildered look as they toweled off.

"Who knew?" Gunner asked.

"I have to tell Alek," she responded.

"You can tell Alek at the game," Finn said.

"Oh my gosh, the game." She paced around the pool deck. "I can't distract him before the game. He hates that."

She plopped back down on the chaise.

"And what if he can't forgive me?" She buried her face in her hands.

"My dad gives my mom chocolate when she gets like this," she heard Gunner say. "Hurry. Do you have any M&Ms left?"

A small hand holding two M&Ms suddenly appeared beneath her bowed head. She sobbed out a laugh before looking up at Finn.

"See. I told you. Works like a champ." Gunner puffed out his chest.

Her laughter came more easily now. She took the chocolate candies and popped them into her mouth before she pulled both boys into a hug.

"You'll never know if he'll forgive you if you don't take a chance and ask him."

The words had come out of Finn's mouth, but it was definitely Jamie's voice she heard.

What was in that pill the doctor gave her last night? Whatever it was, it was making her delusional.

You are worthy of your own joy, Sheridan. Always choose happiness.

Delusional or not, she could feel her brother's words

empowering her. She'd let him down, yet he'd forgiven her. Perhaps Alek would, also. He and Finn were right. She'd never know if she didn't try.

She jerked up from the chaise. "I'm choosing happiness."

"Yay!" both boys cheered.

"What happens now?" Gunner asked once they'd done a little happy dance.

Sheridan grabbed both their hands and tugged them in the direction of the conference room the team had commandeered. "We go find Alek."

They raced inside, nearly tripping over Lori in the hallway.

"Are they still in there?" Sheridan asked her.

"Uh, no. They were headed outside to the bus a minute ago."

"To the bus!" Gunner shouted.

ALEK SAT ALONE on the team bus. His stomach was still a bit queasy from last night's bad decisions. He'd already had the embarrassing conversation with Coach suggesting he put Jordan in goal despite it being Alek's night. Even if he felt better in the next two hours by some stroke of luck, he doubted he could concentrate on keeping the puck out of the net.

I'll never, ever be able to forgive myself for Jamie's death.

It wasn't her fault. She should know that. Hell, he should have told her that right then and there. Except he'd been too absorbed in processing everything he'd learned in the past twenty-four hours to get the right words out. Rather, he'd been sulking, thinking about all the time he'd lost with Jamie this past decade.

He needed to shoulder some of the blame, too. Alek had let

his pride get in the way. He could have confronted Jamie. Or Madison. Especially Madison.

And, Christ, the things Sheridan had overheard him say. He pinched his forehead so hard it was painful. Much less than he deserved, however. The truth was, he'd encouraged Sheridan's attention all those years ago. He liked having someone who hung onto his every word. Who smiled at him with such adoration when he was having a bad day. Who believed him to be faultless.

Alek slammed his fist onto the empty seat beside him. He didn't deserve her.

"Is he going to be okay?" Junior whispered from a few seats back.

His teammates had been giving him a wide berth all afternoon. They were still tiptoeing around him as they found their seats on the shuttle.

"I'm fine!" he shouted. "Fan-fucking-tastic, in fact!"

He wasn't. And every guy on the bus knew it. Only he wasn't sure how to make himself whole again. He slammed his head back against the high seat back.

The doors closed, and the bus lurched as the driver put it into gear.

"For crying out loud, Ice-Berg," Gus shouted from up front. "Did you tell her you loved her?"

A heavy silence fell over the bus. Everyone froze. Even the driver.

"Well? Did you?" Valentine demanded. "Maybe if you took your own advice once in a while, you wouldn't be so hang-dog right now."

"It's not too late," Picard threw in.

Alek felt like all the air was seeping out of the bus. He watched as Henrik moved in what looked like slow motion, reaching over the driver to grab the handle for the door and pulling it until it opened.

"Do it," the big Swede commanded. "You are no use to us on the ice until you do."

He did love Sheridan. Alek loved her with every fiber of his being. She'd admitted to loving him. Hell, she'd shown him in multiple ways. Yet, for some reason, he hadn't been able to get out of his own way and take that final leap of faith.

"Are you willing to risk losing her?" Gus asked.

He shot from his seat. She wasn't taking Finn to Spain. Neither were they "figuring out logistics later." His makeshift family wasn't splitting up because one or both of them felt guilty about what happened to Jamie. They'd work through that together. Not apart.

Alek stormed up the aisle to the front of the bus. He and Sheridan were meant for each other. And no way was he rolling over and letting her walk away.

His teammates remained quiet. Their silent confidence propelled him forward and down the steps—where he collided with Sheridan.

"Oh," she cried when he slammed into her.

Alek gripped her elbows, steadying her so she didn't tumble backward down the steps. Finn and Gunner waited on the curb wearing matching smirks. Lori swept in and guided both boys back into the hotel.

"I found you," she said.

"I was coming back for you," he said at the same time.

Her eyes were bright with enthusiasm. A marked change from the dejection weighing them down earlier in the day. He took some confidence from that.

"I have something to tell you," she insisted.

"No." He tugged her body up against his. "Me first."

He could have kicked himself when her smile deflated slightly. Pressing his forehead against hers, he softened his tone.

"Were you serious when you said you loved me back then?"

She nodded slowly. "Yes."

"Do you—" He swallowed roughly. "Do you still love me now?"

"Yes," she murmured. "Even more so."

His chest felt like it was exploding when he kissed her. She laughed into his mouth while wrapping her arms around his waist. He would have stood there kissing her forever had Henrik not jabbed him in the back with a hockey stick.

"Don't you have something to say to her, Ice-Berg?"

Sheridan pressed her palms to Alek's chest and leaned back in his arms, arching an eyebrow at him as she did.

"I love you, Sheridan." He surprised himself with the volume and ferocity of the words. "I was a fool not to tell you sooner. You and Finn make me a better person. And there is no one else I'd rather go through life with than you."

"Well done," Henrik said. "Finish this somewhere else. We need to get to the barn for a hockey game. You catch a ride with the ladies and the kiddies on the next trip. Put your skates on."

Alek helped Sheridan down from the bus. A chorus of catcalls and wolf whistles filled the valet driveway when the bus pulled away.

"It's about time," Valentine called from an open window.

It was definitely about time for another kiss. Sheridan let him have his way with her mouth for several heartbeats before she pulled away.

"I have something to tell you," she repeated.

"If it's about you feeling guilty about what happened in the past, forget about it. There's nothing to forgive. You acted out of love." He dropped another kiss on her lips. "But if you need to hear it. I forgive you."

"Thank you." She kissed his chin. "That means a lot. But I'm talking about Jamie."

Not this again. Alek was starting to get agitated. "No. You did nothing wrong. There is no way you caused that accident. You hear me? That's all on that guy, Sergi."

She nodded. "I know that now. This is about me not setting him straight about you and Madison. He figured it all out. At the reunion, one of the guys told him you'd bought Madison a ring and you had intended to propose. And that I knew all of that." She waved Finn's phone in front of his face. "He made a video for me. He said he wasn't mad. In fact, he wished things had worked out between us."

He dabbed his thumbs at the tears welling in her eyes.

"Jamie forgave me," she whispered. "It's all going to be okay."

"It's going to be better than okay, Sheridan. We are going to have the love Jamie wanted us to have. And we are going to shower that love on his son."

"He'd like that."

"What about you?"

"Mmm. I could get behind that after a little more convincing."

Alek proceeded to convince her until they were nearly late for the game.

EPILOGUE

ALEK IGNORED the stinger in his hip as he climbed the grassy bluff. He welcomed the soft breeze that lifted his hair off his neck. Hiking the New Hampshire countryside with Hattie and Finn in the July heat had him working up a sweat. Luckily, his destination resided beneath a decades-old black walnut tree.

He came to a stop in front of a granite headstone. A layer of walnuts and leaves were scattered over its top. Alek sighed as he brushed them away. He bent over and pulled several weeds from the ground in front before sliding down and resting his back against the cool stone.

"Jesus, Jamie, you're still a slob."

Stretching his legs out, he crossed them at the ankles and took in the view in front of him. Down below, Finn and Hattie were chasing a hacky sack ball. Sheridan was busy arranging flowers into two outdoor vases that she would stick in the ground next to her parents' and her brother's markers. She took her time, giving him several minutes of privacy with his best friend.

It had become a habit over the past eight months. Whenever he could carve out time during the season to venture to New

Hampshire, they brought Finn back to the picturesque little cemetery to visit with his parents and grandparents. Finn would leave the perfunctory rock on top of his father's grave and run off with Hattie to explore after a few minutes. But Alek always liked to spend time filling Jamie in on their lives.

"Well, another season ended without me hoisting the Cup," he announced. "The New York Guardians knocked us out in the second round."

Alek was surprised how the bitter aftertaste of being eliminated from the playoffs hadn't lingered as long this year. He let out a resigned sigh.

"There's always next season. Everyone's coming back. Gus, Twos, Picard. Even the Swedes. The kid, Dern, is a Swiss Army knife on the ice. He can do it all. Defense, offense, you name it. And he hasn't even grown into his body yet." Alek shook his head just imagining the star Parker Dern was going to be someday. "Although Junior was skating on thin ice with management for nearly the entire second half of the season. He turned things around come playoff time, though." He chuckled. "It certainly helped that his sister was running interference with Kellogg."

Hattie barked at Finn to throw her the ball.

"My dad got into a drug trial in Boston. He's actually taking a position in Dartmouth's history department as a visiting professor while he's in the trial. Talk about full circle. It's a good thing he wasn't there the same time we were." The dread he'd constantly felt about losing his dad had dissipated somewhat with the slow progression of the disease. "My mom has promised not to redecorate Barn Burner while they are here."

Finn laughed when Hattie nearly did a backflip trying to catch the ball.

"Your son is the only nine-year-old I know who got his own bar for his birthday," Alek continued. "The corporate types drove a hard bargain, but it's Finn's legacy. I would have paid a ransom to get it back if that's what it took. You did what you had to do to protect your family. I get that. I'm sure it hurt to do it, though. Rest easy, my friend. It's back in the family where it belongs." He scoffed. "Of course, knowing kids these days, Finn won't want it. I'll end up running it after I retire."

He took in the pastoral panorama spread out before him. It was quiet and peaceful here. Relaxing. The idea of running a bar didn't sound that bad.

A cardinal glided to a landing on the gravestone two away from where Alek sat.

"Finn and Gunner are going to Valentine's camp next week. Can you believe that? Your kid passed on my camp." He grinned as he shook his head. "We haven't told him about the baby yet. I know we put the cart before the horse, but you can put your shotgun away. The wedding is in two months. No matter the order we did things, Finn is going to be a great influence on this kid."

He glanced back down to where Sheridan was putting the finishing touches on the flower arrangements. She flashed him a radiant smile as if she could sense him looking at her.

"And your sister is going to be a remarkable mom."

The cardinal cocked its head in Alek's direction.

"Thank you." Alek patted the granite. "I'm not sure what I did to deserve the gift of your sister and your son. Know this, though, they will always be safe and loved."

Alek swore the bird nodded before it flew off.

Sheridan weaved her way up the little hill. He hopped up and met her halfway, taking the metal vases from her. She swatted at the grass sticking to his jeans on his ass.

"Save it for later, lady," he teased before nipping at her lips.

He positioned one of the vase's pointed stakes into the ground next to Jamie's headstone. "Here?"

She nodded. He pressed it into the turf with the heel of his sneaker. Moving over to her parents' plot, he repeated the process with the second flower arrangement.

Sheridan's eyes misted up. Alek stepped behind her, wrapping his arms securely around her waist and spreading his fingers over the gentle swell of her belly. She was growing a life inside her. One who was already so loved. He nuzzled her neck.

"I love you," he murmured against her soft skin. "Have I told you that today?"

She relaxed against his chest. "Hmm. Let me think."

He spun her around and took her lips in a searing kiss. God, he would never get enough of this woman. She tangled her fingers in the hair behind his neck and responded with equal amounts of passion.

"Gross!" Finn moaned when he and Hattie joined them.

Sheridan smiled as she rested her cheek against Alek's chest.

"Look." Finn held out his palm, exposing a round, flat rock." This one looks like a puck, doesn't it?"

Alek kept his arm around Sheridan's waist as he inspected Finn's rock. "It certainly does."

Finn hesitated. "Should I put it on Dad's or Grandpa's?"

Sheridan exchanged a look with Alek. It pleased her that he kept the memories of both men alive by sharing stories about them with Finn.

"How about you put it on Ed's marker today? We can run back here tomorrow before we head up to Quebec for camp and move it to your dad's," he suggested to Finn.

"Great plan." Finn set the stone down on the granite. "Can we get lunch now? Hattie and I are starving."

Sheridan rolled her eyes. "What's new?"

"Bye, Dad," Finn called as he raced down the hill, a barking Hattie at his heels. "See you tomorrow!"

Sheridan blew a kiss to her family. Alek adjusted the rock

one last time, making sure it was secure. Hand in hand, they strolled down the hill toward their future.

I hope you enjoyed Alek and Sheridan's story. Are you curious about their wedding? Well, I've got you covered with a bonus scene exclusive to my readers. Scan the QR code and it's yours.

Alek was first introduced in ***Catch and Release***, the slow-burn, enemies to lovers, second chance romance between Milwaukee Growlers quarterback Trey Van Horn and *the-one-who-got-away*, London Headley. It was fun catching up with Trey and London again, along with Collin Slater. You should definitely check out their story.

If you want more day to day details about my books, my crazy writing life, and opportunities to name places and characters, come hang out with my reader group, the X's and O's, on Facebook. Scan the QR code to join:

And please, don't forget to tell other readers how much you enjoyed ***Keeping it Real*** by leaving a review on the site where you purchased the book. It's the best way to show an author some love and I ALWAYS appreciate it!

If you like sports romance books, check these out:
Game On – a grumpy hero romance
Foolish Games – a secret baby story
Risky Game – a fake relationship romance
Sleeping with the Enemy – a second chance romance
Gossip Game — a fake relationship novella

Meet the Milwaukee Growlers:
Just for Kicks – A marriage of convenience rom-com
Double Dog Dare – An enemies-to-lovers rom-com
Catch and Release — A second chance romance

How about a little suspense with your romance?
Recipe for Disaster – a mistaken identity Secret Service romance
Shot in the Dark – a forced proximity Secret Service romance

Between Love and Honor – a second chance Secret Service romance

Do you enjoy books about small towns and big families—including some sports stars? Be sure to check out my Chances Inlet series:
Back to Before – a forced proximity romance
All they Ever Wanted – an enemies-to-lovers romance
Second Chance Christmas – age gap romance
It Had to Be You – a nanny romance
Take Me Home for Christmas — a friends-to-lovers romance

ACKNOWLEDGMENTS

As always, this book would not be possible without the help of an extensive supporting cast. I am not a doctor, nor do I play one on television. Lucky for me, Dr. Kristine Sufcak came to my rescue with the medical jargon needed for this book. Thank you, Kristine. Any mistakes are mine and not hers. And thank you to her mom, Kathy, for answering my endless questions about Canadian colloquialisms.

Thank you to Melanie, Tina, and Kim for the beta reads. Your insights always make my books better. Thank you to Jenny Sims at Editing for Indies whose careful and thorough reviews make my writing better. And, as always, a great big thank you to my assistant, Rachael, who knows what needs to be done even before I do! Thanks to all the bloggers and bookstagrammers who share my books. And to the indie bookstores who support the genre we love.

My family puts up with a lot while I'm in full author mode and I'm grateful for their support—especially when they go above and beyond and show up for readings and signings. Love you guys!

Finally, thanks again to all of you who take the time to read the crazy stories I write. I'm still pinching myself every time I think about it. Thanks for coming along for the ride.